FREE HAND
IRONS AND WORKS
BOOK ONE

E.M. LINDSEY

Free Hand
Irons and Works Book One
E.M. Lindsey

Copyright © 2023

All rights reserved. This book or any portion thereof may not be reproduced or used in any manner whatsoever without the express written permission of the publisher except for the use of brief quotations in a book review.

This book is a work of fiction. Any events, places, or people portrayed in the book have been used in a manner of fiction and are not intended to represent reality. Any resemblance is purely coincidental.

Cover by Amai Designs

EM LINDSEY LINKS

[EM's Discord](#)
[EM's Patreon](#)
[EM Lindsey's Website](#)
[Free Short Stories](#)
[EM Lindsey's Amazon Account](#)
[EM Lindsey on Instagram](#)
[EM Lindsey on Bookbub](#)

CHAPTER ONE

"I'm surprised you took your boyfriend's cock out of your mouth long enough to check up on your old man." The cruelty in the voice didn't faze Derek much anymore, though tonight his defenses were low. He'd woken up late, took a bad spill in the shop hallway, and work hadn't been great. A client from the week before came in on a rampage because someone had made fun of her new ink—something she'd printed off the internet and asked him to trace onto her skin in spite of his warnings that it would be better for him to design something based on the image rather than copy the image itself. She'd insisted however, that he provide, and so he did. Because that was his job. And when it didn't pan out, it was also his fault. The insults spilling from her lips had echoed around his head the same way his father's often did, and it was just...a lot. "What the fuck you doin' anyway, boy?"

Derek dragged a hand down his face, squinting at the way his window started to fog up. The rain was getting heavier as he tried to navigate the streets toward the bank. "I uh...I'm just heading to the bank. Dad, you get your meds today?"

"Fuck you, you little shit. What gives you the right to ask me questions? Who the fuck do you think you are? You prance around in your little pride parade like a goddamn homo and they come knocking on my door asking why I have a faggot son goin' straight to hell inna handbask—"

"Mr. Osbourne?" came a softer voice after his father was cut off.

Derek pulled into the parking lot of the bank and took a breath before he answered the nurse. "He get his meds tonight?"

"They were a little late. I'm really sorry, I didn't know until after he'd dialed," she told him.

Derek let out a tiny sigh. "It's fine. Trust me, I've heard worse."

"This can happen in the late stages of cirrhosis. I'm sure the doctor explained it. They're just...not themselves."

Except Derek's father was very much himself, and it seemed like the old man would be the angry, hateful, bigoted old dickhead until his liver finally gave out and he took his last breath. But that would probably be years away. This was Derek's personal hell, knowing that he'd suffer these calls weekly, unable to escape this fate in spite of having chosen it. When the hospital asked both Derek and his brother to act as caregivers, Sage had simply laughed and hung up on them. Derek, for whatever reason, couldn't bring himself to say no. Call it self-hatred, call him a martyr, he accepted it was his fate and ran with it. It wasn't like the old man could do any more damage as it was.

"Just call me if he gets any worse," Derek told her. "And I'll talk to the doctor in the morning and let him know about the slip with the meds."

"Sounds good, Mr. Osbourne. You have a good night."

"You too." Derek hung up, then let his phone drop to the empty passenger seat.

He stared at the waterfall of rain beating down on his window. The bank was less than twenty feet away, but that was twenty feet of torrential downpour, which frankly would put the cherry on the cake of this fucking day. His arm still ached from where he'd landed when Kat had forgotten to lay down the wet floor sign, and the echo of his angry father's voice would sound in his ears all night when he let himself have even a moment of silence. He desperately needed to make his deposit so the auto-debits from his account to pay monthly bills wouldn't cost him a shit-ton in over-draft fees, but the prospect of getting drenched for it was almost worth the repeated thirty-five bucks the bank would level at him for taking too long.

He sighed, pressing his forehead to the wheel, murmuring out a few curses and a couple prayers. "Alright, Osbourne," he said aloud, last-naming himself in hopes of providing some sort of external motivation, "just get your ass out of the fucking car. You can dry off later, and even eat half that tub of Ben and Jerry's waiting for you in the freezer."

It wasn't ideal, but it was enough. He grabbed his keys, grabbed the envelope which he shoved under his shirt, then bolted. Halfway through the drenching rain, he remembered he'd left his phone in the car, but it wasn't going to take long. A quick stack of cash shoved into the ATM hole and then he could kiss his shit-ass day goodbye.

The room where the little ATM kiosk sat tucked away in a corner was at least warm. The bank gods smiled on him enough to keep him from going hypothermic as his trembling hands pushed into his pocket and pulled out his wallet. Though his fingers were stiff, he managed to withdraw his card and shove it into the slot.

The machine clicked, and at the exact same time, the door swung open and he was blasted by a sudden wave of icy-cold air. Derek glanced over his shoulder at the man who entered, shaking his umbrella as he hovered near the now-closed door. Derek was rarely intimidated by other people. Hell, he was usually the guy in the room everyone else was afraid of. Six-two, two-ten, both arms covered in tattoos. His ears were gauged, his face in a permanent resting-murder face, though that was hardly his own fault. He was one of the nicer guys with a stall at Irons and Works, he just didn't always look like it.

The man didn't really seem to notice him though, his face tipped down toward his phone as he waited a polite distance for Derek to finish up. He took a deep breath as he went through the steps, punching in his code and shoving the cash into the machine before the stranger got any ideas about trying to rob him—it was late, after all, and the street corner was shady as fuck. The machine chirped out what he imagined to be a thank you, then coughed up his receipt. He shoved it into his pocket, fumbling with his card as he awkwardly stepped away from the ATM to give the other guy some room.

He got a better look at him in the dim overhead light and was immediately startled by how attractive he was. The guy was wrapped up in a thick coat, but his face above his high collar was round, full of soft edges and a natural smile. His dark eyes flitted up to meet Derek's for just a second, and when a trail of rainwater dripped down the side of his neck, Derek had the inexplicable urge to reach out and swipe it away with his thumb.

What the fuck was wrong with him?

Shaking his head to try and get some of his damn sense back, he turned to reach for the door.

It all sort of happened at once, then. There was lightning, and immediate thunder which was strong enough to rattle the windows and rumble the floor beneath their feet. The lights flickered and then plunged them into almost total darkness. The only thing Derek could see was the faint glow of the man's phone, and the only sound was the rushing heartbeat of panic in his ears.

He was half a foot away from the front door, so he reached for it, giving the door a tug. When it didn't budge, he tried again—pushing and pulling and falling into damn-near hysteria because apparently the automatic locks had engaged, and he was stuck.

Claustrophobia wasn't exactly one of Derek's secrets. When he first started at Irons and Works, James had tried to haze him a little by locking him in the supply cupboard. Derek's PTSD had been at an all-time high, and to this day, he couldn't entirely remember what happened apart from blanking out with his hand against the door and coming to in Antonio's office with a cool cloth on the back of his neck and Katherine murmuring something soft and comforting into his ear.

James' black eye was apparently his fault, but the guy was contrite and overly-apologetic which likely meant Antonio explained a little bit about Derek's past to the guy. It never happened again, and everyone at that point knew that the back room doors needed to stay open if Derek was in there looking for supplies, and that Derek always—always—got the stall closest to the front desk.

In that moment, Derek immediately walked himself through the steps his therapist taught him. Mostly because he was in a strange place with a strange man, and the last thing that guy needed was to watch Derek completely fall apart. He didn't always get violent, but he couldn't control what happened if he totally lost it, and he didn't want to add assault charges to his already-shit day.

"Ten," he murmured to himself, pressing both palms to the glass door. "Nine. Eight. Seven..." He swallowed thickly as his throat began to grow tight and his fingers began to shake. "Six. Please, god," he whispered. He didn't often invoke a deity he hadn't believed in since he was a kid, but right now it felt like a ballast. "Five..."

His voice faded to silence when a hand touched his arm, and then a bright light was in his face. No, not a bright light, a phone screen. It was a notepad app and one short sentence was written there.

> You OK?

Derek shook his head. "No. Fuck, I'm sorry, I'm super not okay. I can't...we're stuck, and I feel like I'm about to lose my goddamn mind and I don't..."

The stranger interrupted him with an impatient noise, pulled the phone away for a second, and he could hear the faint sound of the default iPhone keyboard clicking as the guy typed. After what felt like a short forever, the phone returned.

> Sorry, can't understand. Deaf. I'm Basil.
> Please type. Help you, OK?

Derek stared at the words, trying to make them make sense in his scrambled-eggs processing, but he couldn't seem to figure out what to do next. His hands stayed pressed against the window, and his breathing got tighter. Squeezing his eyes shut, he felt an all-too familiar wave of dizziness and the room felt tilted.

Then, just when he thought he would lose all sense of reason, a hand pressed itself to his sternum. He was gently turned from the window, and the man—Basil—took his right hand and laid it on his sternum. Derek couldn't begin to understand, but after a beat, he felt the guy's chest rising and falling with a slow, steady breath. Basil was counting off a rhythm with a tap on his forearm.

One. Two. Three.

One. Two. Three.

Derek let himself release the air in his lungs, drew in another when Basil's chest expanded, then held it for one, two, three. He released it the same time as the stranger in front of him—the man he'd never met before, but who was somehow keeping him from falling apart.

One. Two. Three.

His head began to clear, bit by bit, and the room began to still. He was hit by a sudden wave of humiliation at the way he'd just fallen apart. He was still trapped, the electricity was still out, and the storm was still raging, but he was calming down and reality began to set in.

"Shit," he said aloud, "I'm so sorry." Then he stopped, remembering what the guy had typed on his phone. In the very faint glow of the phone, he could make out the guy's frown of confusion.

There was another moment he could see Basil typing, then he handed the phone back to Derek and took a step back.

> Panic attack? I have before. Your name what?

Derek frowned at the wording and deeply wished he had bothered to learn more sign. He knew a handful of words, all of them baby related since Antonio and Katherine had been taking beginner's classes once their daughter had been diagnosed with hearing loss. The entire crew knew enough to make Jasmine laugh and understand when she wanted her bottle or her parents, or a cookie. But that was about it. Tony and Kat had been on them about starting up in the beginner's ASL, but all of them had been dragging ass, which was now coming back to bite him.

At a loss for any other way to respond, he tapped the return button a few times, then typed his response.

> My name's Derek. I'm claustrophobic and being in a closed space unexpected gives me panic attacks. I'm really sorry if I freaked you out.

He handed the phone back, watching Basil's expression soften a little as he read the message. When he looked up, he waved off Derek's apology, then pointed to the ground near the door and made a sign Derek did recognize. 'Sit.' When Derek nodded and moved to sit, Basil looked surprised. In the light of the phone, he saw Basil make a series of signs, but only recognized two. 'Sign, you?'

Derek made grabby hands for the phone. My boss' baby girl has hearing loss and I know a few words, but not a lot. When he handed the phone back for Basil to read, he demonstrated. 'Milk, cookie, mom, dad, sit, no.'

At the last one, Basil laughed, a low sound, coming straight from his chest which Derek found fitting for some reason. He grinned back, hating that he couldn't see the guy properly, but it was still comforting to have him close by. The fact that he was trapped in a closed space was awful, but not being alone was helping. The storm was still raging outside, with no signs of slowing, but they couldn't be trapped forever.

At some point, tomorrow morning, the bank would open. Or

security would come by and see them. Something. Hell, he could use Basil's phone to call the cops if it got dire. For now, he was safe. He was drying, and the air was still warm, and nothing in there could kill him.

Derek's thoughts were interrupted when Basil made an inquiring noise, then touched his arm, then handed the phone over.

> Tattoo? What meaning?

Derek glanced down at his left arm, curled over both crooked knees, which he'd drawn to his chest as a way of comforting himself. He was asked that question a lot, and the funny thing was, there wasn't some deep meaning behind most of his ink. They were a flood of images he just liked, things he saw and wanted on his body in a permanent way. Some of them were cover-ups from younger days of bad line work and piss-poor shading and a few stick-and-pokes. Some of them were new and still bright, and some had faded into something soft and quiet.

Their real meaning was rebellion. Was taking charge of his own body after having spent years and years taking abuse from the people who were supposed to love him. And his twin brother, Sage, had grown up the sons of a military-rigid politician whose idea of spare the rod meant literally taking a rod to them any time they stepped out of line. He didn't like closed spaces because he'd spent the majority of his formative years being locked in a tiny shed for hours upon hours until his father felt he had 'learned his lesson'.

He and his brother dressed in collared shirts and pressed slacks and never had a hair out of place. For all appearances, he'd been a well-dressed, strait-laced boy with high aspirations of a lucrative career, end up as Dr. Osbourne in some field or another. His obedience and clothes hid all manner of his father's sins, and he didn't dare step out of line.

Except when he had. Except when he was fifteen and exhausted and ready to break. So, he'd stolen his father's car and ended up pulled over and detained by the local sheriff who laughed it off as, 'boys will be boys.' The sheriff didn't miss the terrified look on Derek's face when his father laughed too, with a cruel sort of mirth. It wasn't until he'd spent thirty-six hours in the shed, no water, no food, that a panicked Sage had disobeyed the rules and broken him out.

The two of them ran that night. They took Sage's cash savings and they ran, and they didn't look back. Derek knew his father had called the police, begging to have his boys brought home, but Derek was sure that police chief hadn't looked for them very hard.

They landed in Oklahoma City and worked as day-laborers to get by. They squatted with a group of run-aways in a surprisingly nice warehouse, and Derek got his first stick-and-poke next to an old camping stove where a boy named Pepper had sanitized his needle over the open flame. It was the only tattoo Derek would never cover up. It was a shitty, off-center hand holding up a middle finger on his right hand's middle knuckle.

Every bit of ink after that had been a fuck-you to his dad. The day he got the call that his dad was in the hospital—liver failure putting an expiration date on his life and in need of care—he'd gone to visit him in the hospital, then returned to the shop and lay on Antonio's table and begged him to just make it hurt. He had a crow on the inside of his elbow, filled completely with black, only an eye shaded red staring out with its stark splash of color.

His tattoos were proof he had survived it and moved on. That he'd gone from an abused kid to a tattoo artist and full-time student determined to get his work into galleries and studios and into the hands of people who really and truly understood him.

Derek realized he'd taken way too long to answer, and with shaking fingers he quickly typed up a response.

> I had a rough childhood and I got tattoos to remind myself that I survived. I work at a tattoo shop called Irons and Works. You know it?

Basil read over his shoulder, but instead of taking the phone back, he just smiled and shook his head.

> If you ever want work done, come see me. I'm also an artist though. Is it okay if I show you my gallery?

At Basil's confirming nod, Derek typed in his site address and pulled up his online gallery. He was mostly into nature work—he loved realism, but he wanted to draw and paint things that held life. Even though most of his animal work was in oils, his favorite was of an octopus curled around a rock surrounded by a bed of coral done in charcoal. There was no color, but for whatever reason, the drawing always looked the most alive to him. He had it hanging in his station, but more than anything, he wanted someone to appreciate it.

Maybe it shouldn't have shocked him when Basil's long finger tapped the screen, bringing the octopus to full image, but Derek still felt his heart stutter in his chest. With Basil leaning this close, Derek got a whiff of something heady and overwhelming, like the first wave of scent when you walk into a florist's fridge to see the cold bouquets.

He dared a glance over, and he felt his heart beat even harder at the look on Basil's face. His eyes were wide, lips slightly parted, a curl of black hair falling over his forehead as his eyes took in the image. When he pulled back, Derek switched back to the notepad.

> That one's my favorite, but it's never sold.

> You want selling this?

Derek shrugged. I want someone to love and appreciate my work. I'll miss it when it goes, but I can wait. The right person will come along.

Basil smiled at him, leaning into his shoulder gently as he reached for the phone.

> Beautiful. I make flower bouquet, sell in shop with sister. Older. Bossy.

Derek chuckled and shook his head in sympathy.

> I have a twin brother, five minutes older, just as bossy.

> Look like you?

Derek wished he had his phone with him, because yes, Sage was the mirror of him. Apart from a few tattoos and Sage's shorter undercut, they could fool almost anyone. In fact, the third time Derek's hook-up accidentally kissed his brother, Derek insisted Sage get something visible to declare who was whom. Sage settled on a shark riding up his neck toward his left ear, letting Derek do the ink, and if he was a little bit heavy-handed, well, Sage didn't complain about it.

> We're identical.

Before he could write anything else, there was another flash of lightning, and thunder so close and so loud, it made his ears start ringing. When Basil jumped along with him, Derek turned to look at the guy.

> Are you able to hear that?

Basil shook his head, then pressed his palm to the floor before typing.

> Feel it. Noise make vibrate.

Another crack of thunder and that time, he noticed the rumble beneath him. It was enough to keep him distracted so he didn't start to panic again, though there was the pressing threat of it at the base of his spine he didn't entirely want to acknowledge. The truth was, having Basil pressed up against him in that empty bank was enough to keep him grounded, and it wasn't something he would have ever expected. With the panic at bay, he started to feel the fatigue of the day creeping up on him, his limbs heavy, eyes stinging. He wanted some hot food and his comfy bed, and he wanted to forget about this day completely.

Or well, most if it. Because this part was maybe one of the best things that had happened to him in a while and that was a little horrifying to think about.

Before he could reach for the phone again, the overhead lights started to flicker. They went on, off, then on again with a steady hum which sent both men jumping to their feet. They faced each other, and it was strange to be looking at Basil full in the face, in the dim light of the faded halogen bulb above them.

He was startlingly good looking, his wet hair in ringlet curls which had ceased dripping at some point during their conversation. He was thin under his thick coat, his skinny jeans hugging his legs, his converse making his feet look long and narrow. Derek stood at least four inches taller than him, but for whatever reason, he didn't feel monstrously huge the way he normally did. Derek had the inexplicable urge to put his arms around Basil, kneel low, and bury his face in the guy's neck, and he had to force himself to take a step back to keep from doing it.

Basil's eyes flickered to the ATM which had rebooted, then to Derek before lifting his hands and signing, 'You OK?'

It took Derek a minute for his brain to register the sign alphabet which he was just starting to memorize, but when it did, he offered a little smile. 'OK,' he repeated. 'Thank you,' he went on, then stopped because he wasn't sure how to say what he wanted to next. 'FOR HELP,' he spelled.

Basil's grin was wide and gorgeous, making Derek's stomach flip. 'Help,' he said, mouthing the word as he showed him the sign, and when Derek copied it properly, he offered him a thumb's up.

"I should let you uh…" He gestured to the ATM machine, unsure if Basil could read his lips, but when the other man nodded, he figured he'd gotten the gist of it. 'Thank you,' he signed again.

It was painfully awkward and unsure, but eventually Derek turned on his heel and marched out of the building. Where the rain had been annoying and unwanted, now it was a sweet relief, proof of freedom, that he hadn't been trapped against his will. He glanced through the window again, to see Basil at the ATM punching in his code, and he forced himself to finish walking to the car.

It started right away, and the blast of hot air told him he'd only been trapped for a handful of minutes—nothing like the eternal hours it had felt like in the moment. He hesitated one more time before putting the car in reverse, letting himself wonder if he'd ever see the guy again. But it was too late to do anything about it now. Turning onto the street, he decided he'd just let fate have at it. If it was meant to be, then it would be.

BASIL GOT BACK to the condo, shaking the water off his coat and swiping his feet on the mat a few times before heading into the foyer. He could smell something cooking, which made his stomach growl, and he pressed his hand to it as he made his way down the short hallway and into the kitchen.

Amaranth was already at the stove, her back to him as she stirred something in a huge pot. He could feel vibrations through the soles of his shoes which meant she had her music on loud, and he reached for the light switch, giving it a flicker to let her know he'd finally made it back.

She turned, smiling at him as she tucked a strand of hair behind her ear and dropped the spoon against the counter. 'You're late. Did you get a huge rush after I left?'

Basil rolled his eyes, shaking his head as he walked to the fridge to get himself a beer. He cracked the top and took in a few long drinks before he could bring himself to answer. Mostly because he didn't know what he was going to say.

It was simple enough. He got a last-minute order for a wedding which had taken a hundred years since the woman—the mother of the bride—hadn't wanted to communicate through his notepad and pencil. She spent twenty minutes insisting he try and read her lips, no matter how many times he jotted down that he was very bad at it, and after a long day it was almost impossible.

He had been seconds away from throwing her out and having her patronize some other business when she finally relented, and they got the preliminary order, date, and arrangements settled. He took her deposit and was damn glad to see the back of her. The drive had gotten complicated when the rain started coming down in a massive downpour. Being that he relied entirely on his vision to navigate the streets safely, having that compromised through every window but the front had been only slightly terrifying.

His plan had been to hunker down a little inside the ATM vestibule until it let up a bit, but he hadn't anticipated what had come right after slipping inside. Not just the absurdly attractive man and his intense panic attack, but the feelings it had invoked in Basil who had long-since stopped having immediate feels for random hearies he met in public. No matter how huge and attractive they were.

And the guy was both of those things. He hovered nearly half a foot above Basil, his arms covered in ink so intense he could make them out in the near pitch black when the power went out. He was also sweet, and he could sign a little for his friend's deaf daughter which stirred something in him he didn't want to feel. At all.

Then the guy—Derek—had gone and shown him his art page. A page Basil had not-so-subtly saved on his browser, and he knew then he was in trouble.

The worst part about it was that if he told Amaranth about it all, she'd be fine with it, she'd encourage it, even. Because in spite of knowing what Basil had gone through with Chad, in spite of having gone through her own bullshit with men who could hear, she always looked for the best in people. She didn't necessarily want Basil to end up with a hearing guy, but she didn't want him to give up in the idea of finding love wherever it might find him.

She was an absurd romantic and always had been. He wanted to hate it, but it was one of the things he loved most about her.

'You look like you're trying to solve some complex equation,' she said after waving her hand to get his attention. 'What happened?'

He gave her the bare bones version, but when her eyes lit up like a menorah, he knew he was screwed. She latched on to his vague description of Derek and demanded more detail. 'He was fine. Freaked out,' Basil told her. 'He was okay by the end.'

'Did you get his number?' she demanded.

Basil pushed himself up from the table and snapped, 'No,' in her face before walking to the stove to peer into the pot. Chicken soup. Their mom's recipe, probably, and it made him want to cry. After the long day, the obnoxious mother of the bride, and his strange draw to the tattooed guy, he needed something to comfort him.

Ama punched him on the shoulder to get his attention, and he turned, glaring at her. 'Why didn't you get his number? That's like straight out of a rom-com.'

'I hate rom-coms,' he retorted before turning his back, a pointed gesture he knew would set her off. He felt her stomping behind him, but he ignored her in favor of getting a bowl from the top cabinet and filling it. He ate a few spoonfuls before finally turning around, and he tried not to laugh at the sight of her furious expression.

'Asshole.'

He shrugged.

'You have to stop shutting people out just because they slightly, and barely, resemble Chad. At this rate you've cut out hearing guys, blondes, guys with beards, and guys who wear shirts with collars.'

He shrugged again, eating a few more bites before putting his bowl down so he could address it properly. 'If I was sure the guy was nothing like Chad, I'd give him a chance. But I'm not ready to trust anyone. Every time I think about him, I think about that night and I just don't have it in me to take that risk.'

Ama's face fell and she took a step forward, reaching for his shoulder to squeeze. 'I'm sorry,' she signed with her free hand, then pulled away. 'I do understand, Basil, and I never want you to go through something like that again. I'm not asking you to put yourself at risk, I'm just asking you to remember that not everyone is like him.'

He appreciated that she didn't mention what shit luck he'd had dating in the Deaf Community, either. He was starting to think the whole thing wasn't other people—it was him. Someone far back in their family's history had cursed the second-born sons named Basil or something, and he was doomed to suffer the consequences. Still, being single wasn't the worst thing in the world. He hadn't dated for three months and the loneliness was starting to ease. He was a happy guy, generally, and he enjoyed being on his own.

So naturally, he didn't want to acknowledge the pressing absence he felt after Derek had left the vestibule, or how he had practiced shaping the letters of Derek's name on his lips on the drive home. Or how the moment he slid into bed, his thumb tapped his phone screen to pull up the gallery.

And if—just if—he let himself click on the 'buy now' button sitting under the gorgeous octopus sketch, well, no one would be the wiser.

CHAPTER TWO

"Oh no, no no no," Derek groaned at the shrill ringing of his phone. His one open, bleary eye peered at his phone and saw it was just past six in the morning. Which meant he'd managed a solid three hours of sleep before this nonsense. If the name on the caller ID had been anyone but Sam, he would have thrown the phone across the room and let it shatter. "What the actual, ever-loving fuck do you want right now at six in the morning?"

"Beth just called."

If there was a way to take him from dazed sleep to wide awake like he'd just downed a gallon of espresso, it was saying the phrase, Beth called. Because Beth was the social worker handling Maisy's case. And Maisy happened to be Sam's burn-out cousin's daughter who had been taken by CPS, from the hospital, and bounced around the system for nine goddamn months before they managed to locate someone in her family to take her.

Sam immediately stepped forward to take care of the infant, but he'd been initially rejected on appearance alone. Sam was a lot like the twins—incredibly large and intimidating with bulging muscles from the sheer amount the guy worked out, most of his skin covered in ink, but the real kick in the balls was that he'd been officially turned away due to his disability. The original case-worker had rejected Sam's petition to take the little girl in because she wasn't convinced he would be capable of giving a baby the care she needed while also using a wheelchair.

For Sam, he'd been paralyzed for longer than he'd been walking. At fifteen, he and his friends had gone for a joy-ride in a truck, the driver having a little too much to drink. It ended with the truck rolling down an embankment and Sam waking up days later being told he'd never walk again.

He was thirty-six now, and ran a successful company providing classes for rehabilitation centers, private fitness lessons, and his absolute favorite, Wheelchair Zumba which he taught every Saturday before starting his late afternoon shift at Irons and Works. Sam was only a part time artist, but he was a full-time family member to each of them, and when they'd heard about his rejection, the entire studio banded together to ensure Sam would get this little girl.

Maisy had been living with him for three years now, and he was finally allowed to petition for her adoption since Sam's cousin hadn't come forward to claim her. Derek had not only been one of Sam's closest confidants in the whole mess, but he'd been labeled unofficial babysitter since Maisy seemed to like him best of everyone. A badge he wore proudly—even if it did get his ass up out of bed at six in the goddamn morning.

"What do you need?" Derek asked, swinging his legs over the bed and scrubbing a hand down his face.

"Can May come stay at your place for a bit? They want to do another invasive inspection and I don't want her here while they riffle through my shit and force me to take however many steps on my walker."

Derek felt his teeth grin together, and he forced himself to take a few calming breaths. "Of course, man. I'll come pick her up so you don't have to worry about transport." Standing up, he groaned at the unexpected tension in his limbs. He always felt like this after a panic attack, but he hadn't realized how bad it would be that morning. "Shit."

"Der?" Sam asked softly. "What happened?"

"God, it's the longest story in the world," he confessed, shuffling to his bathroom to dig around for his scope and tooth brush. "I'll happily spill everything once this stupid song and dance is over."

"How about I bring lunch when I come to pick up May-Day?" he offered. The phone went muffled, and Derek could just make out the sound of Sam cooing Maisy awake, which made him grin as he stuffed his toothbrush into his mouth and began to scrub.

"Whatever you get, make it good. And fried, preferably. That one deli over on ninth with the falafel I like? That place isn't shit for you to get in and out of, right?"

"Nah, it's good. Plus, it'll give me a chance to go flirt with Abram. It's been a while," Sam said, a grin in his voice. "I'll throw some frozen waffles into May's bag so you don't have to worry about her breakfast, alright? She's…having a thing right now about cooked food."

Derek chuckled softly. "Got it. Give me fifteen and I'll be there." He hung up without saying goodbye, then wriggled into his too-tight jeans and a ratty old t-shirt that was damn-near see-through from too many washes. It felt good though, comfortable, the way he should feel in his own skin. He glanced at his reflection and sighed, dragging a heavy hand through his hair in a vague attempt to order the mess.

He slipped into his work boots, leaving them untied, then hurried down the stairs to find his car. It was a little damp from the leftover rain, but he'd managed to remember getting all four windows closed, so he called that a small victory considering what a mess he'd been by the time he got home.

It was only ten minutes to Sam's place, a little ground-floor townhouse in a neighborhood mostly filled with old, middle-class white couples who oddly enough loved the inked-up guy in the sporty wheelchair. It helped that Sam liked to take his dog out for a stroll every morning, and his obnoxiously sweet Schnauzer loved the attention from the old folk. It also helped that Sam was a freakishly good baker and tended to win the hearts of most people around him. He'd managed to amass a group of sweet little old grandmas for Maisy, so the girl was never without cheek-pinches, hard candies, and love.

Derek was always amazed that Sam hadn't been snatched up already. Sam wasn't a socially awkward, panicked mess the way he was. He was bright and gorgeous and made even the surliest strangers fall half in love. But then again, it was probably the fact that Sam had a schedule which didn't compromise itself with anyone. Work, the shop, and Maisy—not in that order.

All the same, Derek was jealous. If he had even a fraction of Sam's charm, he might have walked away with more than a vague memory of Basil's hand on his chest, and the echo of his laughter, and the ghost of that intensely floral scent in his memory bank. He would have been brave and a little reckless and would have done more than just offer a quick sign of thanks before running off like a goddamn coward.

This was why he was going to die alone, surrounded by cats who probably wouldn't want to eat him even if they were starving.

Chasing away his weird melancholy, Derek hauled himself out of the car and trudged up to the front door, tripping a little over the edge of the ramp but righting himself before he smashed into the door. It would be just his luck to break his nose right before trying to show he was a responsible caregiver and friend, and he straightened his shoulders in some pathetic attempt to look like he had his life together. Yes, I am fine, please trust me with your child.

He didn't bother knocking—none of the family did—and he stepped into the foyer. He turned the first corner to find Sam sitting on the floor, packing up Maisy's little Moana backpack as she played with her dollhouse a few feet away from him.

He glanced up when Derek entered and frowned. "Why do you look like someone just killed your fish?"

"First of all, I've only ever had a fish once in my life," Derek said as he slid down to the floor next to Sam, "and Sage murdered them when he got stoned and decided to share his Oreos. Secondly...it's been a really fucking bad twenty-four hours."

Sam's brows dipped low in a frown and he pushed his hands to the floor to adjust his position so he could face Derek a little better. "Your dad?"

Derek dragged a hand down his face. "That was part of it. But don't tell Sage, okay? That old fuck has been leaving him out of it—I mean honestly, I'm not sure he even remembers there's two of us, and I'd like to keep it that way."

Sam pursed his lips, but he didn't argue which Derek decided to take as a win. "The rest of it?"

"Oh, just your basic run of the mill bullshit. Wrenched my arm at the shop, some woman came in freaking out because she decided her tattoo was wrong six weeks after I finished it, then my dad called to tell me what a useless homo I am. Uh...and then I turned into disaster human last night after I got trapped in this ATM kiosk thing and had a claustrophobic meltdown." He didn't want to admit the whole story, but Sam knew him better than that.

"A vestibule? How the fuck did you get trapped in one?"

Derek leaned his head back against the sofa cushions, groaning. "I went in to make my deposit last night because I had a bunch of shit getting ready to clear, and I had almost all cash clients this week. Right after I got my receipt, lightning hits something nearby and the power just goes out. There's some auto-lock mechanism on the door because it fucking locked me inside and shut everything down."

At that, Sam reached for him like he couldn't help it, his hand falling on Derek's shoulder with a tight grip. "Why didn't you call one of us?"

"I left my phone in the car," Derek said with a sigh. "It was pissing rain and it was bad enough my entire everything got soaked.

And anyway, if I had any idea that shit auto-locks I would have taken it with me."

Sam didn't look entirely convinced though and moved his hand down to Derek's thigh. "Panic attack?"

Derek shrugged, glancing away, but he knew he couldn't lie to him. He was never a great liar, and Sam was kind of like the shop's human lie-detector anyway. "Yeah, bad one, but it was fine." When Sam looked skeptical, Derek waved his hand. "Seriously. There was a guy in there and he helped me breathe through it. Once I had calmed down, we sat, and he kept my head busy so I couldn't think about being stuck."

Sam smirked at him and lowered his voice so Maisy wouldn't hear. "I sure as hell hope you don't mean the head of your dick, man. Those things have cameras. With back-up generators. Last thing you need is some kinky, tatted up douche bag sex tape going viral."

Derek punched him in the arm. "My brain, fuck you very much. Communicating was a little difficult so it was like...you know when you give Pepper one of those puzzle balls to keep her from getting all worked up and bored?"

"Are you comparing yourself to my dog?" Sam asked with a huge grin.

"Oh, you know what," Derek started, but Sam squeezed his thigh again, quieting him.

"I get it. So, what was he like?"

Hot like burning, sweet, amazing, and I'm torturing myself for letting him go, he let himself think. "Uh, he was really nice and helpful. He was also deaf, so we had to type on his phone, and it kept me distracted. I showed him my gallery."

Sam's grin spread further. "Yeah, I bet you did."

"Jesus Christ," Derek whispered. "I'm leaving before this can get any more absurd." He started to push to his feet, but Sam's hand caught his wrist and dragged him back down. He frowned at his friend. "Seriously, don't you need me out of here?"

"Yes, I do," Sam told him, "but I also need to know you're okay."

Derek licked his lips, then felt pretty good about the fact that he knew he could be honest. "I'm beat down, and I only got a couple of good hours last night, but I'm way better than I was the last time I had a break-down. Seriously, the guy really helped."

"Okay," Sam replied after a beat, then let him go. He finished packing up Maisy's bag, then handed it over before reaching for his chair and using his arms to lift his lower half into it. "Come here, munchkin," Sam called to her.

Maisy immediately dropped he doll and launched herself into Sam's arms. It was in the moment, with the two of them together like that, Derek could see the intense familial resemblance between them. Maisy shared Sam's dark brown hair, and high cheekbones—though hers were still hidden under a soft layer of baby fat—and the heart-shaped mouth. For all anyone might have guessed, she was his biological daughter. And for as much as Sam loved her, she may as well have been.

"You need to be good for uncle DeDe, okay?" Sam told her, stroking a few stray waves back away from her forehead. "I'm going to pick you up when I'm done, okay?"

Maisy appeared to consider this, looking between Derek and Sam, then nodded. "Yeah. I could behave."

Sam kissed her forehead. "I know you will, sweetpea. I'll see you in a little bit."

Maisy slid off Sam's lap, then marched up to Derek and held both arms up in a demand to be picked up. Derek obliged—generally unable to say no to her which was probably why he was her favorite—and he hitched her up on his hip. "Can we go in your twuck?" she asked.

He shook his head. "Uncle Sage has the truck today, so we're going in the zoom car." He drove a Mini which she found delightful—like some sort of old Roger Rabbit-style cartoon car kids couldn't get enough of. "Is that okay?"

She thought about it, then nodded. "Okay. Can I bwing my oh-fant?"

Derek shrugged and let her slide to the floor so she could race to her room and collect the elephant she couldn't live without. He caught Sam's grin and he fought the urge to flip him off. "At least I get to give her back," he snarked.

Sam shrugged. "Hey, I'm not complaining here. If I didn't have you guys, I don't know what the fuck I'd do."

"But you do, so there's no point in letting this freak you out," Derek reminded him. "We've got this. All of us."

Sam relaxed a fraction, and even managed a smile by the time Maisy came out of her room with her arms stuffed full of dolls and animals. With a sigh, he unlocked the brake on his chair and rolled toward her. "One," he said in a stern voice.

Her bottom lip poked out in a pout sad enough that Derek almost cut in on her behalf. "But..."

Sam shook his head. "You're not going for very long, May. One doll. We talked about this."

She looked furious, and in a fit of toddler rage let them all tumble to the ground at her feet. "Fine!" She turned on her heel and started running for the front door. It was Sam's clever thinking and a lot of experience which had prompted him to have installed child-safety locks on all the doors, so neither of the men hurried to go after her.

"Want me to help tidy before I go?" Derek offered.

Sam rolled his eyes and shook his head. "Nope. It'll give me something to do before Beth gets here."

Derek shrugged, then leaned in to give him a quick one-armed hug. He could hear Maisy stomping by the door and attempting to pull it open, so he grabbed her pack and elephant and headed after her in an attempt to stave off the toddler tantrum. She didn't cry as he got her out the door and buckled into the seat, and by the time he had her zooming down the road, she'd calmed down almost completely.

For all that Derek wished he could have slept most of the day away, he was grateful for the call. Not just because it was one more step closer to Sam being able to finalize the adoption, but also because he was starting to realize that every time he stood still, he pictured Basil in his mind. He could still smell those flowers, still feel the warm weight of his hand pressing Derek's to his chest. He could hear that laughter, and he could see his deep, rich eyes staring at him once the lights went back on.

Derek hadn't felt this way in too damn long—frankly he wasn't sure he'd ever felt like this before—and it was getting to him. They'd been ships passing in the night, nothing special, nothing destined. It would be a miracle if he ever saw the guy again.

By the time he arrived at his house, Maisy was sleepy and let Derek carry her into the house and set her on the sofa with some princess show on Netflix. She declined her waffles, so he threw them into the freezer, then grabbed his softest blanket and laid it over the both of them. She curled up against his chest, a warm, comforting weight, and he started to drift off.

Derek jolted awake some time later, unsure how much time had passed. It took him a second to realize what had roused him, and he realized after a second it was his phone. Trying his best not to jostle a still-sleeping Maisy, he managed to dig the phone out of his pocket and saw Sam's number on the ID.

"Yo, everything cool?" he asked.

Sam sighed quietly into Derek's ear. "If you mean being forced to drive to fucking Denver to sit through another psych eval, then yeah. It's peachy with a hefty side of fucking keen."

Derek pinched the bridge of his nose in an attempt to clear the sleep-fog from his head. "Seriously? Again?"

"Beth's boss wasn't satisfied with the initial report, so they want me to sit through a psych eval, they want my OT records, and she thinks they're going to make me sign up for some sort of like...coping with paralysis and how to live your life class in spite of the fact that I've been like this for an eternity and have taken care of May since she was nine goddamn months old."

Derek felt a slow, simmering rage burning in his gut, but he swallowed it back. Sam had warned them all they'd need to get on board and help him jump through hoops rather than fight the system which would have been their first instinct. "I'm sorry," he said eventually. "What can I do?"

"I called Kat. She has two early appointments today, but she said she can take May off your hands before your first booking if you want to just meet her at the shop."

"I'll give her a call," Derek said, "but that sounds fine. And if she needs me to cancel," he started.

"Dude, no," Sam said in a rush. "You're not going to cancel on anyone because of this. If Kat gets booked for whatever reason, Mat said he was only doing walk-ins today so he can cover, too. We've got this, and I'm going to breeze through and get the hell home."

"Alright," Derek said. He didn't tell Sam that he would have almost welcomed an excuse to clear his schedule for the day. His head was still in a little bit of a post-panic fog and though he could work through that just fine, he could use the break. "Just drive safe and get home when you can. You know she's in good hands with us."

"The best hands," Sam told him, his voice warm. "Kiss her for me and tell her to be good. I'll call when I'm back on my way."

"Will do. Talk later." Derek ended the call, then pulled up his texts and shot off a quick one to his brother.

> Derek: Where u at?

> Sage: Work, u lazy fuck. Why?

> Derek: I have May for the afternoon, more fuckery for Sam. Wanna grab lunch?

> Sage: Hell yes, I miss the munchkin. Come in at 12. I'm helping Kat with Jazzy so we can get something.

Derek checked the clock and saw it was just gone eight, which would give him enough time to ease her awake, get her some breakfast and play time so she wouldn't be a total monster when he took her down to the shop. Easing out from under her, he settled her against the cushions, then wandered into the kitchen to start his coffee maker. By the time his pot was brewed, Maisy was shuffling into the kitchen, her bare feet padding along the tile. She scrubbed at her eyes with one small fist, her other arm raised for him to pick her up.

Derek didn't hesitate as he lifted her up, propping her against his hip as he walked to the freezer for her waffles. "You hungry, munchkin?"

She shrugged, yawning. "I want chocowat."

Biting back a laugh, he said, "How about I toast them with a little butter and syrup?"

Wrinkling her nose, she squirmed in his arms. "Noooo. I wan' it wike dis!" She made grabby hands at the open package, and before Derek could stop her, she'd seized one of the frozen discs and immediately started chewing on it. With vague horror, he let her slide down and stared at her before grabbing his phone and sending Sam a text.

> Derek: This so-called child ur raising is eating a waffle frozen.

> Sam: LOL yeah she does that. It's fine. Pick your battles, man, and this ain't one of them, trust me.

> Derek: Gross, but ok.

It was the simple fact that Sam wouldn't let Maisy do anything that might put her at risk that he let her continue eating the frozen breakfast, though he turned his attention to his coffee instead of the way she was tearing it to bits with her tiny little gremlin teeth.

When she was done, she skipped out of the room to play with her dolls, and Derek poured himself cereal just to keep his energy up. He stood in the doorway between the kitchen and the living room and stared out the window. The morning was grey, the pavement still wet from the rain before, but it looked like it would clear up. It meant the day would be humid and a little ugly as they were hurtling from spring to summer faster than he cared about, but it also meant his semester was almost over and he wasn't sad about that.

He felt a little weird being as old as he was and sitting in a classroom full of eighteen and nineteen-year-old kids. He understood, on a fundamental level, that there was nothing wrong with it. He and his brother had both been dealt a shit hand in life, and he'd just taken longer than Sage to reach a place he could be around large groups of people and balance both school work, his art, and his clients all at the same time.

It was still tough, and he still relished his freedom during summer, but he was starting to feel like he was making real progress. Even nights like last night, which even just a year ago would have made him felt like he'd gone ten steps backward, didn't weigh on him the same way. Likely it was due to Leila, his therapist, giving him coping skills that were actually working, but it was also a testament to his own strength and desire to move on with his life.

He'd always have trauma, but he didn't have to let it rule him.

"DeDe?" Maisy asked, pulling Derek out of his thoughts as she tugged on the bottom of his shirt.

He grinned down at here. "Yes, sweetpea?"

"Can we pway outside?"

He shrugged. "Why not. You wanna walk down the street to the pond and feed the ducks?"

She jumped with excitement, then tripped over her own feet in a haste to reach her shoes. "Yeah! Yeah I wanna...I wanna go!"

CHAPTER THREE

Derek convinced Maisy to leave the ducks after an hour, and only when he promised that Jasmine would be at the studio when they got there. He parked his car around the back, then carried her inside through the employee entrance and found Katherine in her private room prepping for what looked like her next client.

Her head popped up from where she was cling-wrapping her supply table and she grinned. "Hey, baby girl! You come to see me?"

"Yeah," Maisy said, wriggling out of Derek's arms. He kept a hold on her so she couldn't dart into the clean space, but Katherine quickly shed her gloves and walked out to lift the toddler into her arms, kissing her cheeks.

"Are you and DeDe gonna take Jazz and uncle Sage to lunch?"

"I want chicken nuggets," Maisy said dutifully.

Derek rolled his eyes with a grin before taking the girl back into his arms. "And maybe something green?" he added. "Is my brother here?"

Kat nodded, jutting her chin at the swinging door which led to the open floor. "He's out there getting Jasmine's bag ready. Tony's at the doctor's today so Sage is literally saving my life."

Derek frowned with worry. "Is he okay?"

"Yes," she said with a sniff. "He has an ingrown toenail and didn't fucking listen to me two weeks ago when it started getting disgusting, and now he gets to suffer through the pain of removal because he apparently knows better than his wife."

Derek backed away. "Staying the hell out of that one."

Kat laughed. "Wise. Anyway, I checked your schedule and it looks like I'm good to take the girls off your hands at two. You got someone at three, right?"

Derek nodded. "Yeah, it's just a consult, then I have some line work to get done on one of my regulars which I think will be about two hours? Then I have my shading appointment at five-thirty, and that's going to take up the rest of my afternoon. Why, you need me?"

"Nah," she said, waving him off. "Tony will probably want to come fill in once he's done. You know how he gets when someone fucks with his routine."

"He has only himself to blame," Derek said dutifully.

Kat winked at him before waving him off, and he walked through the doors, still holding Maisy's hand. A head of soft lavender hair knocking against short, black spiked locks told him Emily and her husband Marcus were working on their sketch sheet together, and he spotted Mat bent over his drawing table next to his already wrapped tool bench.

"Hey, man," Derek said to Mat, dropping a hand on his shoulder.

Mat looked up with a grin, reaching out with a hand to tickle Maisy under her chin. "Hey little one. Did you miss me?"

"No," she said plainly.

Mat's eyes widened with shock, making him looked like a kicked puppy which Derek found far too endearing. He and Mat were probably closest, as they had apprenticed together and shared a very similar style and some of their clients. Mat wasn't the typical sort Derek was used to—soft-spoken and nonconfrontational. But he'd grown on him like stubborn moss, and apart from Sam, was the person Derek trusted most with his own issues.

It helped Mat had his own. Years back, Mat's car had been crushed by a drunk driver and he'd been in a coma for six months. He'd come out of it only to find himself needing to relearn nearly everything. And not everything had come back. During his hospital stay he'd managed to get back on his feet and regain his ability to speak, but he found himself still unable to understand written words and numbers—he claimed they all looked like an alien alphabet, and no amount of therapy had been able to get him back to where he'd been. The one thing he could do, though, was draw, and it had been a huge part of his therapy in the rehab center.

He had been married at the time too, but the stress had been too much for his wife who ended up leaving just as he was being released to live on his own. He'd moved to Fairfield after his divorce—needing to be away from a bigger city, but needing the comfort of knowing he could blend into a crowd. That was where he met Tony and Kat, and the rest was history. Tony and Kat's shop was perfect for a tatted-up artist whose brain wouldn't allow him to do his own accounting or book his own appointments, and he had fit into Irons and Works almost like he'd been around from the beginning. Mat mostly kept his personal life to himself, and no one pushed him to move on, though Derek couldn't help but worry that his friend was starting to buckle under the weight of loneliness. It wasn't his place though, so he kept his worry to himself.

"She's just in a mood," he told him. He gave Maisy a nudge toward the swinging half-door which led to the lobby. "Go on and see Sage," he told her. "He has Jazzy waiting for you."

Maisy perked up and hurtled herself out of the room and to the lobby where Derek heard his brother greet the toddler with enthusiasm. When he was sure the girl was in safe hands, he turned back to Mat and smiled.

"Don't take it personally, dude."

"I'm not," Mat said, though his tone told a different story. "How are you doing? You have that look."

Derek sighed, hating how much of his heart he wore on his sleeve, but he made it a habit not to lie to his family at the shop. "I had a rough night. Got stuck in one of those little ATM rooms at the bank after the power went out and had a nasty panic attack."

Mat rose, taking Derek by one shoulder. "Shit, are you okay? Do you need me to take some of your clients tonight? I can move stuff around if you need time off."

Derek smiled at him. "Thanks, but I'm good. I wasn't alone, and the guy who got stuck in there with me kept me distracted. And anyway, watching May will help with the rest. Sam got called to fucking Denver to jump through more hoops for these fuckers, so I'll have her for most of the day."

Mat's brows dipped, his expression going dark. "Seriously?"

"Seriously," Derek said from behind a sigh. "They're making him sit through another psych eval, and he said May's case-worker—or her boss, or something—wants him to do another like life skills class to prove that he can parent with a disability."

"Those fucking fucks," Mat growled.

"Trust me, I know." Derek unclenched his fists when he felt his arm muscles begin to burn with the tension. "But I promised not to say anything. I have a feeling they're going to send a few more suits in here to make sure we're not like dealing drugs or sacrificing virgins, so we should be prepared."

Mat rolled his eyes. "I'll tell Tony when he gets in."

"Alright." Derek laughed when Jasmine's loud squeal pierced the quiet of the room. "I should head out before the princesses start a revolt against how long it's taking to get their lunch. You working late?"

"All-nighter. Sage asked me to take walk-ins for him this evening, so I'll be around."

"I'll bring you something later if you want. Just text me." Derek cupped the back of Mat's neck and squeezed before stepping away and heading for the low swinging door. He found his brother holding Jasmine by her ankle, two inches above the soft leather couch cushion, and the little girl was giggling her head off. "If Tony saw that, he'd cut your...walnuts off and give them to you in a jar."

Sage laughed as he righted the girl and smacked a kiss on her cheek. "Tony trusts me with his life. Anyway, who's hungry?" he signed the words with one hand, and both Jasmine and Maisy clapped their hands as he led the way out.

BASIL POINTEDLY IGNORED his sister as he lost himself in arrangements. Spring was their busiest time—they had Mother's Day, graduation, spring weddings, and religious celebrations which kept them working from open to close. Being able to make money like this helped his ire at living in such a quaint little town. It was modern and trendy, but had the small-town feel to it which for him meant the over-enthusiasm of locals who were doing everything in their power to pretend like they were cool with deafness. It always amused him the way that hearing people thought he would benefit in any way from their yelling, or the way they would speak without sound and exaggerate their words, or the way they just couldn't accept that he didn't read lips.

He could catch a few things, but people didn't want to accept that being Deaf from birth made it a little difficult for him to understand the concept of speech, and frankly he found English confusing and frustrating. There were just too many goddamn words that could easily be said with expression instead, and why all of the plurals and tenses and conjunctions and articles?

He never really understood his sister's desire to assimilate. They'd both been raised by Deaf parents, in the Deaf Community, but he figured it had something to do with just how social she was. She hated being left out of any conversation, hated not being included in everything. His parents had always told him not to worry about it, that she'd find her own way, and he tried not to feel betrayed when she began living her life mostly verbal and rarely taking out her hearing aids, and applying to universities on the west coast.

Frankly, if it hadn't been for the accident, for the death of their parents and their aunt and uncle, and being left the flower shop, she might have just stayed in LA and made herself a comfortable life there amongst the people she'd grown to love. He couldn't help but wonder if she resented him for it, when he'd asked her to help him get the shop back up and running.

He wouldn't have blamed her. Hell, he resented it enough himself that in the end she'd been right when she pointed out he was going to need help from someone who could communicate with most of the town. And he couldn't help but appreciate that she'd been the one to stay, because the idea of hiring some stranger to work with him made his stomach twist in ugly ways.

He just didn't trust people. He'd dropped his guard once—and only once—and it had left a big enough scar he wasn't anxious to do it again. Ama was forever giving him shit about it, for the way he shut down and just stopped trying, but she had never let humiliation stop her from moving forward.

Basil just wasn't that kind of guy.

He'd met Chad when he was at University. Chad was interning for some Senator in DC but was staying near campus because he'd found a sublet with cheaper rent, and he ended up frequenting the coffee shop where Basil was working. He was attractive, which Basil had to admit even to this day Chad had a charismatic charm about him that was hard to ignore. Up to that point, Basil had never given a hearing guy the time of day, but he watched Chad navigate the mostly-Deaf run coffee shop with ease, taking it in stride when they didn't bother to accommodate him, and watched week after week as he picked up more and more of the common signs thrown around the place.

He also watched Chad watch him—it was blatant, there was no way to miss how Chad's deep blue eyes followed him around every time he moved from the coffee bar to the ice bin to the pastry window. And the way Chad would sometimes wait until Basil was at the register before ordering. And he'd been charmed the day Chad had raised a shaky hand and looked as nervous as a newborn foal when he curled his fingers into the letters of his name.

His friends encouraged him to go for it, not deterred by the fact that Chad was one of them—the hearing people who outside of this insular community and campus, would treat him like a second-class citizen. Chad was trying, they told him, and he was hot, and he obviously liked Basil.

So, when Basil carefully signed, 'Go out with me,' mouthing the words as carefully as he could so Chad might understand, he'd been over the moon when the answer had been yes.

Then they dated. And Basil was young and stupid and thought maybe it wasn't such a big deal when Chad's signing skills plateaued at basic customer service. Or the way he kept pushing Basil to learn lip-reading better, or the way that he pushed for Basil to sign up for speech therapy.

It still made Basil feel sick to his stomach when he thought about the way he'd just signed up for the therapy, and the way he knew that deep-down it was wrong because he'd hidden it from both Amaranth and his parents.

He was losing sleep, and his grades were falling, and he was unhappy, but it didn't matter because his boyfriend was hot and wanted him, and he was a special kind of guy. He had a way of looking at Basil like he was the only person in the entire room, and it was enough to warp the mind of a twenty-year-old who had never really had much luck with dating before.

It got ugly so slowly, Basil hadn't realized it until one night he was having beer and pizza with some of the other interns Chad was working with. Basil had been working his ass off in therapy and lip reading, but he had been struggling so he'd kept it to himself. In the end, maybe it was best, because Chad felt safe in front of his friends when he started talking about Basil like Basil had no hope of understanding what was going on.

"Dude, it's fucking hilarious. He barely understands me. I have to talk like a fucking child to get him to understand that I just want a beer from the fridge. The best part though is that I can say that shit right in front of him and the only thing he'll pick up on is if I'm like, baby I love you." He angled himself more at Basil then, but it hadn't mattered.

Basil had understood it all. Just like he understood the laughter booming through the room so loud he could feel it in the palms of his hands which were resting on the arm of his chair. Part of him wished he'd done better in speech therapy just so he could use Chad's own language to tell him just what he could do to himself, but instead he went with a very universal gesture.

The beer dumped on his head was just a bonus after shoving his middle finger in Chad's face. He didn't need any formed language to tell the guy, 'Fuck you, I never want to see you again.'

For a lot of years, he wondered if the worst part wasn't the fact that he'd been sitting in a room for nearly two years as a bunch of hearing assholes had been mocking him to his face where he couldn't understand them, but the fact that Chad hadn't come after him. He'd just stayed there in that weed-saturated apartment while Basil stormed off and let himself cry—just once—before packing his shit and leaving.

He stayed on a friend's couch and checked his phone every day in some absurd hope that Chad would reach out and apologize and beg for forgiveness. Not that he'd give it, but he just wanted proof that Chad had been actually interested in him as a person, and not just some sort of social experiment to see what he could get the 'deaf retard' to do for his own amusement.

It never came. Chad never looked him up again, never returned to the coffee shop after that. Maybe he was just afraid he'd get the shit beat out of him—and he likely would have, so it was probably best. Eventually Basil moved on with his life and got a master's in computer science, and worked some bullshit menial job doing online tech support because in spite of having a higher education degree, no one wanted to hire the deaf guy.

Then his parents and his aunt and uncle died, and out of the blue he was the owner of a flower shop so similar to the one he and Amaranth had grown up in, it almost hurt. To this day, it left him a little achy inside when he stepped into the cooler and smelled that rush of floral fragrance that had once clung to his mom's hair and skirt no matter how many times she washed it. But this was better than wasting his life in front of a computer screen without any hope of doing more.

This, at least, was his. It was his hard work and toil, and he didn't have to deal with the Chads of the world because Amaranth had agreed to be his buffer. It felt a little pathetic to rely on his big sister for it, but in the end, it was worth it.

It would have all been fine, too, if Derek hadn't waltzed into his life and forced him to feel things he hadn't ever wanted to feel again. He woke up that morning feeling a mixture of loss and regret. Loss, because in spite of it being a small town, he'd never actually seen Derek around before and doubted he would again, and regret because he'd put himself out there in a way he hadn't meant to.

He'd purchased the drawing on a whim, unable to erase the soft, far-away look in Derek's eyes when he'd opened the page to show him something important to him. It was absurd, the strange, bubbly feeling in his gut when he thought about owning something that was part of Derek—something that had been ripped out of him and put onto paper—but it was there all the same.

He nearly cancelled the order when he checked his email, but he realized he'd been using Ama's PayPal which meant in all likelihood, Derek wouldn't recognize him anyway. The delivery address was to the shop and he didn't think he'd given Derek his last name. So, he could keep this piece of the man he couldn't stop thinking about without taking any real risks.

It was ideal, really.

And he could live with it.

His stomach rumbled near eleven, so he poked his head around the corner and saw Ama holding the phone to her ear, writing something down on paper she was reading from the caption screen. He waited until she was done, then walked out into the blissfully empty show room.

'Finished?' she asked when he'd caught her attention.

He shook his head. 'Going to stop for lunch. Do you want anything?'

She considered it a minute, then waved her hands in front of her. 'Whatever. You know what I like. But get me a coffee on your way back. I need a boost.'

Basil sighed, peering over the top of the counter to the order sheet and saw three new ones. 'We're going to be overbooked,' he reminded her. 'I'm not pulling anymore midnight shifts.'

She fixed him with a flat look, and he knew what it meant. The busy season carried them through the slow one, kept them in the black, made sure that his aunt and uncle's hard work didn't go to waste. The sad part was he hadn't known them well. Sharon was his mother's only sibling—she'd been studying botany along with her sister and Basil's dad at University. Michael had been invited in as a guest speaker—a hearing man who was fluent in both British and American sign language and had just finished his Ph.D. in Plant Genetics and had been traveling around the world to share his recent findings. Somehow it ended with Sharon leaving halfway through her senior year to settle in Fairfield with Michael. It had put a rift between Sharon and Basil's mother for years, and it wasn't until he and Amaranth were well into adulthood that the two of them had become close again.

It had startled him to know Sharon had considered him and his sister worthy of taking on her store's legacy—and not just because they were the only family left, but because in the will she said she had wanted to be able to give them more, but it was all she'd had to pass on.

Basil took his parents' own research and stored it in the attic of the home he and Amaranth took over, storing away most of Sharon and Michael's things as a way of trying to make it their own. Still, he couldn't help feeling like he was living with ghosts. Ghosts of his own past, ghosts from those he had loved and had left him, ghosts of his lost bravery and willingness to live life. But he still wanted this to work, still felt obligated to keep Sharon and Michael's dream alive.

So, he gave in to Amaranth's annoyed face and headed out the door so he could fuel up before another long night.

Two years before, when Amaranth and Basil showed up to open the doors to Wallflowers after a four-month mourning period, the community had been a mixture of relieved and confused. And it was a testament to how well Sharon had blended in that they didn't seem overly concerned the shop was run by a Deaf man who refused to even try their way of communication, and a murder-faced woman with a strong deaf accent and a penchant for talking longer than people were willing to listen. He supposed it was a family trait—he had a feeling Sharon could be all of those things rolled into one person, and every so often he felt a pang of regret that he'd never really gotten the chance to know her. If she was anything like his mother, he would have loved her so, so dearly.

Shaking himself out of that melancholy, he patted his pocket to make sure he had his phone, then headed straight for the sandwich shop he liked which was tucked away inside a little outdoor mall. Even just two years ago, the place had been quaint and small—a clothing boutique, a wine bar, a sushi restaurant, and a dry cleaners. The sandwich shop had come next, then a Korean barbeque, all settled by a little tattoo place tucked in the far corner which had been there possibly forever.

It was only when Basil realized that there was only one tattoo shop in Fairfield that he started to feel a little panicked. Because where else would Derek work, if he was a tattoo artist? Possibly Denver—it was only a half hour drive up the twenty-five, or forty-five minutes if you wanted something scenic, and he could see a guy like Derek flourishing in a big city. But with his luck, he'd only ever been a few degrees of separation from the one person who made him feel in so damn long.

Swallowing back his panic, he stepped onto the carefully molded brick pathway and started toward the shop. His steps stuttered though, when he saw the tattoo shop doors swing open, and two identical men walked out. Two identical men that Basil recognized, because he'd never forget that face. He felt his heart thud in his chest, and confusion took over for only as long as it took him to remember Derek typing about his twin brother.

Identical, and he was not kidding about it, either. The one who was not Derek, because Basil didn't need any sort of specific mark to tell who the man was that consumed his thoughts, had shorter hair with a sharper undercut, and he wore far too much gel to slick it back. They were both dressed casually, t-shirts and tight jeans with boots. Not-Derek had a tattoo on the side of his neck, though he was turned slightly so Basil couldn't make out exactly what it was, but it suited him.

The most shocking thing, however, was the fact that the twins weren't alone. They were accompanied by two children, a toddler walking between them, and a small baby on Not-Derek's hip. As he ducked beside a large tree barrel and tried to stay out of sight, Basil felt his heart stutter at the idea that Derek had a spouse and kids. Not that it would have mattered but...

But it didn't sit well. His gut twisted and his previous appetite dwindled to nothing. He backed up further into the lush green that lined the sidewalk, peering through a break in the tree branches. The brothers were talking fast to each other as they breezed past him, and for a moment he wished desperately to know what they were saying. Had Derek remembered him at all? Was it a blur? Had Basil made any kind of impression on him when the night was over?

He thought he might have. The way Derek had looked at him right when the lights went on, the way his expression broke a little, and the way his eyes didn't move from Basil's face. Basil took that opportunity, in that short moment before Derek left, to study every inch of him. The color art on his arms, the slight dip downward of his large nose, the way his wet hair seemed to want to form into little curls in spite of the way he kept brushing it back.

But maybe he was just delusional. Maybe he was developing feelings for a man who would never want him back, simply because he was protecting himself.

He wanted to believe it, truly. But he didn't think his mind liked him all that much.

It turned out, the Universe hated him, or at the very least found it amusing to see him struggle. He got his sandwiches from the sweet college kids at the shop who never really thought twice about him using his phone to ask for what he wanted, and there hadn't been a line at the little parking lot coffee kiosk for Ama's drink. There was no sign of Derek or his brother when he was done, and he was ready to call it a win.

Then, as he turned the corner and Wallflowers came into view, his shoes came to a skidding halt on the pavement. He panicked for a split second, worried he'd made enough noise to be noticed even this far off since he never really quite understood how far sound could travel. But the two familiar men and the two small children who were busy talking to Amaranth didn't turn around and look behind them.

It gave Basil the opportunity to duck down the alleyway of the Italian place and watch surreptitiously from behind the exposed brick. He could make out Derek's profile, the easy way he was smiling at Amaranth and the way he spoke with wide gestures which told Basil he'd probably be a natural signer if he ever tried to pick it up.

The brother, Not-Derek, had the baby in the crook of one arm and Basil noticed with some surprise, both twins were using a few rudimentary signs whenever they could. It was when Not-Derek turned that Basil caught the flash of sunlight off small hearing aids tucked behind the baby's ear, and he remembered Derek telling him that his boss' daughter was hard of hearing.

It had to be her, though it didn't explain the toddler. She had no passing resemblance to the twins at all, though that didn't rule out relation. Mostly, Basil wanted to focus on anything but the sweet way Derek held the little girl's hand, or the way he knelt down to her level to encourage her to take the flower Amaranth handed to her. Derek encouraged her to use the sign for thank you, and then almost absently copied, 'You're welcome,' that Ama signed back.

Basil's heart was thudding in his chest and he pressed himself to the wall as Derek and his brother eventually took the kids and moved along. He didn't dare move until they turned a corner, and until his sister went back inside. Even then, his steps were at a near-run, and he didn't breathe easy until he was safely back inside the shop.

'Should I pretend like I didn't see you throw yourself into the alley?' Ama asked as she reached for the paper sandwich bag.

Basil waited until he had her attention to reply. 'Yes, please.'

She threw her head back in a laugh, and he knew if he'd had a hand to the center of her back, he'd be able to feel how loud and deep the sound was. 'Nice try. Did you know those guys?'

The problem was, Basil had always been a shit liar. Being a native signer meant that a poker-face didn't come naturally. His language all-but demanded he give true, intense, honest expression to every word exchanged, and it took real skill to be able to hide that. A skill he never possessed.

So when Ama's eyes went wide with understanding, he wasn't surprised. Annoyed, maybe, and even a little irritated, but not surprised. 'That was the guy. From the ATM.'

Basil rolled his eyes to the ceiling, praying for the patience to deal with his sister's meddling before he finally looked back at her. 'Don't.'

'What? You think I'm going to chase him down and bring him back here?' she asked, a coy smile playing on her lips.

His hands curled, then uncurled before he replied. 'I wouldn't put it past you, but I'm going to ask you nicely, please don't. It's bad enough he works so close.'

'He said he and his brother work at the shop near the coffee cart,' she told him.

'Yeah,' Basil said, realizing there was no point in hiding it now. 'I saw them coming out of the shop. Irons and Works,' he spelled the name, but he was pretty sure she'd seen it before. 'I hid then, too.'

'Of course you did.' She took a long drink from her coffee, her eyes fluttering closed with happiness before she set it back down on the counter. 'I told them to come back any time, that we'd be happy to do an arrangement or two for the front of the shop. They said they'd talk to their boss about it, but I'm pretty sure they were just trying to be nice.'

He let out a breath and felt something shift in him, though right then he didn't know if it was relief or disappointment. 'Just leave me out of it.'

Ama studied him for a long moment, then came around the counter, though she left plenty of space between them as she leaned her hip against the polished wood. 'I'm not going to meddle. Forcing you to date before you're ready isn't going to do anyone any good. But you might want to consider that you've been ready for a while and you're just used to shutting people out.'

Basil dragged a hand down his face, forcing himself to consider her words, mostly because they were probably true. At least, they had some measure of truth to them. 'You could be right, but I don't want to date a guy who doesn't speak my language. And baby signs don't count,' he clarified before she could come to Derek's defense.

'What if he learns?' she pointed out.

'Like I haven't been through that before,' he reminded her, though he knew at this point bringing up Chad might have been the tiniest bit of a cop-out. 'I respect that you're fine dating in either community, but I'm just...not.'

She looked a little sad then, but her eyes showed an understanding and she gave a nod. 'Okay. So, what about we check out a couple Deaf events in Denver, then? You know they'll have some shit—single's night or something equally lame. Bet you could snag a date there. At least let me help you try to get out there again.'

Basil wanted to argue, wanted to point out that she wasn't dating anyone and didn't seem to be in a hurry to sort her own romantic life the same way she was with his. Except the truth was, she could have easily been dating someone now and he wouldn't have known. He loved her, but he never wanted her private life to be his business.

'Please,' she begged.

He finally threw up his hands in surrender, then grabbed his sandwich without answering her, but he knew she'd accepted that as a defeat. He didn't know what the hell was in store for him next, but he supposed it was time to try getting his feet wet again.

CHAPTER FOUR

Something about the flower shop lingered, even long after they'd returned to the studio and Derek had passed May over to Katherine for the rest of the afternoon. He was in his station prepping for his first appointment, but his mind kept drifting over to the open door, to the woman smiling at the kids and signing, and the smell drifting on the breeze that had been so much like Basil.

It wasn't exactly a far stretch to assume Basil either worked there or was related to the woman who had introduced herself as Ama. She spoke to them and understood without an issue, but she wore hearing aids and her accent gave her away as deaf. In a town this small, he let himself assume. It also didn't hurt that she looked like Basil in the way that siblings often resembled each other. The same nose, same dark curls, though hers fell long down her back. Mostly though, it was her eyes, intense and piercing like she could see everything.

He had that same feeling when the lights had gone up and he could see Basil for the first time. Right before he walked out. In fact, it had taken nearly every ounce of his self-control not to ask her if she knew the guy. The last thing Derek wanted to do was stalk some stranger who hadn't offered to keep in touch. He may have been somewhat infatuated, but he wasn't a creep.

"Dude," a voice to his right said, and Derek's head whipped over to see James smirking at him, toying with his septum piercing with the tip of his finger. "You've been wiping that same spot for like ten minutes. Did someone fuck your actual brains out last night?"

Derek felt the back of his neck flush. "No. Not that I'd tell you if I did get lucky. I'm just tired. Rough night last night."

James' face fell a little and he leaned forward in his chair. "Want to talk about it?"

The truth was, no, he didn't. He was sick to death of having to explain every low mood—even when there was a reason for it. He did appreciate that these guys were his family and would do anything for him, but he also wanted to be treated like a person and not some fragile mess prone to falling apart any time one little thing went wrong.

He'd had PTSD for most of his formative years, and well into adulthood. He'd survived being homeless, and every single day since then. He could survive a little panic attack and the emotional hangover that came with it the next day.

"I'm good," he finally said, moving on to wrap his table with the big roll of cling wrap he'd stolen from Mat's station. "Are you on tonight?"

"I'm doing the shading on my mermaid at nine tonight, and Mat's going to finish carving my left leg up during his downtime," he said, leaning back in his chair and stretching his legs in front of him. Carving him up was essentially Mat's pet-project. James was a double-amputee, both legs just below the knee, and more often than not he wore prosthetics that were just a titanium rod which ended with his shoe, but Mat had gotten a wild-hair to do some steampunk design in James' cover which was made out of some type of flesh-colored foam Mat found intensely satisfying to carve up. His left leg was nearly done, and the design on the right was already being sketched out to match.

"Are you going to help out with walk-ins?" Derek asked as he started fishing through his bottles, mentally chiding himself for how damn disorganized his drawer was.

James snorted. "Dude, it's a Wednesday. We'll get maybe—maybe—some stoned sorority chicks who looked us up on yelp and decided to drive out. I'm not dealing with that nonsense. If I have to tattoo one more infinity symbol on the side of someone's finger…"

Derek grinned, shaking his head even as he all-but buried his face in his ink drawer. "Come on man, it doesn't hurt to take one or two. Coffee cash, you know?"

"I want steak and lobster dinner cash, asshole. Infinity symbols don't pay my rent."

Which, true. They didn't. They were the sixty buck shop minimum walk-ins, but then again, no one in the shop made less than one-fifty an hour for their standard work apart from the two apprenticing, so it's not like any of them had room to complain. Derek hadn't stressed about bill paying in years, even when shit like government shutdowns threatened to choke all their business to death. But he also understood how annoying it was to have to swirl a lemniscate on a nineteen-year-old who was terrified of needles and trying to find some deeper meaning in a symbol that didn't have any significance outside of coding these days.

Derek did his best not to judge people's decisions though. That wasn't his job, even if he did occasionally pull a face when some obnoxious, popped-collar asshole strolled in and asked for a camel on his big toe. His job was to just provide the ink to the best of his abilities—which was worth his one-seventy an hour—and to pocket his cash and move on with his life. He liked his regulars, and he liked his family there, and there wasn't too much to complain about.

"Yo," came a voice from the front. Mat and Sage walked in holding a couple of pizza boxes and Derek wanted to groan because Sage always got fucking anchovies which would make everything smell like fish ass for half the night. "Do you want to eat before your client gets in?" Sage asked Derek.

"Nah." Derek glanced at the clock and saw his client would be walking in within the next ten minutes. "I don't want to get all nasty before I get working. Besides your nasty fish juice probably leaked on everything."

"Ha," Sage said, leaning down to grin in his face, "joke's on you, I got artichoke hearts and feta this time."

Not that it sounded any better, but at least it might smell less. "I'm still good. I'll probably order Thai or something later. Last night kind of killed all sense of appetite." That was nothing new, and no one really reacted apart from a couple of careful looks which he purposefully ignored.

"Okay, well I'm going to eat and get a few of my drawings done for next week. Let me know if anyone comes in." Sage gave his brother a long look before taking the pizzas back into their makeshift break room.

Derek sagged back in his chair and rubbed both hands over his face. When he looked up again, James and Mat were giving him a tentative stare. "Can you please not?"

"You know we just worry," Mat replied quietly.

Derek waved him off. "I know, but that's not necessary. It's...it's not even the stupid panic attack, okay? I got over that sometime around midnight."

James frowned. "So what has your panties all twisted?" He grunted when Mat dragged his leg over a little harder than normal—punishment for the panties comment which Derek appreciated. They didn't do gender-role shaming there. Ever.

"I met a guy," he finally said, knowing that the moment Sam got back, he'd blab anyway so he might as well head it off. "He was stuck in the little ATM kiosk thing with me and helped me through it. And I'm a fucking moron and I can't stop thinking about him."

The two idiots across from him lit up like a house on fire, and before he could head them off, Mat looked like he was ready to start planning a wedding. "Are you going to see him again? What was his name? Did you have some gross-ass romantic kiss in the rain after you were rescued?"

Derek fought off the urge to rip open his package of needles and stab Mat in the neck with the tight-liner he was about to prep. "First of all, fuck you, this isn't a Disney rom-com. Second of all, we didn't exchange numbers or anything. He just helped me out and then we moved on with our lives."

"Well," James said with a small grin, "one of you did."

Mat smacked him at the same time as Derek flipped him off and said, "It was a rough night and I'm not used to strangers being nice for no reason, okay? I'll get over it."

The pair of them looked like they didn't want him to get over it, and frankly if he thought he had a chance with Basil, he wouldn't want to get over it either. But it was what it was. He set the needle package down just as his phone buzzed, and he saw it was an email from his online shop alerting him that a sale had been officially processed.

It had been a while since he'd sold anything from his gallery, so he quickly opened the page and his heart leapt into his throat when he realized what it was. He couldn't stop himself from glancing up at the wall in front of him, where the octopus sketch had been hanging for nearly two years. He hadn't ever intended to keep it, of course. He didn't create to keep, he created to share with the world, but something in him felt a little bereft at the thought of packing it up and shipping it off.

"Dude, are you about to cry?" Mat asked, interrupting Derek's thought spiral. His tone wasn't mocking, it was concerned, and it shook Derek right out of his head.

"No," he said quickly. "No, someone just bought..." He nodded his head at the octopus and James' eyes went wide.

"Someone bought Kevin?"

Derek sighed. "His name isn't Kevin, dude."

"It is," James argued. "I named him, and it's not like you ever picked anything else. Plus, it suits him. Shit, dude, if I knew you were really going to sell him, I'd have bought it."

That made Derek's stomach twist a little, and he wasn't sure if that was a good or a bad thing. He hated selling to his friends, mostly because they felt like pity buys, even if he knew his work was good. He wanted strangers to own those pieces of him, wanted to know that bits of his soul were scattered around the country—maybe the world.

"Where's it going?" Mat asked as he pulled out his scalpel to get to work on James' leg.

With a frown, Derek bent over his phone and scrolled to the shipping address. "Wallflowers Florist, C/O Amaranth Shevach," he said. "That's here."

"That's the chick who gave May a rose," Sage said, coming up from behind Derek. "She bought your painting?"

No, Derek thought, because it wasn't her. It was Basil. Basil had saved the gallery on his phone and had bought the painting because Derek had lamented that no one wanted it in spite of it being his favorite. And it probably was a pity buy, but more than that, it meant Basil had thought about him. Basil was asking to keep a piece of him, even if he didn't want anything more.

He looked back at the octopus and let out a tiny sigh. "Someone at their shop bought the painting," he finally corrected.

Sage raised a brow. "Don't you have like...an entire series of floral work? Why would they buy a fucking octopus, dude?"

Derek bristled, though he knew his brother wasn't trying to be cruel. "I don't know, and I can't say I'm supposed to give a shit. People buy something, I send it. Simple as that."

"Testy," Sage complained as he flopped down into an empty chair on the edge of Derek's stall. He moved to kick one foot up on the bench, but Derek knocked him away.

"My client's about to walk in and I'm not going to goddamn start this whole thing over," he snapped.

Sage raised his hands in defense. "My bad."

Rolling his eyes, Derek spun away from his brother, then startled a little when his phone rang. He glanced at the screen and saw Sam's name, quickly answering. "Hey, man. How'd it go?"

"Do you want to come over tonight and chill? Alice is out of town for the next few days and being in the car this long fucked me up. I'm spasming and I need to get in the bath. I can bribe you with beer and take-out."

Derek smiled to himself as he reached for the stencil he'd drawn out and set it on the table. "You don't need to bribe me, also I've eaten out both meals so why don't I cook?"

"You're a god amongst men, you know that?" Sam said with a breath of relief. "May's going to stay over with Kat tonight so I can get my back to calm down, so it's just the two of us."

"I'll stop over at Wild's and get something to cook up," Derek told him. "What time will you be back?"

"God only knows. I'm on a half hour break, then I have another hour or two. Then she wants me to meet with the rehab specialist regarding the class they're making me take." He sounded exhausted and run down, and it made Derek want to get in his car and haul Sam's ass far away from this mess. "I'm guessing after seven."

Derek glanced up at the clock. "I can be there around then. My last appointment's at four, but it's probably only a two-hour job. Sage and Mat can handle any of the walk ins. And James is here letting Mat carve on his leg, so we're staffed."

"Thanks, man," Sam said, then yawned loudly. "Fuck me. Okay. I gotta hit the head before I get back into this shit, so I'll see you when I get home."

"You got it." Derek hung up, but before he could explain anything, the little bell on the front door sounded and his client walked in. Derek wanted nothing more than to talk about Sam's shit, and to contemplate why Basil had bought the painting, but instead he put on his best customer service face and cracked his knuckles, ready to get started.

. . .

It was half six when he finally got his station sanitized and his shit put away. He wrote himself a note to stock his needles and to organize his ink, then he stared at the octopus painting a few minutes more.

"You really gonna throw that in the mail?" Mat asked, leaning back in his chair with his hands behind his head.

The shop was dead, and the only booking they had was the nine o'clock, and there hadn't been a single walk-in all evening. James had gotten a call with a request for an emergency car repair job which he immediately snatched up, and Wyatt had come in to work on some of his pig skin since he had his first booking that weekend and he was feeling all the nerves.

Derek shrugged. "I mean, I kind of have to, don't I? Wouldn't it be weird if I walked it down to the flower shop?"

Mat gave him a careful look. "Why would that be weird? Unless they paid a shitload for shipping."

Derek bit his bottom lip, considering his options. Refunding the eight bucks he charged for shipping wasn't a big deal. But he didn't know if Basil would appreciate him just showing up. It seemed presumptuous and a little creepy, if he was being honest. "I don't know."

"I bet they'd be happier if you walked it over," Mat said thoughtfully. "I mean, no risk of it getting all fucked up in the mail. They're like two blocks away, dude."

It was a good point, but not one Derek wanted to explore right then. "I got a couple days, I'll figure it out. Anyway, I'm off to Sam's for the night, so if you guys get slammed, just call me."

Mat offered him a mock-salute, then turned back to his drawing table and Derek took the opportunity to slip out without being dragged into further conversation. As he headed to his car, he heard footsteps and turned to see his brother jogging after him.

"Hey," Sage said, trying to catch his breath, "I wanted to grab you before you head out."

Derek stopped, raising a brow. "What's up?"

"This weekend," Sage said, as though Derek really did have that fake-ass twin ESP people always assumed they did. "I…it's four years now and I just…uh. Could use the company."

Derek felt his entire body sag with remorse because how the hell could he have forgotten that this weekend was the anniversary of Sage's fiancé's death? Granted, it had been getting easier, enough that no one really thought about Ted on the day-to-day, but Derek had been more attuned to the loss since it was Sage suffering, and he didn't want to let himself get complacent.

"I have no plans," Derek said. "Come home with me Friday after we close up."

Sage looked somewhat relieved. "Thanks. I kind of have a proposition for you anyway, but I want to talk after you've been able to unwind."

Derek bristled a little at that. Frankly, Sage's ideas were kind of the worst, especially when his emotions were high. But right now, this weekend? He wasn't going to turn down anything. "Yeah, of course."

Sage gave him a cautious smile, and maybe once upon a time, this would have been a moment they hugged, but neither of them had really sought comfort with each other like that in years. Not since they lay huddled together in a rundown, squatter's paradise with no heat and a single sleeping bag as they fought to get by night by night.

Too long since then had passed, but there were moments Derek couldn't help but miss being able to take that small comfort when he needed it. For now, though, the smile his brother offered was enough, and they quickly parted ways.

The drive to Wild's was short, and though Derek hated browsing aisles that smelled overwhelmingly of ground wheat and patchouli, he was able to load up and check out in only a handful of minutes. He loaded the bags into the back of his car, then parked next to Sam's truck which was still making the faint clicking noise as the engine cooled from the long drive.

He slung the bags over his arm, using his free hand to grab the case of beer and lock up the truck, then let himself in the front door and went straight for the kitchen. Most of the lights were still off which probably meant Sam was in his bedroom, so Derek threw everything together in the dutch oven, covered it with a little water, the lid, then wandered off.

He found his friend on the floor with his legs propped up on his exercise ball. Derek could see the vicious tremors in his muscles, and the way Sam's face was contorted in pain. "How bad?"

"Maybe like a six," Sam told him, which in Sam-ese meant he was probably at an eleven. "I just got in and I figured I'd let my legs work themselves out a little before I try to balance in the tub.

"Want me to start it?" Derek asked.

Sam waved his hand toward the bathroom. "There's some of that citrus salt under the cupboard, the one Tony always gives me shit about smelling like the farmer's market. Throw a couple cups in there for me."

Derek was old hat at this. Sam and Tony had grown up together, had been like brothers, but for whatever reason, Derek was better at all this shit. Maybe it was the fact that he'd seen things most people hadn't which left him unbothered by all that Sam required to get by, but there had never been any awkwardness about it. Sam had a carer who usually helped out, but one winter a handful of years back, her sister had gone into early labor and she'd flown across the country for two weeks to help out.

Sam hated the replacement the home-health company had sent over, and after watching his spiraling frustration, Derek had offered to help. Sam was hesitant about letting it happen at first. He tended to keep the more unflattering parts of paralysis to himself—like the bladder control issues, and the spasms, and the times when his entire lower half just wouldn't respond and he needed help with even the simplest transitions from chair to sofa, or chair to bed. Derek had simply put his mind to the task, and after a while, Sam had stopped hesitating to ask.

"Did May behave for you today?" Sam's voice came from the doorway, and Derek turned to see the guy had stripped down and was bare-ass naked in his chair.

"She was perfect, as usual," Derek told him as he arranged the bath seat at the side of the tub, and a towel resting on the edge. "Sage was watching Jaz, so we took them to lunch and fucked around at the duck pond for a while. She also got a flower from that little shop near the bookstore. The owner was outside making some arrangements and of course the girls charmed her."

Sam chuckled as he wheeled to the edge of the tub and set his brake. Derek tested the water, then carefully helped Sam to shift from the chair, to the edge of the tub, and then into the water. He let out a small groan as he laid back, and Derek slid to the floor, grateful to have a moment of peace, even if it was on cold bathroom tiles.

"Kat took her pretty early though, so I'm not sure if she stayed in a good mood. You know how much she hates it when you're away," he finished.

Sam let out a tiny sigh. "I know. She's getting better with the whole attachment thing, but her therapist was talking about this pre-memory trauma she's got goin' on from the foster home bullshit and she said it could last for most of her life."

"God," Derek said. He'd never known Sam's cousin—the fifteen-year-old who'd gotten in way over her head with a too-old boyfriend. The guy was in jail now for assault and robbery, and the girl had sunk so deep into heroine Sam confessed he wasn't sure she was even alive anymore. "Well I've noticed a difference the past few months at least, so that means something, right?"

"It does," Sam said with a smile. He pushed himself up to sit, holding the side of the tub for balance, and used his other hand to massage his still-trembling legs. "How are you feeling?"

"Fucking sick of being asked that," Derek confessed. "Apparently it was all over my goddamn face today and everyone decided to try to play mom with me."

Sam shook his head. "It's out of love, dearie."

"Fuck you," Derek said cheerfully. "I uh...I sold Kevin." He hated himself for using James' stupid name for the octopus, but it meant Sam knew exactly what he was talking about.

"Seriously?"

Derek sighed internally. "Seriously. I think the guy from the bank thing last night bought it."

Sam sat up straighter, almost slipping before he caught himself. "You're shitting me. Dude, that's like..."

"If you say rom-com, I will punch you. I don't care if you're naked and in the bath," Derek warned him without any real heat. "I think he might work in that flower shop we passed by today. The owner had hearing aids in, and she knew sign language, and she...she looked like him. A lot like him."

Sam was grinning and Derek hated himself for confessing it all, though he couldn't help but admit having the weight off felt good. "Did you go in?"

"Nah. The girls were getting restless and we didn't have a lot of time to screw around. But I was...the thing is...Mat pointed out that I might want to hand-deliver it since throwing it in the mail would be such a waste. It probably won't mean anything but...yeah."

Sam's grin softened a little, and he leaned over the edge of the tub, putting his hand on Derek's shoulder. "Maybe it won't mean anything at all, and maybe it will. But it can't hurt to try, can it?"

Derek worried his bottom lip between his teeth. "I guess not. I'm just such a mess still, I don't know someone like him would want to put up with all this shit. It's a lot."

"It is," Sam told him bluntly, "and it might be a little exhausting, but if he feels the same way about you, he'll think it's worth it."

Derek shrugged. "I don't even speak his language."

"Well clearly there's not an easy fix for that," Sam snarked at him. "I mean, it's not like Kat and Tony haven't been up our asses about starting ASL or anything."

Derek flushed, knowing he was right, and knowing he ought to do it for Jasmine no matter what happened between him and Basil. "Yeah. I...I guess."

"I get being afraid," Sam told him. "You can't guarantee happiness forever."

Derek was half-sure Sam was talking about Ted now, and there was a moment of slightly awkward silence between them. "I know that. And I feel like I owe it to myself to at least try. I think maybe I'll adhere the sketch to a canvas and throw some varnish on it, then I can walk it over."

"Maybe write him a love note and tuck it in the back so he finds it years later when you two are married with five kids," Sam said, waggling his brows.

Derek stood up. "That's it. I'm leaving you to drown."

CHAPTER FIVE

Basil jumped, startled when a hand fell down on the desk in front of him. Under Ama's flat palm was a bright orange post-it with sharpie scribbled on the front. A name—Jay—and a number. He stared at it for a minute, then looked up at his sister's smirk.

'What is this?'

'A phone number.'

Rolling his eyes, he pushed his chair back away from the desk. 'Thank you, I had no idea. Seriously, what is this?'

'You'll hate all the Deaf events they have going on in Denver this month. It's all stuff for young kids—bowling, coffee house meet-ups, I think there's like a D and D game in a card shop?'

Basil pulled a face. 'Sounds like my nightmare.'

'I know,' Ama told him with a grin. 'But one of the event coordinators and I were emailing, and I asked him if he had any LGBT events planned? Something for actual gay grown-ups. He said they tried to do that a few months ago but the turn-out was really small. Then he said maybe the two of you could get together and get a drink. And talk. He thought you were hot.'

Basil blinked at her. 'When did he see me?'

'My profile picture is us on the trip to San Francisco,' she reminded him, though he was fairly sure she was lying and had probably let the guy Facebook stalk him. Which, whatever, considering he hadn't used it in two and a half years. 'But I think you'd like him. He has an MBA, he works for a tech company, he's kind of boring, doesn't have any feelings about sports or boats,' she signed that with a grin only because she knew how much Chad loved both, 'and he has Deaf parents.'

Basil's eyes narrowed. 'But is he...'

'No,' she said, her fingers interrupting his own. 'He's CODA, though, and he's cute and kind of uptight. Just the way you like them.'

Licking his lips, he stared down at the paper again, then looked back at her. 'I don't think this is a good idea.'

'One drink,' she begged, then leaned over the desk and touched his chin to make sure she had his attention. 'Please, just one drink. I promise if you hate everything about him, I'll never bother you again. I'm just tired of you not letting yourself get out there just because you're afraid. Not everyone is cruel. Most hearing people would never, ever do what Chad did.'

'Enough of them do,' he reminded her. He wasn't the only person who had dealt with hearing ignorance, but the fact that she so readily chose to ignore it, or to overlook it, got under his skin.

Her cheeks pinked and she shook her head. 'Please.'

After a long moment, he finally relented. The trouble was, he had been happy. Or at the very least, he'd been content. Every single day up to the moment he walked into that fucking vestibule, he'd been satisfied with his single life. Then, in the sweep of rolling thunder, it all changed. Now his entire being was consumed with wanting someone he couldn't have because Derek was a bad idea all around.

But this guy—Jay—this CODA tech guy who ran Deaf events, might have been the answer he was looking for. Because he'd take just about anything to get his mind off the one man he wouldn't let himself consider.

The problem with Denver was the same problem Basil discovered in Chicago, and in DC—you couldn't escape the pretension of people's desire to impress. No matter how down to earth or relaxed the community was, there was always something like this—a upstairs wine loft which served obscure labels and cheese boards covered in meats he didn't like, and fruits dried beyond recognition. The fact that he could sit and converse with the relatively attractive man in his own language without having to worry about going slow or dumbing down his slang should have been a relief.

Instead, Basil found himself staring at the guy's exposed forearms, bared from rolled up shirt sleeves, and thinking about how all that pale flesh was just…boring. Basil hadn't ever been a tattoo guy before—he'd never really thought about it, hadn't paid much attention to people who sported them except to find himself occasionally distracted when he was trying to pay attention to their words, but now…

'Are you okay?'

Jay's waved hand in his line of sight jolted him out of his thoughts, and he flushed a little, giving him an apologetic smile. 'Sorry. It's been a really long week,' he told him. He forced himself to really look at the guy one more time, to search for a spark which wasn't there, but maybe it could be if he tried hard enough. Ama hadn't been wrong, the guy was good looking and intelligent. He was taller than Basil by an inch or so, thin but lithe enough he probably ran in the mornings, and his suit fit him like a second skin. His light brown hair sat styled in a prim part just to the side, and when he smiled, Basil saw neat and pearly white teeth.

Nothing about him was offensive, but on the flip side, nothing about him was intriguing. He'd spent the first half of the date talking about his work at the tech company and how much good they were doing for the Deaf community as far as being offered access to relay devices, captioned phones, and devices to make the trips to the cinema easier. And Basil should have been thrilled by it all. Hell, he'd spent his first half of Freshman year attending every single protest he could make it to, demanding better accommodations and recognition for the Deaf. But something about Jay was exhausting, and even a little boring. Basil felt a little guilty for judging—it's not like he'd gone into his own chosen career field, but the guy was as exciting as biting into a dry saltine.

'How do you like the place?' Jay asked him.

Basil raised his brows in surprise, then shrugged. 'I don't usually eat at places like this, but Fairfield doesn't really have a lot to offer.'

'Small town life,' Jay signed, and there was something like disdain on his face which made Basil bristle. 'I've been there a few times, no Deaf community at all.'

Basil wanted to argue that Fairfield didn't have much of a community period. The people who lived there were either retired or owned businesses, and the rest of their busy life came from the bigger cities who wanted to drive out for the quaint ambiance. Still, Jay wasn't entirely wrong. 'It's been a challenge,' he admitted. 'I could never figure out why my aunt liked it so much.'

Jay pulled a face when he signed, 'Your sister said she married a hearing man. Maybe she just wanted to assimilate.'

The truth was, Basil didn't know her well enough to even begin taking a guess, but the fact that Jay would feel he had the right to be judgmental over a member of his family that he had not only never met, but who had died, made his stomach feel twisted and sour. 'Are you saying that's bad?'

Jay looked a little startled. 'I thought you were against it. I mean, your sister seems bad enough, but from what she said about you, I figured we were on the same page.'

Basil blinked at him. 'You're hearing.'

'I'm CODA,' Jay corrected, looking put out.

Basil couldn't help his snort of laughter. 'But you're still hearing. You don't really have the right to decide if it's a good or bad thing.'

Jay's jaw tightened and his hands flexed like he had an argument all prepared. Then, after a moment, he relaxed and his face gentled into a smile. Basil wasn't a fool though, he could see the coldness that remained in his eyes and he knew this was doomed. Guys like Jay—guys who felt they had a right to speak where their voices weren't wanted—they were a dime a dozen. He was wealthy and arrogant and dull, and nothing like the man Basil wished he was sitting there with.

Hell, he had a feeling if the night had gone on with Derek, they wouldn't have come to this place at all.

'I didn't mean to offend,' Jay told him.

Basil shrugged it off. There was no sense in fighting with him about it. 'It's fine. The truth is, I didn't know my aunt very well, but she seemed to love it in Fairfield, and it's started to grow on me.'

Jay smiled, but it was a little tight. 'So, no plans to get out?'

Basil felt another wave of irritation at the question. There was a sort of condescending tone to his signs, an arrogance in the way he had said it, as though a small town wasn't worthy of long-term plans. He hadn't grown up in the place, but it was home for now, and he felt oddly protective. 'I'm not sure,' he finally answered.

Jay looked at him, then laid one hand on the table and signaled to the server for the bill. Basil turned his gaze away, knowing that Jay knew how rude it was to do it right there in the middle of their dinner conversation, but he wanted to make a point.

Suddenly, out of the corner of his eye, Basil caught a flash of bright color on skin, and he whipped his head around without thinking. A group of three people—one man and two women, all of them sporting colorfully inked skin—were being sat two tables over. When the man turned, Basil's breath caught in his throat.

Derek. It was Derek. Their eyes met and the guy smiled a little, but there was no recognition there. Before Basil could panic, he suddenly became aware of the different hair, of the tattoo on his neck and it hit him.

That was Not-Derek. The twin.

Relief hit him like a sack of bricks, and he forced himself to turn away before he made a spectacle of himself. He returned his attention to Jay who was staring at them openly with a look of disdain.

'Disgusting,' he signed. 'How could a person do that to themselves?'

'Tattoos?' Basil asked.

Jay's expression deepened. 'It's trashy. Why would someone ruin their future like that? Someday they'll want a real job and then where will they be?'

Basil couldn't help it, his laugh bubbled up and he felt it vibrating in his chest loud enough to draw attention from people around them, but he didn't care. 'What year are you living in? No one cares anymore. And I'm willing to bet those people aren't miserable fucks like you. Thanks for dinner, I have to go.'

He felt Jay swipe at him in an attempt to get his attention, but Basil was a lot faster and a lot more fit than he was. He managed to bob and weave through the crowd and he made it out of the loft and down a dark alley, hurrying to a long string of bars where he could get lost in the crowd for a while.

He could make it to his car no problem, but he had a feeling Jay would be waiting, and after all that shit, he needed a drink. He picked the place with the loudest vibrations, then slapped a ten into the door person's hand and went in. The dance floor was crowded, but the bar was nearly empty, so he whipped out his phone and typed his usual.

> Hi, I'm Deaf. Can I please have a vodka tonic with a lemon twist?

The bartender glanced at his phone, then smiled up at him. 'I know sign language if you want to sign with me?'

Basil felt the tension in his chest unknot and wondered if the universe was doing him a kindness after that bullshit date. 'Thank you. That's great. It's been a bad night.'

The bartender—a good looking guy, tall and skinny, dark tawny skin and thick, straight hair combed into an elaborate pompadour—gave him a sympathetic smile. 'Want to tell me about it? I can sign and work.'

'You deaf?' Basil couldn't help but ask.

'HOH,' the guy signed with a shrug. 'You?'

'Deaf. My name's Basil, and if you don't mind, I would love to complain.'

The guy chuckled as he twisted a lemon peel into Basil's drink and handed it over. 'I'm Amit,' he signed, then offered his sign name. 'Were they a local? Some of them aren't so bad, but we get some awful ones from time to time. Too much mountain air.'

Basil laughed as he took a drink and let the burn of alcohol soothe him. 'He took me to a wine loft.'

Amit pulled a face. 'Terrible.'

'The worst. He's CODA, hearing, spent the entire date telling me what a gift he is to the Deaf Community for his tech work. Then he insulted Fairfield, then told me that everyone with tattoos is trash.'

Amit's eyes widened. He was called over to make a few more drinks as server's tickets came pouring in, but he kept Basil's gaze and signed fluidly with one hand. 'I have twelve. You?'

Basil shook his head. 'None, but I met a guy who works in a shop in Fairfield and his work was gorgeous. The guy was a dick.'

Amit's face brightened and he pulled up the side of his shirt to reveal a bright red and orange phoenix cascading up his ribs. 'I had this done there. Guy named Sage did it for me. Hurt worse than anything, but I love it. I know the place and they're amazing guys.'

Basil bit his lip, but he couldn't help asking, 'Did you meet a guy named Derek?'

He wasn't expecting Amit to smile and nod. 'Yeah. Sage's brother. Twins, but Derek does more Neo-Traditional work and Sage does a lot of geometric and abstract design. Sorry, I'm a tattoo nerd.'

Basil shook his head as he let that information slowly sink in. Sage. Not-Derek was named Sage, and he had once had his hands on the man right in front of Basil. And Amit had known Derek, knew some intimate details about him. The coincidences were starting to worry him, because nothing had changed his mind about Derek. Not yet. It still wasn't going to work.

'I have to go make a couple of blender drinks,' Amit said, waving to get his attention. 'Do you want to start a tab?'

Basil looked down at his drink with the single sip missing, then shook his head. 'I need to drive.' He laid cash on the counter, then waved off the change before Amit moved to get his receipt. He took another sip but knew he didn't want this. He didn't want to be drunk in Denver and stuck waiting to sober up before he could get the hell out and go home. He just wanted this night to be over.

He glanced up when Amit slid the bit of paper toward him, and as he walked away, Basil noticed there was a number and a little note scribbled at the bottom.

Call me some time if you ever want to hang out, I could introduce you around. All my friends are inked, and none of them are douchebags.

IT WAS OVER THE TOP. It was too goddamn over the top and he was going to get laughed right out of the flower shop. And then the next day he would probably get served with a restraining order because all the guy had done was buy one of his art pieces. Not just that, either, because Derek didn't have tangible proof that Basil was the one who'd done it at all.

The account was in his sister's name and there was every chance Basil had just shown her the site and she found Kevin interesting. Or something.

Fuck.

"Fuck," he murmured to himself. He stared at the octopus which was now glued to a canvas, covered in varnish, and framed, and he pressed his palm to his forehead. He was such a fucking moron.

"Are you just going to stare at it all day, or are you actually going to take it over there?" James asked. He was half-bent over a woman's lower back, giving her a string of cherry blossoms.

"I'm going to rip that machine out of your hand and stab you in the neck with it," Derek growled.

The woman twitched—not enough to fuck with James' lines—he was one of the steadiest hands in the shop, but it was enough to make him look up and glare at Derek. "Can we not terrify the newbies, dude?" He gave the woman's shoulder a firm pat. "Don't worry, darlin', this one's all bark, no bite. He'd never stab me in the neck."

No. Derek would save it for his balls if he didn't shut the entire fuck up. He was well aware he was making this a bigger deal than it was, but anxiety didn't ever have chill, and neither did he. He started to drag his hand through his hair, then realized he didn't want to fuck it up completely because even if Basil told him to fuck all the way out of the shop and never come back, he at least wanted to make his retreat look good.

"Just go, dude," James said. "You've got two hours before your appointment comes in. That's plenty of time to suck his face or his dick or his a—"

"Seriously, man," Derek said. He grabbed the folded note he'd spent two hours writing and decided to go because anything would be better than sitting there and listening to James give him shit for it. "I'll be back."

"Don't hurry on my account," James said, looking up and giving him a wink.

Derek flipped him off, tucked the note into the back of the frame, and hurried out. The walk was less than three minutes, but he took five in a pathetic attempt to give himself a moment to calm down. It wasn't working, and he was getting more worked up, so he decided that just jumping in was his only real option.

From the front window, he could make out that the shop was empty. The owner, Amaranth—the woman he'd met before—was behind the counter tapping away on her phone, and there was no sign of Basil anywhere. He wasn't sure if that was good or bad, but it gave him the smallest amount of extra courage to walk in.

The door gave a loud ring as it opened, and he noticed a light in the back flashed. As he stepped in, Amaranth looked up and smiled. "Hey. Tattoo guy," she said, coming around to greet him. "From the other day. Which one are you again?"

"Derek," he said a little shyly. "Uh…"

Her eyes flickered to the painting in his hands. "What's that?"

"He's called Kevin," Derek blurted, then flushed and turned the painting to show her. "Actually, my dipshit friend named him. I just called it Octopus, so you can name it whatever you want."

She blinked at him, staring hard at his mouth like maybe she'd missed something. "Sorry…what?"

"You…this. You ordered this, right?" He said two prayers equally—one that the painting was hers, and the other that Basil had done this. He was such a mess.

She stared, then her mouth slowly curved into a wide grin. "No, but I think I know who did. You're the guy from the ATM vestibule. The night the power went out."

He blushed so hot he felt light-headed. "Yes."

"My brother told me about it," she told him, her tone full of glee. "He told me you were an artist, I didn't realize he tracked you down."

Derek rubbed the back of his neck. "Well I uh…just…during the storm I showed him my gallery online for something to do. He was probably just being nice."

She laughed loudly, shaking her head. "My brother doesn't do, 'just being nice'. Trust me. He either really liked that, or really liked you."

Derek licked his lips nervously. "Well I can just...leave this for him. When he gets back, he can..."

"He's here," she said, interrupting his flow of words. "He's in the back pouting because he had a shit date the other night."

Derek didn't even bother to pretend like he didn't know why hearing Basil on a date hurt the way it did. "Oh."

"Yeah. The guy was an ass, and he's blaming me because I set him up. But he's got this dumbass thing about how he can't date anyone like his ex, and that leaves a very small population of guys to choose from because his ex was basic as hell."

Derek couldn't help a small chuckle. "Yeah?"

She nodded sagely. "Trust me, total bro. It was gross and I was glad when they broke up, but it kind of fucked him up a little bit. He's starting to get over it—I mean, at least he's trying to now, but it's been a long road."

Derek frowned at her. "Should you be telling me all this without his consent?"

She gave him a careful look, something bright shining in her gaze as she sized him up. After a moment, she shook her head and shrugged. "He'll take one look at you and me together and realize I told you all the dirty details. He expects it. I'm an asshole." She moved to the counter and hit a button a few times, which made the back lights blink. "He'll be out in a moment," she told him with a grin.

Derek began to sweat profusely, holding the canvas with one hand so he could swipe his other on the top of his jeans. He waited, his heart hammering in his chest, and then the door swung open. He wasn't entirely sure how he felt when Basil walked out. Time stopped for a second, and then, when the guy gave him a tentative smile, he felt like he could breathe again.

'Hi,' he signed.

Basil's smile twitched a little bigger. 'Hi.'

Derek stared down at the canvas in his hand and then, like an idiot, shoved it at Basil so hard it made the guy stumble back a step. "Uh..."

"Oh my god," he heard Amaranth mutter under her breath.

Basil seemed to recover quickly, taking the canvas from Derek and gently setting it down against the counter. He crouched to look at it for a long moment, then looked back up at Derek. 'Beautiful.'

Derek stared for a second, then saw movement out of the corner of his eye. Whatever Amaranth had signed, Basil shook his head and told her, 'No.' He stood back up, leaving the octopus where it was, and approached Derek slow, like someone might a wounded animal.

Derek realized he sort of was that. The last and only time Basil had seen him was when he was having a panic attack in a closed room, so it was only fair he think Derek would freak in any circumstances.

'His name is Kevin,' he signed, then pointed at the octopus.

Basil stared blankly, then his shoulders began to shake with his near-silent laughter. 'Kevin?' he spelled, mouthing along.

Derek flushed. 'My friend,' he signed, but that was as far as his ASL skills extended in explaining James' asshattery.

Basil held up a finger, then pulled his phone out of his pocket and started to type. Your friend name octopus?

Derek sighed and took the offered phone.

> Yes, because he's a dickhead, but it stuck. It's been hanging in the shop for a few years. But you can name it whatever you want to.

Basil grinned at him as he typed.

> I like Kevin. When Derek gave him an incredulous look, Basil laughed louder. It look like his name. You bring here why?

Derek felt a little more embarrassed and he shrugged before answering.

> I work down the street, over at Irons and Works. It was safer this way. I know for sure it wouldn't get fucked up in the mail.

When he looked up, Basil was smiling at him. 'Thank you,' he signed.

'You're welcome.' Derek desperately wished he'd listened to Tony months ago about the classes, that he'd paid better attention, that he knew more than 'want milk' and 'sleep' and 'mommy'. He wanted to talk to this man in his own language, to give him an avenue to express himself in a way that was natural and comfortable. Fidgeting, he took the phone back.

> I'd better let you get back to work. I have a client coming in soon.

Basil took the phone, and before Derek could move away, he seized his arm and ran thin, elegant fingers along some of the grey-scale six-fingered hand he had extending up from the wrist. He released him and signed something, and before Derek could ask, Amaranth voiced it. "I like this. Chamsa?"

Derek smiled and didn't look away, even as Basil's eyes moved over to see his sister interpreting. "My mom was Jewish, and uh…" he licked his lips. "as kids, my brother and I weren't allowed to participate in the faith or anything, especially after she died. My father…" He stopped, the words feeling like they were choking him, and it must have shown on his face because Basil reached for his wrist, squeezing as his thumb rubbed gently over the top of his ink. Shaking his head, he took a breath and managed a tight smile. "It's a tribute to part of me that I wasn't really allowed to have when I was younger."

When Basil looked at him fully, there was something in his eyes —sympathy, maybe—but it was nothing like the oppressive mothering he got at the shop. It was just understanding and comfort. He wanted to turn his hand and link his fingers with Basil's, but he let that moment right there be enough.

His other hand raised, and he tipped it from his chin. 'Thank you.'

Basil squeezed his hand once more before he dropped it and signed for Amaranth to interpret, "Thanks for bringing this by. You were right before, it's wrong no one wanted it. Kevin will have a good home here."

Derek blushed but nodded, took one last look at the octopus, then hurried out without glancing back.

CHAPTER SIX

Derek walked into his place, arms full of shawarma boxes and foil-wrapped pita, and immediately unloaded it all onto the coffee table. Sage had been there for a while, having texted Derek when he got in, and he was sitting on the couch with socked feet up, looking better than he had the year before which Derek counted as progress.

"Give me five, but if you're hungry, don't wait," he said, then went into his room to change. He found a pair of sweats that weren't completely covered in dry acrylics, and a white tee, and came out to find Sage opening a couple beers and sorting the food out for easy access.

"Movie?" Sage asked as he settled on the floor, digging his fork into some of the saffron rice.

Derek shrugged. "If you want. I'm not feeling picky."

Sage chewed a moment, then said, "I'm good." He waited for Derek to settle in next to him, and they took a few minutes to just eat and exist before he spoke again. "I went to visit his memorial last week since I knew I couldn't make it up this weekend. Plus, I really didn't want to run into his mom."

Derek put his fork down and looked at his brother. "Why didn't you ask me to go?"

Sage shrugged. "I uh…" He licked his lips, unable to meet Derek's gaze as he spoke. "I've been thinking about dating again. I mean, I haven't met anyone, but the other day when I was grabbing coffee, this super hot guy behind the counter gave me a free scone because he said I looked like I needed it. It wasn't in a creep way either. It was just…it was nice. And I started thinking, shit, I could ask this guy out and he might actually say yes. I've spent the last four years not being ready, and I'm not now. I still can't shake the feeling like I'd be betraying Ted, but there's going to come a point where I am."

Derek reached for Sage's shoulder and just let his hand rest there. He smiled inwardly when his brother moved into his touch just a fraction, making him feel like he was needed there. "I can't know what that's like, but I do know the agonizing panic of letting yourself be vulnerable again, and I know the courage it takes to even consider it."

Sage chewed on his food, swallowed, then took a long drink of beer before he answered him. "He'd want me to be happy. I mean, he'd want me to be picky—because he'd never settle for a douche—but he'd want me to let go, and I want to do that for him. I just don't know how to be ready." Leaning his head back on the sofa cushion, he closed his eyes and let out a slow breath. "I didn't cry today. Or last week, when I was there. It was still hard, but it didn't feel like I was choking on my own heart this time and I realized I am moving on. Stupid little things, like I can't remember what he sounded like first thing in the morning anymore, and I forget if his hands were smooth or calloused, and it doesn't hurt the way it used to."

"I think that's normal," Derek said softly.

"Tracy told me that when I talked to her today. She said I'm going to be scared for a long time, and that I'll probably always be a little neurotic with my future partners, but that someday that suffocating grief is just going to feel like an echo. It's so wrong. I shouldn't just…get over it."

"Except you don't really have a choice. If we were eighty and you'd been together sixty years, I might let you get away with it," Derek said quietly. "But we're not eighty. We're young enough that we can still find the person we're going to spend most of our lives with, and I want that for you."

Sage slowly turned his head to look at Derek with a slight grin. "You said 'we'."

Derek frowned at him. "...okay?"

"You said we, like you're including yourself in that. Like you're not shutting yourself off from the very idea of letting someone else in. Is it the ATM guy?"

Derek felt his cheeks burn. "No. I think the ATM guy is just proof that I might be ready to start looking. My panic isn't as bad as it used to be, the nightmares are so infrequent I don't remember the last time I had one. I just...I still feel like I'd be putting someone second to all my fucking issues, and that isn't fair to anyone."

"I think you have to be ready to let someone decide that for you," Sage replied.

Derek pursed his lips, then said, "I don't know that anyone has any idea what they're getting into, and I know for a fact getting dumped for something I can't change feels a hell of a lot worse than getting dumped just because they got tired of me."

Sage opened his mouth to speak, but just then Derek's phone began to vibrate, dancing across the table with a call. Before he could grab it, Sage snatched it up and frowned at the screen. "It's fucking dad."

Derek felt his stomach twist. The issue with his father was getting worse, and he knew something had to be done, but he couldn't bring himself to sever the connection. "I'll call him back."

Sage gave him a look, then hit the answer button and put the phone to his ear. "Hey, old man. I...yes. Yes. Okay..." Derek could tell by the way Sage's eyes widened a fraction, by the way his jaw tightened and his fingers curled in toward his palm, his dad was shouting abuse into the receiver.

It seemed to go on for an eternity, the rapid hum of his dad's voice, Sage's quiet noises as though he was just making sure his dad knew he was still there. Then, after seven long minutes, the call ended. Sage didn't say much, just set the phone face down on the table and stared at it.

"Sage," Derek said quietly.

His brother shook his head. "He's always like that? Every time he calls?"

Derek shrugged. "It's…I mean, he's not all there and…"

Sage scoffed, looking up at Derek with hard eyes. "He was like that even when he was all there. I just didn't realize he was still at it."

Derek glanced away, taking a shuddering breath. "It's fine. I don't…he doesn't matter anymore. He's dying. And you really don't need to do that, you know. I can handle it."

"He didn't know it was me," Sage replied with a huff. "He can't remember he's got two of us, so you can let me share in this."

Derek shifted, his body tense. "Look, you're already dealing with enough, trying to handle yourself after Ted, and I know that's not easy."

Sage gave him a startled look. "Der, that fuck is entirely responsible for your PTSD. He's entirely responsible for every fresh hell you endure whenever something triggers you. You don't get to be a martyr here just because I'm sad my fiancé died, okay? I'm strong enough to handle that. I couldn't," his voice broke and he cleared his throat, "I couldn't protect you back then, but I can at least shoulder some of the burden now. Just…fuck. Let me take a call or two. He won't live long enough to do real damage anyway."

Derek closed his eyes, breathed in, then opened them as he released it all. "We can talk about it."

It seemed to pacify Sage enough for the moment. "There's something else though," he said, and though his tone was hesitant, he didn't give Derek time to think. "I met someone I think you'd like, and I want you to consider going on a date with him."

Derek sat up a little straighter, his brows dipping into a frown. "You didn't promise him I'd…"

"No," Sage said, putting up his hands in surrender. "I'm an asshole, but I'm not an asshole. He goes to my gym."

Derek pulled a face. "Okay, that's so not my type."

"He's an accountant," Sage replied with a tiny knowing smile. "But he also works out with me a few times a week, and he's hot as hell. I also know for a fact he'd be interested in you."

Derek bristled at that because it meant the guy had hit on Sage, and since Sage wasn't ready to date, he was just punting his cast-offs toward his twin. "I don't know, man. If he's into you, then he won't like me."

"He isn't," Sage told him, crossing his arms. "I mean, he thinks I'm hot, which is a big plus for you, but he and I have been talking over the last few months and he's into all the crap you are. Same music, same art shit, same movies. Here let me…" Sage grunted as he twisted his hips up and dug his phone out of his pocket. He tapped at his screen for a few seconds, then displayed a Facebook photo of a fit guy with tanned skin and dark curls under a backward cap. He was wearing a muscle shirt and tight jeans, and his smile was very bright. Sage hadn't been lying—the guy was very attractive. Unfortunately, Derek's mind was slightly occupied with someone else, and it was hard for him to focus on someone who wasn't Basil.

"You said he's an accountant? So why isn't he into you? You know, with all the math shit?"

Sage laughed and rolled his eyes. "I don't know, dude. I mean, he's cool with numbers, but I don't think he wants to like sit and talk quarterly reports at the end of the night or anything. Just…just think about it, okay? Let me know, and if you want to give it a try, I'll help set something up."

Derek knew he should at least consider it. He had no promises, no prospect of a future at all with Basil. He'd delivered the drawing and the guy had been utterly perfect, but it was the second time Derek walked away without a number. And hell, they could be friendly now, and there was every chance they'd see each other in passing, but he couldn't count on there ever being more.

It was foolish to think he'd stumbled on some epic romance that was written in the stars. It only made sense to let Sage do this for him. He certainly wasn't any good at doing it for himself. He took a breath, then met his brother's gaze. "Go ahead," he all-but grunted.

Sage looked momentarily startled, then chanced a tentative smile. "Seriously?"

Derek sighed, letting his head fall back again. "Seriously. Might as well rip the bandage off, right? So just…if he wants to, yeah. Let's do it. You can give him my number or whatever and it…it could be good, right?"

"Right," Sage said. He reached out and gave Derek's wrist a gentle squeeze, right where Basil had touched him before, and he suppressed the urge to tug his hand away because he didn't want to lose the ghost of that comfort just yet. But he didn't. "It could be really good."

Basil had been dodging both texts and Facebook messages from Jay who seemed to think that although Basil had run out on him, he was owed a chance to do the date over. The very thought made his stomach squirm, and he threw himself into work, staying late nearly every day the week after Derek had brought Kevin by the shop.

It was hanging in his office for now, and he found himself working on some digital arrangements, but mostly staring at the near-perfect sweeps and smudges of charcoal that somehow brought the drawing to life. It was almost as though Basil could reach up, and the octopus would uncurl a tentacle and wrap it around him.

Seeing Derek in the shop like that had startled him in a way he hadn't expected, and his face when he'd been talking about his father had nearly shattered Basil in two. He didn't have to be well-versed in reading expression to see the pain in Derek's eyes, to know that he'd suffered more than a person rightfully should, and Basil had only just managed to suppress his urge to take Derek in his arms and hold him until he smiled again.

Still, he wanted to do something. Not just to cheer Derek up, but maybe to introduce himself to the shop, to meet the others and experience it. He wasn't exactly vying for a tattoo, but he was half considering throwing together a bouquet—something highly fragrant for the front of the shop, and using that as a way in.

Maybe he'd be obvious, but at this point, he wasn't sure that he cared. He didn't think he'd ever go for a hearing guy again—especially one not fluent in ASL, but he found himself wanting to make some kind of effort. Friends for sure. Friends was safe, at least. Friends was far easier to leave when it all eventually became too much.

Without really thinking about it, Basil moved to the back room and began to carefully arrange something to bring over to Irons and Works the following afternoon. He had some white Hyacinth and some Boronia already cut, and he tucked those between sprigs of Jasmine and as an afterthought, added a yellow rose in the center. It was hardly the prettiest bouquet he'd made, but when he tipped his nose low over it, the fragrance was gentle, but lingering. He wasn't sure any of them would appreciate it, but he could only hope.

When he was finished, he tucked the bouquet in the cooler, then resolved to grab it around lunch and sneak out without his sister realizing what he was up to.

DODGING Ama was easier than he anticipated, as they had a large group of bridesmaids come in for some bouquet tests right around noon, and Basil was able to grab the flowers and sneak off to the shop without his sister being the wiser. He felt a little foolish, hurrying down the street with the bouquet tucked in his arms, but he ignored the curious stares in passing cars and pedestrians, and made his way to the little shopping center around the corner.

He could see the tattoo shop from the parking lot, and he hesitated before crossing the pavement and heading to the door. He saw the little glowing orange Open sign in the window which sat next to a horizontal blinking sign which read TATTOO in bold capital letters. The window was all-but covered in pasted advertisements for local bands, skateboarding competitions, tattoo expos, and piercing parlors. But beyond that, he could also make out a quaint shop with a small lobby, a front desk, and beyond that, what looked like partially sectioned off stalls with chairs and tables.

He took a breath then entered the shop, and over the counter, a tall woman with long black hair stared at him curiously. Her mouth was moving, but her wide smile made it hard for him to begin to understand what she was saying, so he quickly set the bouquet down on the table and pulled out his phone for the customary, pre-written greeting he kept saved.

Hi, I'm Deaf, I hope typing is okay. After a second, he added, I'm look for Derek.

She took the phone, read the message, then carefully set it down before signing with beginner's speed, 'My name is Katherine, is it okay to use ASL?'

Basil was startled for a second, then remembered about Derek's boss and his daughter, so he shouldn't have been too surprised. 'ASL is fine, thank you,' he answered.

'My daughter is hard of hearing,' she signed to him. So, she must be the wife, the mother of the child. 'I'm taking ASL 3 now and I'm still slow, sorry.'

'You're perfect,' he corrected her with a smile. 'Your daughter will have great parents.'

She flushed, glancing away for a second like she couldn't take the compliment. When she looked back, her green eyes were a little watery, but he did her the courtesy of pretending not to notice. 'Are you here for an appointment?'

He shook his head. 'No. I met Derek and wanted to bring him...'

he glanced back at the flowers and waved his hand at them. 'Is he here today?'

'He's in the back giving a consultation,' she said, spelling the last word. 'I'll tell him you're here. Can you wait?'

Basil hesitated. This wasn't exactly the plan, but he was also barging in on Derek's work day, so assuming he'd be free at the drop of a hat was unfair. And running again was doubly so. 'I can wait.'

Katherine grinned at him, but instead of heading to the back, she walked through the low swinging door and moved to the tall bookshelf which held dozens of black photo albums. She studied them all carefully before selecting one near the top, then turned and held it out for him. When he took it, she signed, 'That's Derek's work if you want to have a look. He's really good.'

Basil fought the urge to remind her that he wasn't there for a tattoo. He didn't want to commit some sort of tattoo faux pas and shoot this thing dead before it began. 'Thank you,' he finally signed, then sank onto the soft leather couch and opened it to the first page.

His breath immediately caught in his throat. Basil didn't live in a cave, he wasn't a complete recluse, and Derek's tattoo work wasn't the first he'd ever seen. But it was the first time he'd ever been instantly drawn in and captivated. The work in the book was a mixture of sketches on paper and photographs of people's bodies, but every single one of them seemed to come alive on the page. They were almost nothing like his work in his gallery, and yet he could see familiarity in all the lines and shapes and shades that it was like looking at a piece of Derek himself.

When someone touched his arm, Basil jumped, staring up almost guiltily as he saw Derek hovering a foot away. He shut the book with what he hoped was a quiet gesture, then rose to his feet feeling a little bit foolish now. Derek's gaze was welcoming, but a little confused, and Basil couldn't blame him.

Before Basil could explain, Derek held out a little post-it with a note across the top. Was something wrong with Kevin?

Basil couldn't help but smile at the name for such an elegant creature, and he shook his head. He pulled out his phone and quickly typed his reply. I'm want to tell thank you, bring bouquet you.

He watched Derek smile at the message and give a startled glance to the vase on the table, and Basil became distinctly aware that Derek hadn't once attempted to question or correct his terrible English in writing. Basil could do it—he was a college graduate and had gotten by just fine in all his writing exams, but switching in his head from ASL to English was just more effort than he ever wanted to make, and sticking somewhere closer in the middle was just easier.

Hearing people always wanted him to do better, but Derek had simply accepted it for what it was. He hadn't tried to dumb down his own writing either, like so many people did who assumed that because Basil didn't write it the same way, he couldn't understand it. It meant something, and he wasn't sure he was ready for that.

When he finally looked back at Derek, the other man was smiling, then tipped his hand from his chin. 'Thank you. Beautiful.'

Basil felt his cheeks flush, and he reached over to pat the tattoo book and repeated the sign, exaggerating it in hopes Derek would understand exactly what that meant. 'Very beautiful.'

Derek's blush matched his own, and he ducked his head a little shyly, shrugging off the compliment. He held up his hand for a second, then rushed over to where Katherine was sitting, and leaned fully over the counter. Basil couldn't help himself from taking in a full view of the man's ass—gloriously round and looked like it would comfortably rest in both of his palms—before Derek eased back down to the floor and returned with a small notepad and a pen.

Is this okay?

Basil grinned and shrugged, spreading his fingers and tapping his thumb on his chest while mouthing, 'Fine.'

Derek scribbled again. Do you want a tour? I don't have any clients until three. I can show you my stall and my works in progress.

Basil hated that he couldn't just sign, but it was what it was. He took the pen from him to answer. Your art here? You keep here? Paintings?

Derek shook his head. I have my art studio in my apartment, this is just my tattoo work. It's fine if you're not interested.

Basil quickly grabbed his arm and shook his then signed, 'Show me,' hoping he made the right form with his lips.

Derek seemed to understand, because he blushed shyly again, but reached for the swinging door and held it open, gesturing for Basil to step inside. He did, feeling a little like a fish in a bowl with the way Katherine was watching him, and he was suddenly and profoundly grateful no one else was there working.

He turned to see Derek securing the door, then he looked up and smiled so sweetly, it made Basil's chest ache. He took a moment to gather himself, then followed Derek to the first little cubby which was sectioned off by three waist-high partition walls to give a small amount of privacy on the sides. Within the partition walls was something that looked like a folded massage table, a desk with a bright drawing board, then a massive tool box covered in various, brightly decorated stickers. Along the far wall was a pin board and it was covered from end to end with all of Derek's work.

'Wow,' Basil signed as he leaned toward the drawings. He turned to Derek and pointed at him, then at the wall and dipped his brows. 'Yours?'

Derek nodded, looking shy all over again. What's the sign for flower?

Basil showed him and smiled when Derek copied it almost flawlessly. Holding a finger up, Derek turned to a small cabinet in the corner of his stall and came away with another book. It was a large, leather-bound sketch book, and he motioned for Basil to take a seat while he plopped down onto a backless rolling stool.

For a second, it felt a little like a dentist's office, and then he looked up into Derek's soft, smiling face and suddenly it felt like the most intimate thing Basil had done in years. Derek shifted closer, until he was right alongside Basil, and he spread the book over their thighs which had pressed together.

Basil couldn't help the way his breath caught in his chest, stuttering in his lungs. The first page was a cascade to rival even the hanging gardens of Babylon. The outlines of the sketches were pencil, and watercolor decorated each and every bursting blossom, covering so much of the page that the bits of white left over were almost startling.

He couldn't help himself, he traced around the edges of the bright reds, and blues, and oranges with the tip of his finger as though he might be able to somehow feel the petals. He looked up at Derek, and he saw something in his eyes akin to fear or insecurity that Basil couldn't allow.

He scrambled for the paper which Derek had set on his desk and scribbled furiously. I don't know arts, but this…Derek. So beautiful, it make chest hurt, want tears fall. He pressed the center of his palm to where his heart was thudding rapidly against his ribs and made sure he was meeting Derek's gaze fully. 'Beautiful,' he signed.

Swallowing thickly, Derek acknowledged this with a nod of his head, then turned the page to show more of his work. The first few were more flowers, a few birds, a stretch of mountains. The rest were in something like art nouveau, something you'd see in a gallery, and Basil couldn't imagine how he could transfer that onto someone's skin.

He turned to the last page and stopped. There was a single sketch there, nothing spectacular or remarkable. It was a white flower with a stringy center, the thin petals in rows and rows. It was nothing they carried in the shop, but something struck him about it—an old memory trying to claw its way to the surface.

He tapped the page, then looked up at Derek and signed, 'What?'

Reaching for the notepad, Derek wrote for a long moment. It's my favorite. Night-Blooming Cereus. It's a flower on cactus and it only blooms at night, so it's really rare to see them, but their smell is amazing. I saw one once at this botanical garden when Sage and I were younger. When my dad... Anyway, I went home and drew it, but it didn't look right, so I kept going until I was happy. I threw it in my book, but no one ever wants that tattoo.

Basil closed his eyes for a moment against his will, shutting out everything but the moment from his childhood. He'd been five, maybe six, and his mother had pulled him out of bed well into the early, dark hours of the morning.

'I want you to see this, okay?' she told him, her hands flying in the light of the full moon. They crept across the flagstones to her succulent garden and she tugged him to his knees. The cactus itself was unremarkable. Faded green in long cylindrical barrels that reached up from the main stalk. It didn't look covered in thorns like so many of the others, there was a sheen to it like it might be soft to touch. He didn't though. He'd learned his lesson years ago at the hands of her garden that many of the most beautiful were also the most dangerous.

He started to fidget, impatient, and then the half-formed white flowers along the side began to open. It felt like an eternity, but when they did, his mother urged him forward, and he was overwhelmed with the scent. To this day, nothing had compared, nothing had come close, and he hadn't been able to describe it.

'This is you,' his mother had told him. 'Waiting for your chance to bloom, and maybe not everyone will see it, but the ones who do will appreciate the magic you can bring.'

He forced his eyes to open, to shake that off because he was about to become overwhelmed. He felt a fierce, hollow ache in his chest from missing her so damn much right in that moment, because she would have loved this.

He reached out, tracing his finger around the flower, then looked back up at Derek. 'Thank you.'

'You OK?' Derek signed.

Basil almost laughed, only because there were no real words for what he was feeling. Instead he splayed out his fingers and tapped his thumb on his chest, mouthing along with the sign, 'Fine.'

It was obvious Derek didn't believe him, but he didn't push either and for that, Basil was eternally grateful. He carefully handed the book back and started to rise, but before he could take a step away, Derek touched him on the arm and handed over the notebook.

I could give you one, if you ever want. Anything you want.

Basil blinked at the note, then looked back up at Derek and smiled. I'm not sure I could afford your fee. Your work is too good to be cheap.

Derek shook his head, his hand shaking a little as he scribbled back. No, free. I wouldn't charge if it was something you wanted.

For a split second, for just a single beat of his heart, he let himself think about Derek inking that flower on him, giving him a tangible, permanent thing between them, and a visible reminder of the person his mother wanted him to be. Then he felt a wave of irritation because he was not the kind of person who wanted any kind of charity.

Thank you, but no.

Maybe it was the look on his face, or the harshness to the letters, but Derek swallowed and nodded, taking the book back. His mouth opened, then closed, like he was going to say something, but instead he turned on his heel and walked out.

There was a moment, so awkward it was painful, where Basil let himself stand in Derek's stall for another moment. Then he pushed past the little partitions and headed for the door. He was a few feet from the front of the shop when he felt a tap on his shoulder, and his eyes widened as he turned to see Katherine there.

'Wait,' she signed. 'Please?'

He paused, nodding to her a little sharply.

'He upset you.'

Basil licked his lips, letting out a breath, then shrugged and signed slow for her, 'I don't want pity. He offered me a free tattoo, but I don't need it.'

Her face moved through a complicated expression, then she shook her head. 'Not pity, not charity,' she replied. 'Men like Derek, men like my husband, this is their passion. This isn't just a job. If an artist like Derek offers you his work like that for free, it's because he knows you're important, that you deserve it. Tattoos aren't for pity.'

Her signs were uneven and her grammar a little hard to follow, but it was enough for him to understand. He could see it in the way her fingers trembled and in the way her jaw was set tight—she meant it. He'd turned and walked away from Derek because he'd misunderstood.

And maybe that was another sign from the universe that it wasn't meant to be. The language barrier was hard enough, and he might have just ruined something good. 'Sorry,' he finally told her.

Her smile softened. 'He's not angry. The guys are all learning sign for my daughter. Come by more. They'll sign for you, they'll keep practicing. You'd be a good fit here.'

He snorted a laugh. 'I'm not an artist.'

'Yes,' she told him pointedly, 'you are. Not the same as us, but you are. And you're welcome. You fit,' she repeated.

It was...it was a lot, but it was so tempting he nearly burned with it. He hadn't willingly let himself be part of an all-hearing group ever in his life, not even groups of students back in college. Because they never understood, and ultimately, they left it up to him to fit in with them. Yet, for whatever reason, he wasn't sure it would be the same here. He wanted to rebel against that thought, but maybe it was worth a chance. Maybe there was room in his life for both worlds.

Amaranth had never hated it, and maybe he didn't have to either.

CHAPTER SEVEN

"Shit. Fuck. Shit," Derek cursed, staring at himself in the mirror. He ignored the laugh behind him as he ran his comb through his hair one last time, all-but destroying any positive effect the pomade might have had. A few locks of hair flopped down over his forehead and he groaned, turning to a smirking Sam who was lounging on his bed with one leg hooked up under his arm and hugged to his chest. "This is going to be a disaster."

Sam released his leg, using his hands to shift himself to the edge of the bed, and he beckoned Derek over. "Maybe," he conceded as Derek knelt in front of him. He spread a little more product on his fingers and began to fuss with Derek's hair again. "But it probably won't be. The worst that can happen is that you don't like each other. Sage trusts this guy, right? And you know as well as I do, he wouldn't set you up with some asshole." Sam gave both his shoulders a firm pat and sat back a little, but Derek didn't stand back up just yet.

"I just," he started, then shook his head and flopped back onto his ass.

"You just can't stop thinking of your hot florist?" Sam offered.

Derek flushed but couldn't deny it. "I just don't know how I fucked up so bad."

"It was a miscommunication," Sam told him gently. "But you said the guy wasn't interested in you anyway, which is why you're doing this whole blind date thing."

Derek shrugged, letting himself fall all the way onto his back, and he stared up at the ceiling. He didn't look over when he heard a gentle thud as Sam hit the ground, and he shuffled up next to him so they could lay shoulder to shoulder. "I'm trying to be a fucking adult about this, but I feel like some idiot teenager discovering his first crush."

Sam shifted onto his side, propping his head up on his elbow and looked at Derek carefully. "You didn't really get to have that, did you? The simple, easy middle school crush?"

Derek dragged a hand down his face, then turned his head to look at his friend. "I mean, yes and no. I had my first crush—his name was Brent, and he was in eighth grade and the captain of the soccer team. One day in PE some fuck-face threw a dodge ball and hit me on the temple and damn-near knocked my ass out. I came to with Brent holding an ice pack to the back of my neck and gently calling my name. It was like…some shit out of Titanic or something. Music played, Celine Dion was there."

Sam chuckled quietly, nudging him in the ribs with his free hand. "You're such a fucking nerd."

Derek shrugged, unrepentant. "For that ten minutes, I felt like a normal kid. Til I got home and my old man started in on me for being a pussy because of course the nurse called him. I never spoke to Brent again after that. I was petrified my dad would find out and…" He shuddered and didn't let his head go there. "So, I guess yeah. I mean, I did get those moments, but I never really got to hold on to them."

"Maybe you're just making up for it now," Sam suggested.

Derek closed his eyes and sighed out a lungful of air. "I'm a grown-ass adult, Sammy. I don't want some teenage crush on the boy I can never have. I want something normal—something that makes me feel good. All of my relationships up to this point have been for fucking and free tattoos and I'm exhausted. And Sage had it once—all the good shit—the Katherine and Tony shit. Then he fucking died, and I keep thinking, what if we're just cursed, me and him? I'll never find someone who wants me for me and not for what I can give them, and he'll never get to keep the people he loves."

"I don't believe in curses," Sam said after a beat. He laid back down and let his head rest against the side of Derek's shoulder. "And trust me, a guy like me—paralyzed as a kid, now fighting to keep the child I rescued—I'm prone to falling into those black holes. I don't know if this Basil guy will ever mean anything to you in the long run, but I do know it means something right now that he's getting you to feel things you wouldn't let yourself feel before. And the fact that you're going out tonight on this date? You have no fucking idea how proud I am."

Derek felt his chest tighten, so he rolled over and punched Sam lightly. "You're so gross right now." He pushed himself to his feet with a grunt, then pushed Sam's chair over to him before walking back to the wall mirror and staring at himself all over again. "I guess this is the best I'm going to do."

Sam wheeled up behind him and slapped him on the ass. "Your worst is every other man's Vanity Fair cover, dickhead. Go have fun, okay? And if it sucks, come back here and you can watch The Emperor's New Groove with me and May for the six-hundredth time this week. Deal?"

Derek couldn't help but grin. "Deal."

THE GUY's name was Niko, and he'd been texting Derek off and on for the last two days leading up to the date. He hadn't been pushy when Derek was busy, tired, or just not in the mood to be chatty, and he hadn't seemed like a martyr about it either which was a huge tick in the positive column for this guy. Derek tried to use Sam's pep talk to psych himself up as he approached the little Italian bistro, but his nerves were still on high alert.

He was grateful Niko had picked a place that had a calm ambiance, and he wondered if maybe Sage had warned the guy that loud noises and chaotic atmospheres were too much for Derek to deal with in public. Or maybe the guy was just perceptive. He wanted to think the latter, mostly because he was ready to start feeling like a normal, grown adult man who dated and socialized.

Walking in, he approached the hostess who quickly led him back to the table where Niko was waiting. He was dressed casually—jeans and a polo shirt—but he looked elegant in a surprising way. His arms were toned, his glasses added another layer of appeal to his already gorgeous face, and when he smiled, his eyes lit up with it.

He extended his hand as Derek approached, then waited for him to sit before he did the same. "Hey. Can I just say that this is a little weird?"

Derek froze halfway to reaching for his napkin. "Uh...why? Did my brother bribe you into this or something?"

Niko laughed which showed off a twin pair of dimples in his cheeks. "No, man. Of course not. Just...he talked about you so much, and it's not like I haven't met twins before, but you two have the same face."

Derek felt his cheeks heat up and a pang of worry flare to life in his gut because generally, people who liked Sage weren't into him once they got to know him. The two of them were identical twins, but their bodies were exactly where the similarities ended. Sage had always been quieter, and more reserved, and definitely more well behaved. It was probably why his father hadn't noticed him as often as he noticed Derek. Sage had always been more level-headed, had always dealt with things better.

Even after the death of Ted, he was living his life, and Derek didn't know if he'd ever be that strong.

"Sorry," Niko said at Derek's continued silence, "was that super offensive?"

Derek huffed a laugh. "No, no, it's not that. Just...Sage and I aren't exactly alike. Apart from the whole identical twin thing, our personalities are like night and day."

The corner of Niko's mouth twitched up. "He did mention that, you know. Part of why I agreed to go out on this date."

That gave Derek pause, and he looked at the guy over the rim of his water glass. "Yeah?"

Niko shrugged as he sat back. "Yeah. Don't get me wrong, your brother is a great guy. He's the perfect gym buddy and he's hilarious. But he's not my type. Physically...I can work with that, but we don't really mesh well on things that matter."

"How so?" Derek asked, a little nervous, but more curious than anything.

Niko bit his lip in thought, then smiled a tiny bit as he said, "He keeps insisting on calling a tomato a fruit."

"Oh my god," Derek groaned, dipping his head forward, "he so fucking does that. Like okay technically yes, but it's not a fucking fruit. A few years ago, we had this huge argument and to prove his point, he grabbed one off the counter and ate it like an apple because he's a fucking monster."

Niko threw his head back, laughing. "He didn't. That should be considered treason."

"I know!" Derek said, feeling his cheeks ache with how wide his grin was. "I won't change my mind either."

"Well," Niko said as his laughter began to die down, "he mentioned that you agreed with me about his shitty opinions. And that was intriguing enough to give this a chance. What about you? How'd he convince you to come?"

Derek bit his lip, debated about the truth, then said, "He said you were a great guy, and...I've been kind of looking for one of those. I guess I didn't take much convincing."

Niko's smile softened, showing all the way to his eyes.

. . .

The date was good. It was so good. They got along better than Sage told him they would, and Derek found himself smiling more than he had in what felt like years. When the server offered dessert, Niko shook his head and leaned in toward Derek. "Trust me?"

Derek shrugged. "You haven't steered me wrong yet." He wanted to protest about Niko picking up the bill, but it had been so damn long since he'd really done anything on the dating scene and he didn't want to be rude, so he let it go.

Niko lead the way outside and turned the opposite direction of where their cars were parked. "So, this little gelato shop just opened up two blocks down and I've been dying to try it. I really limit my sweets, but I get to indulge since we're on an official date."

Derek wasn't really a sweets guy, but the way Niko looked so hopeful, he couldn't say no. "Sounds good to me."

"And since we're doing the date thing...would holding your hand be out of line?" Niko asked in an even softer voice.

For just a split second, Derek wanted to say no, wanted to say that was too much. But he promised his brother he was going to try, and it was such a small step. After only a beat of hesitation, he held his hand out and felt Niko's fingers slip between his. It was a somewhat awkward fit. Niko's hands were surprisingly thick, and they stretched Derek's to a point of almost pain. His palm was rough too, calloused from where he held weights and it wasn't entirely pleasant, but touching another person wasn't something he got to do often, either. It felt strange and alien, but he didn't entirely hate it.

He ignored the tiny voice in the back of his mind telling him that it was only because he wished it was someone else's hand he was holding, and he distracted himself by following along with Niko's quick pace and listening to him wax poetic about the wonders of frozen fruit flavors vs chocolate ones.

There was a small crowd both inside and at the tables which stretched along the side of the building, but not much of a line, so when they stepped inside to wait, Derek didn't feel too closed in. He busied himself by studying the flavors, not really impressed by the selection, but then again this wasn't really his thing.

"I want every single one," Niko mourned.

Derek almost laughed. "I think that would probably break even the date rules about sugar intake."

Niko pouted a moment, then said, "We could each get one we both want and then share."

Derek didn't entirely love sharing food either, but this night was all about crossing small lines and getting just outside of comfort zones. He let Niko drag him to the counter and they tried five flavors each before Niko settled on the chocolate Guinness, and he went for pineapple. They took their little bowls, and he crunched down on the little tuile while Niko found them a free two-seater.

Derek was about to lower himself into the chair when two pairs of rapidly moving arms caught his attention. He looked over, and couldn't help a hot, ugly sensation from rising in the pit of his stomach when he saw Basil there with a guy who looked somewhat familiar. Amit, one of Sage's regulars, he was pretty sure. Amit was a super nice guy who lived in Denver but came down every few months or so to get new ink done.

Derek let his eyes close a second because he wanted to hate him so much right then. He wanted to hate Amit for being attractive and nice and being obviously fluent in sign which gave Basil so much more than he could offer right now.

"Hey," Niko said, grabbing his attention back, "are you okay?"

Derek let out a shaking breath, then smiled and nodded. "I'm great. Sorry. Just someone I know—he's on a date I guess."

"Someone you know, like an ex?" Niko asked. He wasn't an idiot and he'd been able to track Derek's line of sight. "Do you know sign language? Is he deaf or what?"

Derek found himself bristling a little, but he answered him anyway. "He's not an ex. He's a friend—he works down the street from the shop and we hang out sometimes. But uh...no. No, I don't really know sign. I mean, I know some because of Jazzy—Tony's baby? And I'm going to be starting classes soon. The whole shop is."

Niko frowned. "For what?"

"Well, for Jasmine," Derek said, "but also because it's probably a good language to have. I mean, being able to talk to deaf customers matters, right?"

Niko snorted. "I guess. I mean, how many deaf people are there, really? I doubt it's enough to justify learning a whole language."

Derek's jaw tensed. "Why should the percentage matter? I mean even one deaf person should be enough of a motivation."

"Well, they have ways, right? Writing and shit?" he waved his spoon dismissively. "How do you talk to him if you don't sign?"

"We text and I know some sign language," Derek defended. "But I know it sucks for him, and I'd like to be able to communicate with Tony's baby as she gets bigger."

Niko shrugged. "I guess. They're not going to teach her to talk though? I mean, deaf people can talk if they take therapy, can't they? Plus, there are those implant things she could wear so she can hear like a normal person."

Something hot and angry settled in his gut, and he felt on the verge of either panic or outright rage, and neither one of them would leave the evening on a good note. He took a breath, then set his cup down. "I just...I need to...I have a thing. I'll see you later." He rose and hurried off, not looking back when he heard Niko calling his name, and it was by some miracle the guy didn't follow him to his car.

CHAPTER EIGHT

Derek's head snapped up at the soft knock on the door frame, and when he saw his brother standing there, his eyes narrowed. "Don't."

"Look," Sage said, taking a step into the small room, "he told me what happened."

Derek shook his head, dropping his pencil next to the sheet of tracing paper he was working on for his next client. "You said if it didn't work—if for whatever reason, he and I didn't mesh—you'd leave me alone about it."

"I know, and I meant it," Sage said. He closed the door behind him and leaned up against it. "Is it because of Basil?"

Derek let out a frustrated breath, dragging both hands down his face. "Yes. And Jasmine, and anyone who has to deal with the rest of the world thinking they're not worth some effort just because they're not the fucking status quo."

Sage winced, because he had to know what it meant for Derek to hear that, how short that leap was between a deaf person who used sign, and someone with PTSD who needed someone understanding and willing to do things a little differently. "He didn't understand."

"That's fine," Derek said, and he meant it. "It's fine when someone doesn't understand, but when their default is to shit on someone, I can't trust them to understand what I need."

"I just," Sage started, then stopped and shook his head. He crossed his arms, then uncrossed them, his posture telling Derek he was approaching a possible conflict between them.

"Please don't defend him. I'm not saying he's a monster, I'm just saying he's not someone I could date."

"Do you think maybe he'd like the opportunity to learn?" Sage tried.

"And you think I'm the one who should teach him?" Derek spat. "You don't think I have enough on my plate just getting by? Where the hell am I going to find the energy to hold his hand through all this shit, Sage?"

Sage winced, then grabbed the small chair in the corner of the room, flipped it backward, and sank down. He rested his arms on the back and leaned toward his brother. "I won't ever understand, okay? I get that. You took the brunt of every single moment of dad's cruelty..."

"No," Derek said, putting his hand up. "You don't get to belittle what you went through, Sage. That's not what this is about."

"I know that, and that's not what I'm not doing," Sage argued. "I'm not making this some sort of fucked up competition that you managed to win by sheer bad luck. I deal with plenty thanks to that old bastard, but I didn't walk away with the same scars you did. And I would never, ever tell you that you had to be the one to guide someone through it."

"Then what are you saying?" Derek asked, all the fight draining out of him. His limbs felt heavy, his emotions having him wrung out, and suddenly he just wanted his bed.

"I'm saying that if he tries, if he learns—on his own, maybe with one of us—you might give him another shot? He's not a bad guy, he's just one of the billions of ignorant morons on this planet who were fortunate enough to not know what all of this was like."

Derek wanted to tell his brother to fuck off, to remind him he didn't owe this blind date anything. Except he couldn't help but recall how well the date had gone before, and how somewhere deep-down, Niko wasn't a bad person. Sage was right—he was ignorant. It didn't make him less than a person. In fact, he thought with some sarcasm, it almost made him more.

"I just don't know if I can," he finally admitted.

"That's fair. I'm just asking you to consider it. I'm not even sure he wants to try again. He knows he fucked up when you left the way you did, and he didn't hesitate to take all the blame for being an asshole." Sage scratched the back of his head, then sighed and pushed up to stand. "For what it's worth, I'm sorry I put you in the position to deal with something like this. I didn't see it coming."

"Neither did I," Derek told him. "Up to that point, the date was so good. We were getting along, and I...shit," he breathed out, rubbing his hands over his face again. "It felt so nice to just forget for a little while that I'm this hot mess of a person with no hope of ever being put together in a way most people can deal with."

"Derek, don't—"

"It is what it is, man," Derek told him. "It's fine. I'm sure there's someone interested, and I can be patient until then. At least I'm trying, right?"

Sage gave him a long look, then backed up to open the door. "Yeah. Right. If you need anything..."

"I'm good," Derek said, and he quickly turned his attention back to his work. At least, in these moments, his work gave him a sense of purpose, and ever made him feel like his existence was a burden.

'You talk to your friend yet?' Amit asked later that week over coffee.

Basil sighed, shaking his head. 'I don't know what to say, and I hate writing so much. I saw him heading into the community center for the ASL class, but they're not going to get into anything useful for months.'

Amit gave him a tiny smile, waggling his brows. 'You could always offer to private tutor him.'

Basil felt his cheeks heat up, even as he shook his head. 'He was on a date.'

'One that ended almost as badly as yours, man,' Amit pointed out. 'I'd say a comfort blow-job is always a good conversation starter.'

Basil gave him a dry, expressionless stare. 'Why are we friends?'

'Because I'm amazing, and you're kind of a loner who doesn't like to socialize,' he told him with a grin and a shrug. 'Anyway, I'm just saying it might not be the worst thing in the world that the dude walked out on a date because some gym-rat insulted Deaf people.'

Basil couldn't deny that. That fact had been haunting him since he and Amit had eavesdropped on Derek's date. Amit was a skilled lip-reader which made it much easier for him to interpret what was being said from four tables away, and Basil had been on the edge of panic until Derek all-but told his date to fuck off and then walked away.

It was almost a near echo of Basil's own bad date—the roles reversed, and he couldn't ignore how it made him feel that Derek had just as quickly and just as easily jumped to his defense. He hadn't told his sister about it, who was still feeling contrite and apologetic after the date with Jay, but he'd told Amit everything which was why they were out for ice cream that night.

'He offered me a free tattoo,' Basil eventually said.

Amit choked on his drink, swiping the back of his hand over his mouth to wipe away latte foam. Setting his drink down, he stared at him. Hard. 'He offered you a free tattoo. A free tattoo at Irons and Works?'

Basil flushed a little, shrugging one shoulder. 'Is that weird?'

'Irons and Works,' Amit started, spelling the name out very carefully, 'is not the kind of shop that just gives stuff away. They're expensive because they're good. Every person who works there is employed because they're able to prove their talent is a step above others. This is like getting free music lessons from Mozart.' When Basil raised both his brows, Amit rolled his eyes. 'Okay not Mozart, but close. I'm just trying to make a point that if this guy offered that to you, take it.'

Basil found himself brushing fingers along his forearm, the place he'd get that damn Night-Blooming blossom tattoo if he really was going to go through with it. He'd been thinking about it since Katherine chased after him and explained what Derek really meant by the offer. 'I can't seem to stop thinking about him.'

'I noticed,' Amit replied, a dry expression on his face. 'Are you really set on never dating him?'

Basil shrugged, glancing away for just a second to gather his thoughts. 'No. I want to say yes, because the thought of going through anything like my ex put me through sends me into a panic spiral and I can't live like that. But every one of my instincts is telling me Derek won't be like that. None of them will.'

Amit considered him for a long moment. 'I've spent most of my teenage and adult life in the Deaf Community. I don't have a lot of hearing friends, and the only reason I know those guys is because they were the best rated and I wanted good ink. I'm not the kind of guy who would tell you to start dating outside of our community, or to give hearies a chance, because I don't really feel like that. But those guys are different. I was there when the owner's daughter came home from her doctor's appointment after they were told she was hard of hearing.'

Basil's eyes widened. 'They came to the shop?'

'It's their family, all those guys,' Amit clarified. 'I was getting one of my side pieces done, so I was laying on a table. Sage had been going for a while, and he was in the zone, so he didn't want to stop, but it was obvious there was news. I always take my hearing aids out because the buzzing is overwhelming, but Tony's really easy to read.'

Basil knew this story. He'd seen it a hundred times on social media—parents struggling and crying because their child was deaf.

He'd read a hundred captions on a hundred videos, 'We didn't know what to do when we got the diagnosis, we were heart broken.'

Then some inspo story about finding some amazing speech therapist or audiologist and their baby smiled for the first time after they got CIs or hearing aids or whatever. He didn't need Amit to tell him this.

'I thought it was going to be some bullshit, and I couldn't decide if I was going to get defensive or not, because you don't fuck with people permanently altering your skin. It ended up not being necessary. He sat down at a computer, and when someone asked him what was up, he just turned around and said, 'Jazz is deaf, so you fuckers better be ready to learn sign with me.' Then he found a couple of classes and made some calls, and before I was wiped down and wrapped up, he was registered for ASL.' Amit gave Basil a second to absorb all that. 'I know the guys have been slow about it, but they're nothing like Derek's date. And nothing like your ex. No one's forcing this girl to verbalize. They sign with her all the time. They let me sign with her. They all try.'

Basil knew that. He knew it in the effortless way he'd seen Sage and Derek handle the kids, in the way they were with his sister, and how Derek always used every bit of sign he knew with Basil before resorting to paper and pen. Maybe if he started slow. Maybe if he took up Katherine, and now Amit's, advice and worked with him, gave him time so they could get to know each other without communication creating a barrier between them, there could be something real there.

'Start with the tattoo,' Amit said. 'Go from there.'

AT HOME, Basil paced his room, annoyed with himself and unable to stop replaying his conversation with Amit over and over in his head. Boiled down to the bare bones of the situation, it was simple. He liked Derek, Derek wasn't anything like Chad, and he would probably be safe.

But that didn't erase his fear of what could be, of what it all meant, and the not knowing how serious Derek was about any of it. They could try this—they could move forward and try something more, and then Derek could get annoyed, or bored, or tired of not speaking his own language and eventually they'd reach an impasse. Mostly because Basil would not voice—he would not. He would not compromise that part of himself again for anyone, no matter what they meant to him. A word or two here or there—fine. But he'd never carve away at his Deaf identity because it made some hearing person's life easier.

And he didn't know if there was middle ground between him and Derek with that between him.

Walking to his chair, he flopped down and pushed back, a little too hard. He hit the wall with a thud, and out of the corner of his eye, he saw the octopus painting crash to the floor. With a gasp, he jumped to his feet, terrified that the canvas had been torn, and he yanked it from between the desk and the wall.

It looked fine, and then he saw a scrap of something poking out of the wood frame in the back. For a moment, he thought the canvas had torn, but as he picked at it, he realized it was something else. A folded bit of paper, and he could see ink bleed on one side.

With trembling hands, he unfolded it and stared down at the writing, the surprise of it all preventing him from absorbing the words for a long moment.

Basil,

I don't really know why I'm writing this except to tell you that what you did for me the other night meant everything. Part of me isn't sure this painting is for you. Hell, maybe you showed your sister and somehow she had a thing for sea creatures, I don't know. But another part of me thinks maybe this means something.

That maybe living through dark moments, you get to have something like this. I don't know if we'll be friends—if we'll be more—if we'll be less, but I do know that I'll carry the other night with me probably forever. You're not the first person to talk me down from the ledge, but please you know are the first person who I walked away from without drowning in guilt and feeling like I'd been a burden. You just let me feel like a person, and I can't tell you what that meant. So thank you. If you ever get this note, just...thank you.

Always,
Derek

He stared down at the words, his hands shaking so hard he wasn't able to read them clearly when he went back a second time, but it didn't matter. He'd memorized it from that single pass. Maybe he was a fool for letting it get to him, maybe he should just burn the damn thing and be done with it. But instead, he folded it up and laid it on his nightstand, and he knew that tomorrow would bring a change.

CHAPTER NINE

Basil headed over to Irons and Works on Wednesday afternoon. His own shop was all-but dead, and Amit said that was the slowest day for most tattoo shops that he knew of. He couldn't be sure Derek was working, but he was taking the plunge. His feet dragged on the walk, but he finally made it to the door, and his heart stuttered a little in his chest because he could see Derek inside working in his stall at his drawing table.

He swallowed thickly, fighting the flight urge, and forced himself to walk through the door. It must have had a bell or buzzer, because the moment it swung open, Derek's head lifted, and his mouth parted in surprise. Basil could see his lips form a word, then Derek got to his feet and hurried toward the low swinging door.

'Hi,' he signed.

Basil smiled at him. 'Can we talk?' He hoped Derek's lessons and his work with Jasmine had gotten him that far, and by the blush on Derek's face, Basil thought maybe it had.

Derek gestured for Basil to follow him through, then led him to the seats they'd occupied last time he was there. Nothing looked different, apart from the spread of paper Derek had been working on, and though Basil was curious, wanted to poke and prod and learn Derek from the inside out, he held back. He sat down, then reached into his pocket for the short note he'd carefully crafted before coming over.

I am here for apologize. I didn't understand what you mean about free tattoo. I was think pity, but Katherine explain. So I say yes. If you want.

Derek read the note, then looked up with bright eyes and the curve of a smile on his lips. He carefully set the paper down, then signed, 'Yes. I want.'

'Book,' Basil signed, then pointed to where Derek had pulled out his sketchbook. 'With flowers.'

Basil felt a measure of relief when Derek nodded and reached for it. Their communication was half pantomime and nothing more advanced than the infant he was learning for, but it was something. He handed it over, and Basil wasted no time flipping to the back page where the Night-Blooming Cereus had been sketched. He wanted that, and something a little more, something that was all Derek, and a little bit of him—but not something Derek had pre-drawn.

He motioned for a pen and paper, and Derek handed over a blank notebook and a little golf pencil which barely fit between Basil's fingers. It would do, though, enough to explain what he was looking for. My mother have this flower. I want, but not this, you understand? Want new, but same flower.

Derek read the note, his tongue darting out to wet his lower lip, and Basil felt a hot surge of want he tried desperately to ignore. Friends, he reminded himself. First, they would try for friends. First, he would see if he really had the ability to trust him and let him in, because he owed it to himself to go slow.

Okay, Derek wrote beneath Basil's scribbled note. I have an idea, and you let me know if you like it. Some of my clients, ones that trust me a lot, let me do something free hand. I'll draw it on you with my pen first, but I don't stencil it. I just see where the work takes me.

Would you want something like that, or do you want me to draw it out first?

That, Basil thought. That's what I want, what I need. He laid one hand over Derek's wrist for a second, then signed, 'Yes. Perfect,' and, 'please.'

Derek's cheeks bloomed a soft pink, but he nodded and carefully put the notepad to the side of the desk. After a long moment he lifted his hands. 'I'm learning ASL. Beginner's class. I'm sorry I'm slow, but I'm trying.'

Basil ducked his head a little shyly and he nodded. 'I'm happy. Jasmine,' he used the sign name the twins had showed his sister, 'it will mean a lot to her when she grows up.' He mouthed along with his words, going slow, slower even when he saw Derek's eyebrows dip into a frown of confusion. But he didn't back down, he didn't dumb it down. 'I can help you.'

'Help me,' Derek repeated. Basil could tell from the way he moved his lips, he said the word aloud and he felt an inexplicable urge to lay his hand to Derek's throat and feel the vibrations of his voice. His fingers tingled with the barely repressed urge. 'Sign?'

Basil nodded. 'Every day. We can meet, drink coffee, practice.'

Derek's lips lifted into a grin that reached his eyes, making them stand out gorgeous and almost hypnotizing. 'Thank you. I…' His finger hovered in the air, pointing to himself like there was so much more he wanted to say but didn't know how yet. Which was fine. It was okay. Some day he would have the words, and Basil was almost positive he'd be there when Derek could finally give them.

'You are out of your damn mind,' Amaranth said, though she was smiling at him. She had her legs up on the arm of the sofa, her head pillowed on a folded afghan, her signs a little sloppy from the half-gone bottle of wine at the floor near the edge of the table. 'A tattoo. You?'

Basil scowled at her. 'Since when do you not like tattoos?'

'I love them.' She rolled onto her side, lifting her shirt so he could get an eye-full of her songbirds which bore a ribbon with their parents' names. She dropped her clothes and settled back in. 'You don't have any.'

'Need to start somewhere, right?' he challenged.

'You just want to touch dicks with him,' she said, waving her hand dismissively.

Basil's entire body erupted with a blush so hot he was almost dizzy with it. 'I'm helping him with sign, and he's giving me a tattoo. There's nothing sexual.'

'Yet,' she signed, spelling the word slow and pointed. 'You'll seal the deal with some good old fashion fucking, and I'm happy for you. I wish things hadn't been so ugly with Jay, but I think Derek is a great guy. And he's so hot.'

Basil rolled his eyes, but he couldn't exactly argue with the latter part of her statement. He was a good guy, and he was so hot. More than. There was a beauty about him—something maybe a little vulnerable like his beauty had been part of why life was so shitty for him before now. But he didn't want to read too much into it. Derek deserved to be discovered properly and truthfully, and Basil wanted nothing more than to dive in and start learning him.

'When do you start?'

'Tomorrow,' he told her. 'For sign. Saturday for tattoo.' He dropped his hands, then let his right palm fall to his left forearm and he stared down at the blank skin there. By the end of Saturday afternoon, there would be something there—permanent and bright, and there would be no taking it back. He wanted it though, wanted to see the evidence of someone like Derek on his skin.

His thoughts were interrupted by the lights flashing, and he frowned over at her. 'Are you expecting anyone?'

Amaranth shook her head. 'No. It's probably just soul-solicitors. You want me to get it?'

He grinned at her. 'Nah. They always walk away faster when they realize I don't speak.' Pushing himself up, he walked to the door and flung it open, preparing a flurry of ASL in hands too fast for anyone but the totally fluent to understand.

Instead of people asking for donations, or to test their water, or to sign them up for their church service, Jay stood there looking contrite and hesitant. His hand raised, hesitated, then signed a simple, 'Hello.'

'What are you doing here?' Basil demanded. He figured his total ghosting of the guy had sent the message well enough, but apparently not.

Gnawing on his bottom lip, he fidgeted a moment before he answered. 'I wanted to apologize. I should have before. I should have texted or emailed you, but I wanted to say it in person. I was being really harsh and judgmental without considering they might have been your friends.'

Basil clung to his frustration and anger, because he didn't want to forgive him. He didn't want Jay to pave the way for some sort of reconciliation. 'You didn't need to do that.'

'Yes,' Jay signed. 'You're a great guy and I liked you a lot, and I'd like the chance to maybe start over. It had been a rough week for me, and I wasn't at my best.'

Wasn't there some saying, he thought to himself, about handling someone at their worst to deserve their best? Jay's worst wasn't as bad as Chad's had been, but all the same, he wasn't sure he wanted to continue on with some guy whose default was judgmental asshole. 'I don't know.'

'I understand,' Jay offered. 'Just...think about it and text me? I'd like the chance to prove I'm not actually a bad guy. It was just a bad night.'

Basil could give him that, sure. He wasn't the kind of guy who had unreasonable expectations. He was surly and difficult to get along with even on his good days, but something was rubbing him the wrong way. Maybe it was the fact that for most of the night, Jay had centered the conversation totally around himself. And maybe it was the fact that his apology had done the same thing.

'I'll let you know,' he finally replied.

Jay didn't look overly enthusiastic about the dismissal, but he didn't argue either. 'Thank you,' he said. 'I won't keep you, but please just know I can show you a different side to me.'

Basil just nodded, then shut the door before he had a chance to go on. When he went back to the living room, Amaranth turned the TV off to give him her full attention. 'Who was that?'

'Jay,' Basil told her, sinking back into his chair with a sigh. 'He came to apologize for the bad date and asked me to give him another chance.'

Her eyebrows flew up. 'What did you say?'

'That I'd think about it,' he told her. 'I don't really know if I should. He's self-absorbed. He spent the whole night talking about himself when he wasn't judging me for living here or judging the guys from the tattoo shop and calling them trashy. I'm not sure that's someone I want to date.'

'Did he say why he was such an asshole?'

Basil laughed. 'Yeah, he said it was a bad night. And I guess? But I can't imagine having a day so bad I start talking like that. And then to claim he didn't mean it? Bullshit.'

'Maybe,' she replied, her expression careful. 'Maybe he really was just having a shit time.'

Basil bit his lip. 'Maybe,' he conceded, but he wasn't entirely sure he believed him.

WHEN DEREK WALKED into the shop Saturday morning, he was humming with nerves. He'd already had his first coffee meet-up with Basil where they'd gone over the basics of what he knew, and they'd even managed a simple conversation by the end of the night. It might have consisted solely of talking about family members and what he was studying at the university, but it was still progress. And he got to see that look on Basil's face—the quiet smile filled with something a little deeper than pride—that made him want to do anything to keep it there.

Today, he would start Basil's piece. They'd switched to paper to discuss it, and Basil had carefully explained, using more written words than he usually did, the meaning behind the flower. Was it coincidence or irony that one of the most captivating blossoms Derek had ever seen was something Basil's mother had used to show her son that he was special? He could never figure those two words out, but what he did know was that it was important. That it meant something for him to get it right.

Basil had decided he wanted an entire forearm piece—more than just the flower, but he wanted Derek to design it, to come up with something that spoke to them both. It was a lot of pressure—and as an artist, it was his dream job. Not only to have the freedom, but the trust of the person in front of him to get it right.

His heart had been beating in his throat all morning, and his nerves took the place of his need for coffee. He was running on pure adrenaline as he stepped in through the back door and walked through to the main lobby, and he was ready to get settled in when he saw a familiar face in his brother's stall.

Derek felt a small pang of betrayal when his eyes locked with Niko's. The guy was leaning on Sage's bench, and the two of them were bent over his ankle, discussing what looked like a very old, faded lion's head right near his calf.

The silence and tension were almost tangible between them, then Niko cleared his throat and lowered his gaze. "Derek. Hey."

Derek pursed his lips, looked over at his brother, but he didn't see guilt, only a little awkward hesitation. "Hey," he finally said.

"I swear I didn't know you were coming in," Niko rushed to explain. "I sort of surprised Sage—I figured if it was early enough, I'd miss you, and it wouldn't be weird."

"It's fine," Derek said a little tensely. He glanced at the clock and felt profound gratitude that Basil wasn't coming in for another couple of hours. He turned his back away from Sage and pulled out his sketch pad. He'd been working on a few design ideas, but Basil was set on the entire thing being drawn fresh, on his skin. Derek had only done a couple of those, and only on Sage and Mat. He wanted to have at least some reference, but he realized the idea wouldn't come to life—not fully—until his machine was buzzing in his hands and the image was pouring out through the ink.

Just as he was getting lost in his thoughts, a throat cleared and he glanced over his shoulder to see Niko there, hands fidgeting. "Look," he said slowly, "I understand why you don't want to talk to me again. I don't blame you. I was a real shithead, and I think the worst part was, I didn't realize why until after you left."

With a tiny sigh, Derek dropped his pencil on the table and spun his stool around. He considered just telling the guy to fuck off, but in truth, Niko was a good person and Sage had been right about one thing—he deserved the chance to grow past shitty assumptions. "Not one single person in this shop lives life without some sort of accommodation. We got wheelchair users, amputees, brain injuries, PTSD."

Niko blinked in surprise. "I didn't know."

"I get that. You don't know us. And I get it, because working here, it's easy to forget. Talking to these people every day, you don't really think about it. Everyone's chill and we're family, man. We don't let those things define each other. But some nights, we can't help it. Like when I have a panic attack which fucks me up for days. When I can't let anyone touch me because it sends me to a dark place. Or like when my buddy Sam is fighting the system because the government suits think a man with tattoos and a wheelchair can't properly care for a kid. Like when my boss and the only man who's ever treated me like a real son asks us all to learn his daughter's language because she deserves the world to bend to her, and not the other way around. And it don't matter if she's the only one, you know? She still deserves it."

He was breathing slightly heavy after that, carefully watching Niko's expression as the man took it all in. He wasn't sure what to expect, either. He didn't think he'd deal too well if someone read him to filth without any sort of pull back or remorse, but Niko simply nodded and took a step back.

"I know. I knew it after you walked off and didn't come back. I realized the kind of asshole I was because I had been lucky enough in life I never had to consider shit like that before, and I'm sorry." He dragged a hand through his hair and glanced back, but Derek could see Sage had already vacated the main floor. When Niko looked back, his eyes were droopy and a little sad. "We had such a good time, and I fucked it up, and I'll never stop being sorry for it."

Derek felt a small pang in his chest. "It's not okay, but it's not something I plan to hold a grudge over."

Niko's lips twitched at the corners, like maybe he wanted to smile, though he didn't let himself. "Would you," he started, then stopped and huffed a breath, his eyes darting away for a second. "A drink? Would you go for a drink with me? Let me try again? Your brother was right about you—I like you and we could be good together. Even if it's just as friends."

Derek felt himself torn directly down the middle. Making headway with Basil felt like a tiny triumph, but he had no promise there would ever be more. And frankly, he didn't exactly get along with most people, so it seemed a little reckless to let an opportunity like this pass him by. There was every chance that in the near future, his feelings for Basil would cool and he'd be ready to meet someone else.

That someone else might be standing right there in front of him.

"Yeah I...as friends. For now," he clarified.

Niko's face stilled, then he let himself grin, wide and sunny, eyes lit up with it. "Can I text you?"

"Yeah," Derek said with a nod, then rolled back to his desk and turned around to face his table. "You can text me."

. . .

Niko was long gone before Basil arrived for his session. Derek could feel the nerves on him, see it in the slight tremble of his fingers as he laid back in the chair and rested his arm on the cushioned side.

Derek had his gloves on, and he quickly pulled out his bottles of alcohol, witch hazel, and his tube of ointment. He watched Basil out of the corner of his eye as he dabbed some of the ointment on the little cups, then carefully filled them all with his colors. It would be simple today, he wanted outline and shading on the bloom, and a little shadow around it. And then...well, he wasn't sure. He'd wait for Basil's skin to speak to him, but he knew there would be more. Basil's skin was singing for it.

When he finished up, he switched his gloves and grabbed his razor and bottle of alcohol. Before he began, he caught Basil's eye and signed, 'Nervous?'

Basil's face twitched a little, then he let out a breathy laugh and held his hand out flat, see-sawing it back and forth.

'Pain?' he signed, trying desperately to recall the signs he'd practiced so diligently in order to communicate it all effectively with him. 'You hate pain?'

Basil licked his lips, then signed, 'New,' mouthing the word along so Derek could be sure what he was saying.

'If you want to stop, tap me,' Derek told him, then gave his left arm a pat. 'We will go slow, we can take breaks.'

Basil's mouth eased into a smile, and he reached for the little notepad he'd brought with him. You practice all signs for today?

Derek flushed and quickly wrote back, Is it obvious?

Basil shook his head, but Derek knew it didn't mean no. He was wearing a fond grin and his eyes were soft, like he might have even found it endearing. Ready to begin, ready to break the intensity between them, he carefully took Basil's arm in his hand, sprayed it with the alcohol, and removed as much of the hair as he could. Tossing the razor in the bin, he swiped Basil's arm down, then reached for his pen. He wasn't going to do everything, but he was going to give himself a place to start. The pedals came to life in red ink as he sketched, just the bare outlines, the image more in his head than anywhere else. He could see it forming, taking shape, becoming something more beautiful and alive than the rough lines on Basil's skin now. When he was finished, he stared at just how much of Basil's arm it took up, and it looked right. Glancing up, he saw Basil's gaze fixed on his arm, and it stayed there for a while. When he finally looked up, Derek nodded to him, and Basil's lips stretched into a tight smile.

Derek had the machine prepped and ready, fresh gloves on, his fingers itching to take up his machine and get to work.

He loved this part of the job more than anything, that first line drawn on fresh skin, watching the ink imbed itself into a person as a permanent symbol of his work. And with Basil, it felt deeper, it felt more important. He breathed out, then signed, 'Ready?'

Basil's own breath was a little shaky, but he shifted downward in the chair to get more comfortable, then nodded and motioned with his free hand for Derek to start.

Closing his eyes for a moment, just to ready himself, he switched on the machine and it whirred to life in his hand. Normally his first-time clients jumped a little at the sound, but he knew Basil wouldn't react until he could feel it. He wondered what that would be like, to not know the impact of the first line until it hit your skin. He thought maybe it would be better like that, without the moment of overwhelming anticipation had by the loud buzz just before the needle sank in for the first time.

He smiled at Basil, an attempt to reassure him as he dipped the needle into the ink. He watched it drip down onto the table, then carefully reached over and laid his free hand over Basil's. Their eyes met, and he tried his best to convey a message. *I'll take care of you, it will hurt, but it will be worth it. You're safe with me.*

Basil blinked after a moment, and he seemed to acknowledge it. His arm didn't tense, so Derek brought the needle down and began.

• • •

Basil didn't quite know how to describe the pain, except that it was startling and annoying, but not the agony he anticipated when he considered needles pulsing ink into his skin. The first touch jolted him, and he worried for a second like he'd caused Derek to slip, but the other man merely smiled serenely and met Basil's eyes to reassure him it was fine.

And then he began to work, and it was possibly the most mesmerizing thing Basil had ever seen. Derek's face was rapt with concentration and passion as he made short, clipped lines all around, not like the way he'd looked when he was merely drawing it out. The red lines soon became black. With every swipe of the kitchen paper, pulling away smears of ink, the tattoo started to come to life. The concentrated pain in every drag of the machine kept him consciously aware of what was happening, but he didn't want to stop. Something about it made him want to keep going forever, for the pain to drag him to some place of euphoria and keep him there.

It was absurd, and maybe it was just his adrenaline talking, but really it didn't matter. He was still here, and Derek's free hand pressed to his skin, the glove warm as it kept him grounded like a ballast. Every so often, Derek would look up, their eyes would connect, saying a thousand things between them without voicing, without signing. Then he'd go back to work and lose himself again, and Basil would be helpless to look away.

Finally, when it felt like just short of eternity had passed, Derek stopped the machine. His skin felt numb in some places, stinging in others, and there was an almost visceral relief to have the vibrations go quiet. Derek swiped him down with something wet and a little soothing, then he grabbed some ointment and rubbed it into the skin.

It wasn't done yet, that much was obvious. It was an outline, just the beginnings of what it would become, but already it was beautiful. He looked back up at Derek who was scribbling on a notepad, then he handed it over. Ten minute break, and if you're up for it, we can keep going and I can fill and shade.

Basil just nodded, his hand not really up for moving enough to write a reply.

Derek didn't seem to need one, and he took up the paper again. Do you want some food or drink? One of the guys usually gets dinner around now, and he can bring something.

Basil blinked, then grabbed his phone to tap out, Is it safe to eat during a tattoo?

Derek chuckled, his shoulders shaking with it as he replied, I'm not going to eat a sandwich and tattoo at the same time. It'll be for after. But I can get you water or a fizzy drink. Or we have coffee. Whatever you want.

'Water,' Basil signed, tapping the edge of his W on his chin. He didn't think caffeine would do him any favors being stuck in the chair for however long the rest of it took. Part of him wanted to tell Derek to save the rest for later—not just because his skin ached, but because it meant he'd have a reason to come back. But then again, he was sure this piece was far from over. He'd given Derek tacit permission to keep going for as long as he needed, until it was finished, and he knew this wasn't it.

Watching Derek walk away, Basil studied the shining ink on his skin which was now marked forever, and he couldn't help but smile. He turned on his camera and snapped a shot of the angry red, slightly raised lines, then sent it in a text to both Amaranth and Amit.

> Amaranth: Nerd

> Amit: That looks amazing. You done?

> Basil: Shade flower sometime longer not sure time.

> Amit: Right on, well send me a pic when it's done. We can get a drink later if you want. I'm off at ten.

> Basil: Text you.

He set his phone down just as Derek came back in and handed him a bottle of water. As Basil cracked the top, Derek took his arm and gently twisted it from side to side as he studied each line. When he was done, he gently set Basil's arm down and signed, 'You like?'

'Beautiful,' Basil replied. There was more he wanted to say, but Derek didn't have the signs for it. Someday he would, someday Basil would be able to express just how much this meant to him, and he could be patient until then.

He sipped on his cool drink as Derek donned a fresh pair of gloves, then carefully sprayed something almost astringent onto a new bit of kitchen paper and wiped the ointment away. He adjusted his ink cups, added another shade of grey to the lineup, then looked back at Basil.

'Ready?'

Basil nodded and adjusted himself, laying his arm flat again. He watched as Derek drew his lower lip into his mouth, watched as he carefully extracted a new set of needles—these wider and a little more frightening—and set them into the machine. He watched the way Derek treated every piece on his table with a reverence and care that few people had for anything in their lives, and he wondered what it would be like to be treated that way. Would that be what real love was like? To have someone hold you and touch you like you were something precious?

Chad had said he loved Basil, but he had never touched him with sweetness. Possession, and mockery, and occasional concern—but never the way Derek did, as he gently laid his hand back down on Basil's arm.

'Ready?' Derek asked again.

Basil wanted to tell him he'd be ready for the rest of his life, that he'd sit here and let Derek ink every exposed bit of skin if he wanted, if only it kept them in moments like these. But he didn't say that—couldn't, not in a way Derek would understand. So, he just nodded, and let his head fall back, and let himself feel it all.

CHAPTER TEN

Derek's gloved thumb gently felt over the raised lines of the tattoo as he smeared ointment over the work. It was a practice he did daily—several times a day depending on his work-load, and yet for some reason, it felt hollow right now. Maybe it was because three nights before, he'd finally gotten his hands on Basil's skin. He'd felt him heat up and cool down, tense and relax, pull back then submit as Derek inked his skin.

Every client since then had been not enough. Each session lacked the intimacy of his work with Basil, and it was getting to him. With a heavy sigh, he sat back in his chair, watching the young girl leave. The second the door shut, he spun and eyed Tony who was putting together a new bookshelf for Kat's stall.

"Can I ask you something?"

Tony turned, eyebrows raised. "Of course."

"You've done a lot of Kat's work, right? Like pretty much all of it?"

Tony put his screwdriver down and turned his chair to face Derek. "Yeah. She had a small sparrow on the back of her neck before we met, and the cover-up I did turned into her entire piece. Why?"

"I just," Derek said, trying to find words that would make sense. "Was it different, working on her? I mean, when you started on her, were you two already a thing?"

Tony's mouth quirked into a half smile. "Not quite a thing yet, but we were getting there. And yeah, there was a different kind of intimacy there than with my usual clients." He scratched the back of his head as he looked at Derek. "Something goin' on with you?"

Derek felt his cheeks redden a little as he shrugged. "I've just... there's a guy—a client, sort of..."

"The guy you workin' on for free?" Tony asked.

Derek shrugged. "Might be, yeah. He's just different. It's different with him. At first, I thought it might be transference. He helped me out when I freaked out when I got locked in at the bank and my head can get a little nuts when it comes to that stuff. But it just...hasn't stopped."

"He's the guy you started the class for," Tony pointed out.

Derek felt a wave of guilt. "You know that's for Jazz, Tony. You know she's important to me."

Tony laughed. "Yeah, but it also don't surprise me that it took the promise of good dick to rush you through the door. I ain't mad about it, Der. I know you love my girl. She loves you just as much, and you'd get there no matter what. But why you askin' me this?"

"Because it felt different the other night," Derek told him. "It's never been like that before, working on someone, and I've had some pretty intense regulars over the years. People I know better than I know myself. But today—it's felt all fucked up. Working on other people feels empty and wrong. Like...like..."

"Like you're cheating?" Tony offered, and when Derek flushed again, he laughed and shook his head. "That's normal. And that won't last forever. Hell, won't even feel the same tomorrow. But you damn well know this is intimate shit, here. We're leaving our mark—sometimes on strangers we'll never see again. They'll be carryin' a piece of us for life, and even if they get that shit covered up, we're still there. When you cross that line and mark someone who might be special to you, it changes things a little. Adds a layer you don't feel with anyone else. You learn to separate it, but it takes a little time."

Derek nodded, sighing quietly as he leaned on his table. "I think this could be something. I mean...maybe not. He hasn't really given me any indication he's interested in anything more than friendship and sign language tutoring. But when I'm with him, it feels right."

"Would you be happy, just havin' this?" Tony asked. "Just friends?"

"Any way I can have him in my life," Derek answered, and he was surprised by just how much he meant it. Before Tony could respond, Derek's phone buzzed, and he glanced at the screen. There was a message from Niko, the first after his promise to text, and Derek was a little startled the guy had actually gone through with it.

"Go ahead," Tony told him with a grin and a wink. "I gotta finish this up before Kat comes in here and sees what a fuckin' mess I've made."

Derek chuckled, then opened up his phone to read it.

> Niko: Any chance you'd be up for that drink tonight. It's been a long day and I could use some company.

> Derek: I promised my buddies we'd hang out at our friend's place, but he wouldn't mind if you tagged along. Chill night, beer and food.

> Niko: Can I meet you at the shop?

> Derek: Be here at seven thirty.

He set his phone down, smiling just a little. He wasn't sure he was ready to consider more with Niko, but he really did want, at the very least, to be his friend. Sage had been right about how much they had in common, and he might have thought a few shitty things, but he wasn't sure yet. And frankly, he was testing him. Maybe it was a dick move in a way, but he wanted to see what would happen if he brought Niko into a house with the people he loved whose disabilities were in your face visible.

> Derek: Yo, can I bring a friend tonight? I'll pick up food.

> James: Whatever you want, man. If we can help you bump uglies and get you over this slump, we got your back. Nothing's going down besides Matty working on my leg anyway.

> Sam: Whatever you want, but get bbq, I want slaw on okra so bad I can taste it.

> Derek: Gross, but ok. See you at 8.

Seven-fifteen rolled around, and Derek wasn't surprised at all when Niko strolled through the door. Lucy, Mat's roommate who was just starting her apprenticeship with them, was using Sage's stall, and when she smiled up at him, Derek realized Niko was friendly with more than just his brother in the shop.

"Hey, gorgeous. How's Cale?" Niko asked, surprising Derek that he knew Lucy's younger brother.

Lucy smiled. "Recovering. That flu this year kicked his ass. I can't believe it hit in April."

"Tell him I'm still holding his spot when he's ready to come back. I won't ever cheat on my leg-day guy." Niko winked at her, then leaned over the counter and made eye-contact with Derek. "Sorry I'm early."

Derek shrugged, glancing at Lucy out of his periphery who was watching him with a strange expression. He wanted to ask her what it was all about, but he didn't want to put Niko on the spot. "It's no worries. Do you want to do me a favor though?"

"Anything," Niko said quickly.

Derek fished out the food order on the little post-it and handed it off. "Can you call Jerry's and order all this? Tell whoever answers to throw it on my tab and that I'm bringing my card in tonight."

Niko looked at him for a moment, then glanced at Lucy before nodding. "You got it. Be back in five." He strolled back out the front door, and Derek swiveled in his chair to stare at her.

"What?" he demanded.

She shrugged, twirling her colored pencil between her fingers like a tiny baton. "Nothing."

"Lies," he said, pointing his sharpie at her. He was profoundly aware of how much she looked like Cale right then, in spite of being six years older than him, and only sharing one parent. "What is it?"

"It's just…everyone's been talking about you and the flower guy. Like some epic love story or some shit. Niko is bad ass, I just…I guess I was confused."

Derek sighed, resting his back against his tool box. "It's complicated, but right now, Basil and I are just friends. He's helping me with sign, and I'm doing an arm piece on him."

"For free," she pointed out.

"Yeah well," he said, then trailed off, because the last thing he was in the mood for was to tell the sordid story of his impossible feelings and the struggle of their communications barrier. "It is what it is. I had a date with Niko, and it went kind of shitty, so we're seeing if there's any way to fix it."

She looked startled. "Seriously? I mean, I'm rooting for flower guy, but it's hard to imagine a date with Niko going badly. He, Mat, and Cale have been gym buddies for like a hundred years. Shit, my mom invites the guy to thanksgiving every year. He's a good guy."

Derek bristled a little. "Well, he said a few shitty things about… something," he finished with some hesitance, not wanting to drag Niko, but not really in the mood to listen to someone come to his defense. "Do you think he knows about Mat's head injury?"

Lucy's brow furrowed. "I don't know. I mean, he hates talking about it, so probably not. Why?"

"Just...he had this sort of attitude about uh...about disabilities and deafness and shit. It wasn't great."

Lucy's face fell. "Oh. Well..."

"Look," he said, holding up his hand, "it's not a big deal. We're trying again, and even if it's not going to work out like that, we can still be friends. He really does seem like a nice guy, so I'm willing to give it another shot."

The door opened then, and Derek went quiet as Niko walked back up to the counter and put the post-it down. "Done. He said about twenty minutes."

"Sweet." Derek put his sharpie back in his drawer and then double-checked his stall. There was no point in hanging around, anyway. Kat and Laura were in the back to handle any walk-ins, and Wyatt was coming in later for a touch-up appointment, so they were covered. "We can get going."

Lucy gave him a sunny grin as he got up and headed out the front instead of the back, and he waved before the door swung shut. Neither of them said much for almost a full block before Niko let out a heavy breath and stopped Derek with a hand on his arm.

"Look, if you don't want to do this, I'll understand. Don't feel obligated because Sage and I are friends."

Derek couldn't help a tiny laugh as he turned to look at Niko. "My brother and I might share the same face and most of the same ink, but we're not the same person, and I sure as hell don't feel like I owe him my loyalty to a person I don't know that well simply because we're brothers. I agreed to this because I think you deserve a chance."

Niko's cheeks darkened, the color visible even under the dim streetlight. "I really am sorry about that. I should have known better."

"Maybe," Derek gave him. "But you did listen, and that's the important part." He almost told him then, about hanging out with Sam and James tonight, but he wanted to see his raw reaction when they walked through the door. "Do you want to take your own car. In case it gets awkward?"

Niko shoved one hand into his pocket. "I wouldn't mind if we shared. Uh...unless you think you want your own escape. But I also have no problem calling an uber."

Derek smiled. "I think sharing is great. Come on, before I'm sacrificed to the tattoo gods for being late with the food."

They arrived twenty minutes later, Derek holding the door for Niko who insisted on carrying all three bags. They were at James' place that night, a leftover relic from the thirties tucked back into a grove of trees. He'd inherited the place from his brother who had been thirty years older than he was, and no kids to pass his shit onto. It came with some nice in-law quarters, a little cottage out back which was currently being rented by a blind man who was taking a sabbatical from his teaching job.

No one knew the guy well—no one except James, who occasionally ate dinner with him and played cards—but he seemed nice enough, and he never complained if guys' night got a little rowdy and loud.

The guys were set up in the living room, so Derek took Niko right to the kitchen to unload before they went in to make introductions.

"Is your brother here?" Niko asked as he unloaded the boxes of brisket and chicken.

Derek shook his head. "He's out with a couple of the girls from the shop. Did you want me to call and invite him?"

Niko bit his lip, hiding a smile. "Is it bad if I say no? I just," he went on in a hurry, like Derek might be offended, "I like getting to know you without him there. Siblings make each other weird."

Derek couldn't help his laugh, mostly because it was true. He tended to be a little more withdrawn whenever Sage was around, and it was worse after Ted tied because Derek was always so afraid something would remind his brother of the man he lost and would send him into a spiral.

"I don't think it's bad. You'll like these guys just as much as my brother. They swear a little more, but once they trust you, they'll always have your back." Derek grabbed a beer out of the fridge, and Niko grabbed water before following Derek through the sliding door and into the main living area.

Before Derek could begin to make introductions, he felt Niko freeze at his back, and then take a stumbling step away, gasping, "Holy shit!"

Derek frowned, confused for as long as it took to see Mat carving into the fleshy colored foam of James' prosthetic covering. Niko had all-but crashed into the wall, and his face was turned away and slightly green.

Suppressing a laugh, Derek reached out and touched his arm. "Hey, it's okay. It's a fake leg, dude. It's just foam."

Niko's breath hitched, then he opened his eyes and his face blushed so red, Derek worried he might pass out. "Seriously?"

With barely repressed laughter, James lifted his stump into the air. "Seriously. One of the ladies at our shop actually does scarification, but believe me, she only does that shit at the shop in a very sterile room. I wouldn't let any of these fucks carve me up on this nasty-ass sofa."

Mat rolled his eyes, his scalpel digging into a curve of sharpie-marked foam. "Dude, this is your sofa."

"Yeah, and you fucks know I found it outside the dorms last year. It probably has all kinds of pubic lice," James said with a shit-eating grin.

By then, Niko had calmed, his face fading to a faint pink. He leaned his head in toward Derek and murmured, "I am so mortified."

Derek shook his head, still grinning. "Don't worry about it. If I didn't know better, it would have freaked me out too. His leg looks real as hell."

Niko looked unsure, but he stepped back up to Derek's side and looked around. His eyes immediately found Sam's chair, though Derek doubted it was obvious who it belonged to. Sam was on the love-seat with his legs stretched in front of him, and James was half-lying on the sofa with both of his in Mat's lap.

Derek studied him for a moment, but he supposed any sense of immediate discomfort had been dispelled by thinking one of the guys was getting carved up with a scalpel on a dirty old sofa. "Guys, this is Niko."

"We've met," Mat said with a grin.

Derek rolled his eyes. "He's Cale and Mat's gym buddy, and I guess Sage fucks off there too sometimes. Niko, that's Sam and James."

Sam stuck out his hand toward Niko, though he didn't lean forward since by this late at night, his balance was usually shit. "Sorry, my chair's over there so I'm gonna be rude and not come to you."

Niko didn't hesitate as he crossed the room and grabbed Sam's hand to shake. "No worries. It's really good to meet you, Derek talked about you guys a lot."

Watching Niko carefully, it was impossible to miss the way his eyes lingered on Sam, the way they traveled over his features, down his thick arms, over his chest. There was a spark there that was definitely missing from their first date, and where it maybe should have stung, instead it just inspired him.

"You can pop a squat there next to Sam," Derek told him, grabbing one of the folding chairs and setting it up between the sofa and the love seat. "And the rest of you can get food because I'm not your damn servant."

James grinned, leaning over to slap his thigh. "Nah. Just delivery boy."

"Pretty enough to be a rent boy," Mat added.

Derek flipped them both off. "Fuck you, and go eat before your shit gets cold because I'm not in the mood to listen to you bitch."

"Yes dad, sorry dad," James said with a laugh as he hopped up.

He shook some of the foam from his leg, then slipped it on and led the way with Mat close behind. Niko rose to his feet, then hesitated as he looked back and forth between Sam and the kitchen.

"Would I be an asshole if I offered to grab you a plate?" he asked.

Derek could see Sam was holding back a chuckle. "Nah, that would be cool. I just want like a huge-ass pile of slaw right on top of the okra, and some of the mac and cheese. Maybe a beer, too. I'm almost out."

Niko's hesitance turned into a grin, then he looked at Derek like he suddenly remembered who he was with and why. His cheeks flushed. "Can I grab you something?"

Derek smiled softly. "I'm good for now. Go eat, though. I did promise you food."

Niko looked unsure, but after a beat, he turned and headed off toward the kitchen. The second he was out of earshot, Sam leaned over toward Derek and socked him in the thigh. "What the fuck you doing bringing your date around here before you two are solid? I know you didn't miss that."

Derek bit his bottom lip to hide his grin as he shook his head. "Trust me, it's cool. We didn't get off on the right foot, and I was thinking there might be something there, but he didn't look at me the way he looked at you even before the date went bad."

Sam let out a tiny sigh. "Man, I really don't have time for that right now. Everything's in the shitter with this custody thing. They want to find her dad's family and offer them a chance to petition for custody now."

Derek felt like icy water had been thrown over his head. "What the hell? When did you find that out?"

"Got the call last night," Sam said from behind a sigh. "These fucks aren't going to rest til they drag her out of my arms. I don't..." He rubbed a hand down his face. "I can't lose her. I've had her since she was nine months old, man. That girl is mine."

"I know she is," Derek said fiercely. "Have you lawyered up? Like properly?"

"I have some legal aid help, but shit, I don't have the cash," Sam admitted in a quiet voice. "These classes, these trips, all this paperwork—it's been slowly draining what savings I had."

"Maybe I can help," Derek said.

Sam gave him a flat look. "I know you don't have that kind of cash."

"Maybe not, but if we pool our resources," Derek said, then gave Sam a hard look when his mouth dropped open to argue. "Don't be a shit about this, man. She's our girl too. Tony would cut his arm off rather than see you lose her, and I..." He licked his lips and felt his stomach twist with the offer he was about to make, only because he would only make it for one of his family. "I got connections through my dad. I just have to ask him."

Sam paled. "Dude. No. Fuck that. Fuck that so much. You're not asking that sadistic freak for anything. Do you understand me? Do you know what he'll want from you?"

"Yes," Derek said, because he did. His dad would want to drain him of everything he had left, emotionally, physically, mentally. But he'd do it. The sacrifice would be more than worth it for Sam and May. "I know exactly what he'd want, and I don't fucking care. You're not losing that girl."

Sam looked like he might be sick, but he didn't get a chance to answer when the other guys came back into the room. Niko was subdued as he handed his plate off to Sam, and when he sat, it was a little closer to Derek. There was an obvious tension in the room, but it was clear Mat and James didn't want to bring it up with a stranger there.

The topic turned to other things—Derek couldn't bring himself to pay attention, his mind on calling his father and how, exactly, he'd manage to get the favor. But he'd do it. He didn't care what he had to promise the old man.

The tension died down a little, and Sam began to joke with Niko a little, and in spite of his protests, Derek could sense the spark between them. It would be a good match, he thought. When Sam moved to his chair to go outside for a little bit of air, Niko offered to go with, and Sam didn't turn him down.

The door shut, and both James and Mat rounded on him. "Uh," James said, giving him a pointed look, "isn't the gym-rat your date?"

Derek shook his head. "We had a date and I'm not feeling it. But he's a good guy, and I think those two might actually have something there."

"Sam'll never go for it," Mat said a little mournfully. "I've been trying to get that dude laid for months. I basically offered myself as full time, any time, babysitter. Like three am, don't fucking care if it means he gets his dick wet. But he won't pull the trigger."

"He told me about the update," Derek said quietly.

Both men's faces immediately went stormy. "Those dudes are asking for straight up wrath brought down on them," James said darkly. There was a southern-preacher twang in his voice—reminiscent of his past and his father, though Derek didn't know too much about it. But every now and again, he could hear bits of James' childhood peek through.

"I'm going to help," Derek told them. "I might know someone who can represent him, I just need to make a couple calls."

It was saying something—just how much the other two understood the gravity of what Derek would have to do, but also how important it was for Sam to have this—that they didn't question him. Saying it aloud would acknowledge what Derek would have to put himself through, and feigned ignorance was always best.

The hard part, really, would be to convince Sage to let him do it. It was a battle he wasn't sure he'd have the strength for.

CHAPTER ELEVEN

'You look tired,' Basil signed slowly as Derek took his seat at their now-customary table. The café was all but empty, apart from the owner—an attractive man who had a ten-year-old girl always hanging around. He was newer in town than Basil was, and from what he knew, kept to himself just as much. 'You okay?'

Derek nodded, though Basil wasn't sure he was telling the truth. He knew Derek had ASL every week night, and had clients and art classes and his own private work, but there was something more to his fatigue he wasn't saying. 'Long day,' he finally replied.

He wasn't looking directly at Basil, so he knocked on the table gently, making Derek's gaze lift. 'Tell me,' he said. 'Do you want to stop the lesson tonight?'

'No,' Derek signed in a hurry, shaking his head along with pinching his fingers. He looked almost desperate, which was startling. Derek was making amazing progress with the language, better than a lot of people Basil had known, but he didn't think it was a passion for the language, or even for him.

'Tell me,' Basil repeated.

Derek dragged a hand down his face, then signed, 'I don't have all the signs, but I'll try. My friend Sam,' he then spelled wheelchair and Basil nodded his understanding, 'is having trouble. Custody,' he spelled. 'I want to help him, get him a lawyer, but...' His hands stilled and his cheeks went pink.

Basil waited, then reached over and gently touched his wrist in support. 'It's okay.'

Derek shook his head. 'My dad. My dad was a politician when I was a kid, but he was not nice. Abusive,' he added, spelling most of the words, but Basil had no trouble following along with the stuttered pace. 'Abused me and my brother. We ran away at fifteen, and there was an investigation. They found evidence of abuse from Sage's diary. Not enough to convict, but he lost his reputation. He's sick now, dying. I need to ask him for help, but it means...' He didn't finish what it meant, but Basil didn't need him to.

He had never suffered that kind of treatment, but it didn't take more than a little imagination to know what that would cost Derek, and his stomach roiled with anger and desire to stop him from putting himself in that position. If he had any other way to help, he would have. He would cut himself and bleed if it meant Derek didn't have to feel what he was feeling right then.

'I'm sorry,' he finally offered.

It was such a sad, pathetic, sorry thing to offer, and yet somehow Derek brightened at the sight of Basil's fist circling his chest. His shoulders lightened, and his smile was genuine. 'Thank you.'

Basil glanced around, then decided that they had to get out of there. They could sign together, he could help Derek immerse himself in it, but they didn't need to be formal. Not tonight. Derek needed something else, and Basil could give that to him.

He quickly rose, holding out his hand, and he felt a jolt up his arm when Derek took it. He was profoundly grateful when Derek didn't resist or force him to explain in the frustratingly slow signs, because in all honesty, he wasn't sure what his plan was. He just knew they had to get away.

Derek's hand remained firmly tucked in his, palm to palm,

feeling so right it made his head spin, and he found his feet leading him across the street, two blocks over, and coming to a stop at the back door of his shop. At that point, Derek did pull away and he raised an eyebrow at him.

'Work?'

Basil couldn't stop the laugh which bubbled up his throat, vibrating in his chest with the force of it. 'I have ice cream,' he told Derek.

Derek looked surprised, but the smile on his face was enough to show he was in, and Basil quickly unlocked the door and led the way in. He immediately flicked on the lights, flooding the back room with pale white halogen brightness, illuminating all the buckets of flowers waiting to be wrapped and tied and organized into their final stages.

He shed his coat as Derek took a few steps around, his hand darting out as though he couldn't help it, fingertips brushing along the petals of yellow roses which were waiting to be made into wedding centerpieces. He leaned his face into a bucket of petunias which were still planted in the dirt, and Basil could see the way his shoulders moved up and down with his breath.

When he turned, he smiled at Basil. 'You smell like this.'

'Petunias?' Basil asked, spelling the word slowly, watching Derek's lips form over each letter as he watched Basil's fingers like a hawk.

Derek chuckled, then waved his hand in a wide arc as if to say, 'All of this.' Basil understood what he meant. It was the same way he felt about his parents—the way his mother always smelled like her growing things and the back room of her shop, and the way his father always smelled like his lab and his classroom. The smell of the shop clinging to him now was a new stage in his life—and he wasn't sure if it would last, but it was for now. It was the way Derek smelled of ink and sterile, and something woodsy and soft underneath it all.

Basil beckoned Derek over to the desk, then reached into the little mini-fridge next to it and pulled out two cartons of ice cream.

They were little pints—an off-brand store mixture with an almond milk base and chunks of cookie dough. He dug two little spoons out of the package which rested by the coffee maker, and he pretended like Derek's soft grin didn't make his heart threaten to beat out of his chest.

They moved away, and Derek paused, staring at the array of photos littering the edge of the desk. Most of them were of his parents, and of his aunt and uncle when they were younger. Basil wished he had known them better, wished that his parents hadn't let bitterness and stubborn determination create a rift so the only thing he knew of them were notes left over in ledgers when he and Amaranth took over.

Derek reached out and touched one of the silver-framed photos of his mom and aunt, then looked back up at Basil with his eyebrows raised.

'Mom, aunt,' Basil signed. He pointed to his mom, then made the sign again before pointing to the one of both his parents. 'Mom and dad,' he told him. He set his ice cream down so he could sign slow and clear enough. 'They died. Boating accident with my aunt and uncle. My sister and I got the shop.'

Derek watched carefully, understanding dawning on his face after a beat, and then sadness taking over. 'Sorry,' he replied.

Basil shrugged. 'I miss them.'

Derek swallowed thickly, digging his spoon into the ice cream, but not eating any of it. After a while, he set it down and his hands shook a little when he raised them. 'My mom died when I was twelve. The doctor said it was an accident, wrong medication, but I think she committed suicide,' he spelled the last two words twice because his hands were shaking, and he mixed the letters up the first round. Basil wanted to reach out and stop him, but the moment was too much, it was too big, and he wanted to hold it. 'My dad never loved her.'

Basil let out a small breath as he glanced back at the photo of his parents. He couldn't understand that. Not really. He understood not loving a person, but his parents had been madly in love every single day he could remember seeing them together. He didn't know exactly what happened when their boat sank—didn't know if it was quick, or slow, if they tried to save each other, but he knew they were together, and he didn't think they'd have wanted it any other way. In truth, it was a relief in a way, because he couldn't imagine one of them trying to survive the other.

When he looked back up at Derek, Derek was watching him with a careful expression. 'Why did we come here?'

Basil shrugged. 'You have to do something bad. It's nice here—quiet, soothing, smells good.'

Derek gave a startled laugh, and Basil finally—finally—gave in to his urge and reached out to feel the movement of Derek's throat under his hand. It was a deep-chested rumble, rushing up to his elbow, and he found himself wanting to press his mouth there.

Derek startled under his touch, but he didn't react other than to let his laughter quietly die down. 'Thank you,' he finally signed.

Basil's smile was a little tense, but he nodded an acknowledgement of it, then grabbed the ice cream and motioned for the side door. It opened to a set of stairs, to a little loft above the shop that had once been an apartment, though his aunt and uncle had treated it more like an attic. There was a little sofa up there, though, and a half-kitchen which still worked enough to heat up his lunch and dinner during long shifts, and the lights were soft.

Derek followed behind, Basil could feel the thudding vibrations of his shoes on the stairs as they trudged to the top, and he led the way in. It didn't smell as intensely floral up there—more like sun-soaked pine and old dust from boxes and boxes of archived handwritten orders. Basil didn't look back at Derek as he turned the lights on, but when he turned, Derek was watching him again from the doorway.

'Sit,' Basil said, then pointed to the sofa.

Derek's gaze roamed over the sink which had evidence of the old take-out containers of lasagne he brought the week before, and a couple of empty coffee mugs. He eventually crossed the room in three quick strides and sat, leaving enough room for Basil to join him without touching—but only just.

Basil found he didn't want the room. He wanted to compromise every single thing he'd decided for himself about too-good looking hearing men who didn't know his language well and threatened to sweep him off his feet. He stopped to remind himself that Derek was nothing like Chad. He was trying far more and far better in these short weeks with no promise of sex or even real friendship than Chad had done in the entire time they were together.

On the first date, Chad had asked Basil to say his name, and when he'd fucked it up, he laughed. At the time it had seemed good natured, but he knew the truth about him now. Never once had Derek asked Basil to voice anything, not even when their communication was a struggle and he was frustrated with his inability to understand what Basil was trying to say.

It meant something.

'I had a blind date,' Derek signed to him, pausing to see if the sign for blind and sign for date were the right ones. Basil waved him on, and Derek smiled. 'My brother met him, thought he and I would be good together. We went to gelato.'

Basil bit down on his lip, struggling with whether or not to tell Derek the truth—that Amit had told him everything, he knew exactly what happened. He wanted to wait, to see where Derek was going with it, so he just nodded.

'It was bad,' Derek signed, laughing a little. 'I left and went home, was angry at Sage for the bad date. Then he came to the shop later. The day you got your tattoo.'

Basil's hand went to his arm, a reflexive habit he'd been engaging in lately, feeling the still-raised lines of the image even as the shading began to peel in huge, inky flakes every time he rubbed lotion over it. Derek's eyes followed his motion, and for a second, he looked like he was lost in the sight of the flower.

After a second, he shook himself out of it. 'He wanted to say sorry,' Derek went on. 'My brother thinks he and I would make a good couple, he thinks it's time for me to start dating.'

Basil couldn't ignore a sudden pang of possessive anger and jealousy at the thought of Derek moving on to anyone who wasn't him. He hadn't yet committed, expressed any real outward interest, and yet, he let himself feel it. 'Do you want to date?'

Derek bit his lip as he considered the question. 'Yes. I'm lonely, but it's hard. I have PTSD,' he signed the letters slowly, with only a slight tremble in his fingers. 'The night at the bank, it happens sometimes. My dad…' He stopped again, and Basil didn't dare ask him to go on. He didn't need to, his trauma was more than obvious. 'I don't want to be a burden.' When he spelled the last word, he didn't ask Basil for clarification.

'You're not,' Basil told him quickly.

Derek shrugged. 'I will never be normal. Never be fine. Always afraid, always a little broken.' He hesitated, his hands fluttering a little in front of him. 'My brother fell in love. He was engaged. Then his fiancé got sick and died. Rare disease, they didn't know he had it, and then he was gone.'

Basil let out an involuntary rush of air, unable to stop himself from making a small noise in the back of his throat with it. It was unreal to think about how much Derek and his brother had suffered, and how long that suffering had continued through his life. 'I'm sorry.'

Derek shook his head. 'I'm afraid of that, too. Afraid I'll fall in love and lose him.'

Basil didn't really need to consider what he was going to say next. He never talked about Chad—occasionally with Amaranth but only when she pushed until he was forced to give in. But as he raised his hands, he felt the words come without that familiar resistance. 'I went to University. A Deaf University, you know?' Derek nodded. 'It's in DC, and I worked at a coffee shop by campus. A guy used to come in, he was an intern for a senator, and he liked me. I never dated a hearing person before, but he was nice, my friends told me it was a good idea.' He paused to make sure Derek was following, and though Derek probably wasn't getting all of it, by his face it was obvious he was getting enough. 'We were together a long time. Two years. We shared an apartment. He told me to take speech therapy, he didn't know much sign, wanted to voice and write. He would invite friends over and before I could read lips at all, they would mock me to my face because I couldn't understand.'

"Fuck," Derek's lips said, an involuntary slip that Basil could read easily.

He huffed a laugh and nodded. 'One day I could understand, and I knew. The whole time, it was like that. So, I left, and I promised I would never date a hearing person again.' He watched in that moment a Derek's face crumpled when he fully understood what Basil was saying, his emotions playing out before he was able to control it. And it was in that moment Basil knew without a doubt there was more than just friendly interest.

And he knew he was okay with it.

'I understand,' Derek finally replied, that look still on his face.

'I know,' Basil told him with a half-smile. 'That's why I let myself like you.'

Derek's entire body twitched with surprise, his gaze flickering back and forth between Basil's hands and face like maybe he'd read the signs all wrong. But Basil had gone slow, had spelled the words he knew Derek didn't know yet, had mouthed them, taken his time because he wanted to be understood.

'You like?' Derek's hands repeated.

Basil licked his lips, then took a step in close—not enough to encroach on their signing space, but enough he could just feel the heat of Derek's body. 'I like you,' he repeated.

Derek's entire face pinked, and he lifted both hands, curled them into the I love you sign, then circled them in front of each other. 'Romance.'

It was probably one of those cheesy throw-away signs his teacher had given as a reward at the end of one of their classes. It was how all the hearing people he'd met knew swears and pick-up lines, but this felt different. He could picture Derek practicing the sign, clinging to it, hoping to use it one day.

Maybe that was an arrogant line of thought, but the way Derek was looking at him mirrored the way he was feeling inside. Because if the roles were reversed, he might have done the same thing. Basil's bitterness toward Chad had eclipsed his growing feelings for Derek for a little while, but he was too far gone now to ignore it. The moment Derek had pressed his hand against his arm and marked his skin forever, he was lost.

Basil nodded, stepping in even closer now, making it impossible for them to talk. His hands raised, curling around Derek's neck, watching his face for any signs that he didn't want it. Derek's lips parted and he felt a rush of air hit him. His breath was sweet from the ice cream, and still a little cold, and under his fingers he felt the slight vibration of what might have been a moan.

His dick twitched, and he knew there was no going back now. Even if Derek backed away and said he couldn't do this—didn't want this—Basil wouldn't be able to turn it off. Things had changed, evolved, and he was ready for it.

His hand lifted to his face. 'Kiss,' he signed.

Derek licked his lips, and even if he didn't entirely understand that sign, it was clear enough he got the point. His head dipped low, his hands lifting to press against Basil's waist, and then there was no space between them at all.

CHAPTER TWELVE

It was all happening so fast, his head was spinning so intensely, Derek wasn't entirely sure the moment wasn't a long hallucination until Basil's lips met his. The first press of their mouths together was a little clumsy, not exactly on target. Derek mostly got Basil's stubbly chin and he felt a hot brush of air against his nose. Then Basil's head rearranged, and the grip on Derek's neck got a little tighter, and it changed.

Like a gust of wind hit him, suddenly he felt rocked off center, and he fell down to his back against the love seat cushions as Basil hovered over him kissing him breathless. Derek kept his grip on Basil's hips, fingers digging into his rough jeans, holding them together in a furious press of bodies in desperation to keep it going. Basil's mouth was insistent, demanding, exactly the way he imagined it might be when he let himself.

His head was reeling, body aching with want because it had been so fucking long since he'd let himself be touched like this, let himself touch anyone with this kind of intimacy. And before this, there hadn't been meaning behind it. He'd given in to his body's desire to reach orgasm with another person in the past, but he'd never let himself feel—he'd never wanted to. He hadn't been lying when he said watching Sage break apart and nearly give up had terrified him beyond reason.

And yet, Basil made that fear worth it. The mouth drifting from his own to press searing hot kisses along his jaw, down his neck, sucking at his pulse-point was enough to remind him that some risks were worth taking. His hands drifted lower, pushing Basil's shirt up, splaying wide against his warm skin.

He felt more than heard Basil's soft groan, pressed into the crook of his neck as Basil's hips shifted. He felt the hardness there against his thigh, felt Basil rut up into the V of his hip, and his eyes rolled back in his head. With a gentle pressure, he pushed Basil up just slightly, just enough to see the hand he lifted to sign, 'Home,' against his cheek, then pat himself in the center of the chest. 'My home.' It took him two tries to properly spell, 'Condoms, lube,' because his head just didn't want to focus, but he got it, and Basil's eyes widened.

'Sex,' he spelled.

Derek shrugged as Basil pulled off him a little more. 'I want you,' he said. He knew those words might not be the exact ones a person might use when talking about sex—because ASL didn't share the same structure as English, but the way Basil's breath caught in his chest, his meaning was obvious and plain.

He started to fidget with nerves when Basil continued to stare at him, and just when he thought maybe he'd crossed a line and ruined it all, Basil nodded. His hand lifted like maybe he was going to say something, but then it touched his cheek, drawing him in for another, hot kiss.

Derek lost himself to the sensation, lost time as Basil's tongue dragged across his, and it was okay. They'd been there half the night, a short conversation taking an eternity because Derek still needed them to go slow, still needed most of the words spelled out, but he barely felt it. The bubble he existed in with Basil was enough to make the rest of the world feel so goddamn unimportant.

When he pulled away again, Basil signed something else, but in his daze, he didn't understand until he spelled it out. 'You live alone?'

Derek nodded. He wanted to tell him that yeah, he lived alone, and they wouldn't be bothered because everyone else knew that was his sanctuary and they couldn't just barge in and make themselves comfortable. But he didn't have the words to say it quickly and didn't have the patience to go through the motions of it all.

Basil didn't seem to need all of that explanation right then, and really, it didn't matter. He'd learn it all the longer he was around and got to know everyone. The more he learned Derek's routine and how strict it had to be, and maybe he'd even understand how momentous it was that Derek was asking Basil to be part of that.

Of course, right then, the only thing that did matter was collecting their things and leaving the shop, and not letting go of each other as they made their way down the street to Derek's car. They had to part, but instead of Derek letting him go right away, he crowded him back up against the side of the car. Cupping his face, he felt the warmth of Basil's cheeks under his palms.

Basil made an involuntary noise in his throat, pushing his hips out, seeking friction, and Derek pushed right back. He'd dreamt of this from the moment he became profoundly aware of just how much he wanted Basil, and it was everything he imagined. No, it was better. It was overwhelming his senses, making him drunk on want. He tipped his head down and captured Basil's mouth for a long, drawn out kiss.

It was only when he felt the breeze, heard a bottle break and someone start laughing down the street, that he tore himself away. Panting heavily, he pressed his forehead to Basil's for a moment, then finally stepped back. Basil looked just as dazed as he did, blinking slowly before he reached for the door handle and let himself in.

Derek's feet felt like they weren't even making contact with the pavement as he rushed to the driver's side, and he said a moment of silent thanks to the universe that his place was less than a ten-minute drive away. Basil's hand rested over his on the gear shift, and he wasn't sure if it was a good or bad thing that the dark interior of the car made conversation almost impossible. What he did know was that it was comfortable and as he pulled to his parking space, he didn't regret a single second that led to that moment right there.

Switching the car off, he palmed his keys and turned to see Basil watching him carefully. Without breaking eye contact, Derek reached up and flicked the overhead light on, the car flooding with a dim yellow glow above their heads. Basil blinked, the corners of his lips turning up into a half smile, and he bit down on his lower lip like he was trying to keep his grin from going any wider.

'Nervous,' Derek signed. He didn't indicate it was a question, but it wasn't entirely a statement either.

'Me too,' Basil signed.

He felt a puff of air escape his lungs, then he reached out and Basil reached back, and they were kissing again. It was a slow dance between them, awkward with the console pressing into his stomach as he leaned over as far as he could go, but feeling Basil's warm hands on his shoulders, holding him steady and keeping the little space between them from growing, it felt right.

'Inside,' Derek spelled with his fingers after they pulled away. Basil nodded, and Derek got out, leading him over the walkway and to his front door.

The key in the lock sounded like a gunshot in the profound silence, and he was hit with the all-too familiar scent of drying paint and old coffee. He turned to apologize, but Basil's gaze was drifting around the room, taking it all in.

Derek had always been a minimalist, even long before he left home. Growing up, he never had to clean, his father had employed a housekeeper to do the fine tuning, so their place always looked like a show-room. His bedroom had never contained any of him in it, just the things his father wanted to present to the world, even if no one ever saw it. Derek often wondered if it was simply to convince him and Sage of the people they should be instead of the people they were.

Part of him wished his father was in his right mind now, so when Derek stood in front of him in his glory—inked up and pierced and everything he was told he was never allowed to be—his father would be able to absorb the impact of it. But it was what it was.

He approached Basil, who was standing in front of three canvases which were hanging to set the varnish, and he let his shoulder gently rub along the other man's. When Basil looked, Derek shrugged. 'New,' he signed.

Basil nodded slowly. He reached out, letting his finger drift along the corner of the canvas where Derek would eventually paint a black coating to give it a frame, and his face softened into something sweet and understanding. 'Beautiful.'

Derek turned and studied the painting. He never really considered his art in terms of beautiful or ugly. He never really wanted to qualify or quantify his work, because he could show it to a thousand people—a million people, even—and only get a handful of similar opinions. The only thing that mattered was that it represented what he saw when he closed his eyes.

These paintings were simple—dream-like images of his past when he was a child and he and Sage would sneak off during their stay in Missouri. His mother and father had purchased a little cottage on the banks of the Lake of the Ozarks when they were six. They hired a full-time caretaker for the place, who looked after the cottage and his father's hunting dogs.

Derek and Sage would sneak off into the woods and explore and feel how different it was there to anywhere else they had ever been. Growing up in New York, he understood profoundly the term Concrete Jungle, but it never really made sense until he had something to compare it to. There were trees everywhere, vines growing up out of the earth, wrapping around thick, brown trunks. Moss covered the ground, fallen leaves making a cushion for when one of them climbed to a low branch and fell.

Derek discovered a cluster of trees with branches so close together, they made a hammock between them. His father had been angry one day when Derek was thirteen, the year after his mother died. He'd been frustrated by a phone call Derek had been around for, but he'd taken his temper out on Derek with the edge of his thick leather belt. Derek rested his welted back against those soft branches and spent hours watching the sun through the leaves make strange shapes. He laid there for hours until Sage found him and talked him home.

He didn't think about that trip for years, but right after he met Basil, right after he knew Basil was someone he wanted and didn't think he could have, he dreamt of that day. He closed his eyes and saw those shapes and felt a promise of a life he didn't think would ever be his. Now it was, and the thought almost brought him to his knees.

'You okay?' Basil asked after touching his arm to get his attention.

Derek cleared his throat, then turned to him. 'Yes,' he signed, his wrist hurting just a little from work. 'Yes, I'm fine. These are a memory from my childhood. We had a cottage in Missouri, and we would stay there some summers. It was nice before my mother died.' He licked his lips, then rolled his eyes to the ceiling for a second before looking back at the other man. 'I'm happy you're here.'

Basil's eyes seemed to glow at that, and although he didn't smile, there was something about his lips that spoke of a shared joy. He stepped closer and his hands came out to touch again, and Derek let him. Derek stepped into him and let himself feel every second of that impact.

So few people had touched him with tenderness in his life, and this was almost too much. It was like the softness was painful in a way, but he didn't want to let it go. His hook-ups before had been quick and dirty, never shameful—he'd never let himself feel like that about who he was and what he wanted—but they'd never been kind.

Biting kisses when he let himself be kissed, and harsh thrusts and stinging pain.

But never this. Never a soft mouth at the hinge of his jaw threatening to bring him to both climax and tears. His breath stuttered and shook in his chest, even as he dragged his hands down Basil's arms and linked their fingers together.

He gently tugged him, his chin jutting toward the bedroom and Basil let himself be led away. The walk felt like it took a hundred years, and yet no time at all, and suddenly they were in the dim room with the door closed, and Basil had Derek pressed against the wood behind him. The door knob dug into the small of his back, but he didn't notice it. How could he, when Basil's hands were suddenly everywhere, scrambling for every inch of skin he could reach.

With the faintest groan, Basil shoved his thigh between Derek's spread legs, gently pushing upward as his lips closed around his stretched lobe. His tongue toyed with the ring inside, giving sudden sensation to skin he'd long-since thought was numb. His eyes rolled back, head falling until it thudded against the door, and he ground down on the heavy weight of Basil's leg holding him up.

'Bed.' Basil had to sign it three times before it registered, but when it did, Derek nodded frantically and pushed him back the ten steps before they fell onto the unmade covers. The sheets beneath them were cool, soothing to his overheated skin, and he suddenly felt choked by his clothes.

The sensation lasted only seconds, though, because Basil immediately got to work. He pulled at zips, yanking at buttons, stripping away fabric from both of them until it was just hot, slightly tacky skin pressed together as their mouths melded again.

It was a strange thing, not saying anything, knowing that his groans were felt and not heard. He was profoundly aware of what Basil's hand was doing as it rested on his throat when he gave a particularly loud moan, and part of him wished he could block his ears to experience it that way.

"Fuck," he breathed, unable to help voicing aloud as Basil's other hand snaked between them and cupped his balls. His fingers were gentle but insistent as they rolled his soft flesh, palming their heavy weight in his hands. He was already close—too close for comfort—but he found he couldn't care. He was here, finally, with the man he'd wanted for weeks and weeks and it was happening.

"Uhng," Basil groaned. His voice was rich and deep, muted but so absolutely perfect in the silence of the room that it made Derek's head spin. Basil shoved at him until they were lying side by side, facing each other, and Basil had a hand around both their dicks.

Derek reached behind him, a fumbling hand until he got his nightstand drawer open and pulled out the lube. It was barely used—his night anxiety making it difficult to rub one out successfully and he'd stopped trying a long time ago. But that was the furthest thing from his mind right then. When he slicked his palm and coated both their cocks, all he could think about was Basil touching him again.

He didn't have to wait long as a warm palm closed around him and began a furious rhythm. His stomach clenched, balls already going tight with anticipation, and it was all he could do to reciprocate. Basil carefully grabbed him by the wrist and tugged his hand over his hip, down between his cheeks, and Derek's breath stuttered in his throat as he realized what Basil was asking for.

He looked down at Basil's eyes, almost all pupil, mouth slightly open, cheeks red as he panted and thrust his hips back against Derek's hand. 'Please,' he mouthed.

Derek circled one finger around his hole as he felt Basil thrust their dicks together, the sensation almost distracting. But he wanted this to be good for the other man, wanted to give him every single reason and more to come back, to do this again and again until they simply became part of each other's lives without wondering if this time was the last time.

He pushed the tip of his first finger inside Basil's impossibly tight hole, and Basil let out a deep, heavy moan, his body vibrating with it. He fucked himself backward, Derek's finger slipping in even deeper, and Derek felt his orgasm starting to crest. His dick throbbed, and Basil's hand tightened over him, stroking faster.

"I'm," Derek said aloud. Basil's eyes were frantically moving between Derek's cock and his mouth, like he didn't want to miss a second of anything. "I'm," Derek said again.

Basil nodded, and sped up, and fucked against Derek's hand until suddenly Derek's vision whited out and his mouth opened in a silent cry. His entire body seized, pleasure shooting from his core, into every limb, making him go almost numb for a second as he felt himself spilling and spilling over Basil's hand.

He came back to himself in fits and bursts, realizing he'd somehow managed to slip two fingers inside of Basil now, and was fucking him with a slow rhythm as Basil stroked his own cock. Derek's eyes fixed down at the motion, unable to look away. He saw the tension rising in Basil, the way the muscles in his arms bulged, looking up to see the pulse in his neck beating against the skin.

Basil groaned again, and then huffed, then cried out louder than Derek expected to hear as he fell back and came. He splattered his stomach with it, the dark curls going sticky and off-white, and his hand slowed down, knuckles a mess from the both of them.

Derek's breathing began to return to normal as he gently pulled himself out of Basil's ass and laid his hand flat on the mattress. He couldn't bring himself to pull away, overwhelmed with the sensation to kiss Basil, to hold him, to keep him there because he'd had this now and he didn't want to lose it. He couldn't. It would wreck him.

He became aware of the silence in the room, nothing more than the soft breathing between them, and the gentle hum of electricity somewhere in the front room of the apartment. Derek was still frozen in his position, halfway over Basil, staring down at him when Basil's dark eyes came open and their gazes locked.

After a moment, Basil's mouth stretched into a grin. 'Hey,' he mouthed.

Derek couldn't help it. His head fell into the crook of Basil's neck and he laughed, the sound far too loud for him right then, but he was helpless against it. Happiness was flooding through him, and he knew logically it had everything to do with the orgasm, but it also had to do with the fact that for the first time, a moment like this felt right, and good. He laid several open-mouthed kisses to the warm crook of Basil's neck simply because he couldn't help it.

When he pulled back, Basil was watching him, a small grin still turning his lips up. He lifted his clean hand to Derek's face and brushed his hair back, dragging his fingers down his nose, scratching at his stubble. He went lower, to the ink on his shoulder, tracing the old, slightly faded lines of the face on his left shoulder.

Derek gently fell onto his back, Basil following him, propping up on his elbow to watch him. He didn't stop touching, his finger now tracing the word etched along his forearm. Sinner.

When their eyes locked, Basil raised his hand. 'Why?' he signed. 'Gay?' He signed the word, thumb and forefinger touching his chin before he spelled it to make sure Derek understood.

Derek shook his head. 'No.' He considered it, then spelled, 'Irony.' He struggled, but he wanted Basil to understand him. 'My father,' he began in painfully slow motions, 'hated me. Everything about me was bad.'

'No,' Basil told him, his face going stony.

Derek shook his head. 'I know. Now, I know. But when I was a kid, he said I was bad. He hated me. Hated this,' he tapped his hand over his heart, then at his temple. 'My mind. Hated where I came from. Hated my mother. Jewish,' he spelled.

Basil swallowed thickly. 'Jewish,' he spelled, then offered the sign and pointed to himself.

'My father was catholic,' he told him. 'Just one more thing to hate me for. He said I was born a sinner. So, I took that identity back.' He brushed his hand down along the word. It had been a long time since he hated himself for what he was, a long time since he'd let himself believe anything his father had told him. He didn't love his PTSD, or his sleepless nights, or moments when he was so overwhelmed with his brain that he couldn't leave the house. But he didn't hate himself.

'You're beautiful,' Basil told him.

Derek flushed, which felt ridiculous considering what they'd just done. 'Thank you. I'm sorry my signing is slow.'

Basil shook his head, a fierce look coming over his face. 'No. I want you to understand how much this meant to me.'

Derek blinked, letting Basil go over the signs again and again until he understood. 'Why?'

'Because you're doing this. You don't want more from me. You don't want my voice,' Basil replied.

Derek felt his stomach clench, wanted to find the guy who had made Basil feel this way and beat him until he was unrecognizable. He took a breath, then shrugged. 'Your voice,' he signed, then reached out and touched Basil's hands. 'I like this voice.'

Basil's eyes shined, and he didn't smile, but he leaned in and kissed Derek for far, far more than he was worth.

CHAPTER THIRTEEN

Basil was at the little Mexican restaurant mostly to escape his sister, and because the owner knew some rudimentary ASL from when his aunt had lived there. The one thing he could appreciate was the older shops, those who had been in the community for a while, knew how to talk to him at least a little. It was a reminder that his aunt had made some impact on this place, and maybe if he stuck around, he'd make some difference, too.

It didn't mean he didn't miss DC, or his Deaf friends, or knowing where exactly to go to be surrounded by his people and his language. But he was starting to feel less apart, less isolated, and that meant something.

He picked a table far from the window just in case Amaranth came looking for him—and it wasn't that he was ashamed, but he was still processing and trying to understand exactly what it was he was feeling for Derek without her smug look and constant teasing about him finally getting laid. He understood she meant well, but she didn't understand what it had cost him to finally cross that line, even if it felt more of a relief than a fear or burden.

As he studied the condensation on his glass of water like maybe it held the secrets of the universe, a hand in his periphery caught his attention. He glanced up and noticed a man standing there—vaguely familiar, though maybe it was just the fact that he was covered in tattoos that made him seem like they'd met before. He was holding a small baby in the crook of his arm, and Basil immediately recognized her as the one Derek and Sage had been taking around town.

'Hi,' the man signed. 'I'm Tony. I work with Derek.' His signs were slower, but more fluid than Derek's.

Basil smiled at him. 'Do you want to sit?'

Tony looked a little hesitant, but he turned his head and said something to the hostess who brought over another menu and a small highchair for the little girl.

'Are we interrupting?' Tony asked once Basil had looked up again.

Basil smiled, shaking his head. 'Lunch break. You?'

'Off work today. Baby,' he said, and reached over to tickle his daughter's cheek. She gave a laugh, her feet kicking, cheeks plump with her grin. 'My wife and I switch.'

Basil considered him for a minute. 'Your signing is good.'

'It's slow,' Tony countered, 'but we're on level three now. I want to be fluent before she develops more complex language.'

The fact that he was using ASL—properly, the grammar, the flow, even if some of his signs were a little archaic—meant he was dedicated, and it made something happy twist in Basil's gut. One more child being taught that the way she was born wasn't wrong, even if it was different from her mom and dad.

'She'll thank you,' Basil told him.

Tony grinned, his entire demeanor going soft as he looked at her. Basil had seen that look before—his own parents loved him that much and fuck, he missed them. It also made something ugly rise in his chest, because he was pretty sure no one had ever looked at Derek like that. Not once.

'Derek was smiling when he came into work today. He wouldn't tell me why, but I have a feeling I know,' Tony told him.

Basil licked his lips and debated about keeping it a secret, but he thought about all the ways Derek had been forced to keep himself a secret from the world. His formative years had been shoved into a box and locked away, and he couldn't bring himself to do that, even if this ended up being nothing. 'You're probably right. We had a good time last night.'

'He said you went to his apartment,' Tony said, and there was a look of significance in his face that Basil didn't understand. His confusion must have been apparent, because Tony went on, 'He doesn't let people in his apartment. Only Sam, sometimes Sage. No one else.'

That hit Basil like a physical blow. He didn't understand Derek's trauma—not completely, not the way he wished he did—but he could understand the impact of Tony's statement. 'I don't know what to say.'

Tony smiled. 'Don't let it put pressure on you. He won't break if it doesn't work out. I just want you to know that it meant something to him.'

'I know,' Basil told him, because that, at least, he was aware of. There was no other way to interpret the way Derek talked to him after, and the way he held him. There was no way to misinterpret the gentle love-making in the morning, or the shower, or the sweet way he poured him shitty cereal and made stale coffee in his tiny six-cup coffee maker. It was something more than a fling, and not quite love, but it could get there if he let it.

'He's serious about you,' Tony said. 'It might not seem like it, he's shy and scared, but he's trying. He would have taken sign for Jasmine eventually, but you made him want it more.'

Basil absently rubbed his fingers over his tattoo and considered what that meant, too. 'He makes me want to try.'

'May I?' Tony asked, then pointed at Basil's arm. Basil offered it up, and didn't flinch when Tony brushed his thick, calloused fingers over the design there. 'It's not finished.'

Basil couldn't help his laugh, mostly in wonder at how all the artists at the shop seemed to just instinctively know it wasn't finished. 'No, not yet.'

Tony grinned at him. 'It's beautiful. It suits you.'

Basil felt himself blush because it did, but it was strange to have someone else notice it and understand it without really knowing him as a person. Then he realized if this worked out, if he and Derek made something of all this, Tony eventually would know him. Just like the others would, because they were Derek's family. The thought caused a slight rise in his anxiety, because they were all hearing. Tony and Katherine knew sign for their daughter, and most of the others knew how to understand the few things the baby wanted, but that was it. And he didn't see the same drive in them that Derek had. There was no motivation to try.

And the thought of that level of communication barrier made his stomach twist uncomfortably. He didn't want to speak, he never would want that, but he'd lived that life before. And maybe they wouldn't be cruel the way Chad and his friends had been, but there would be a wall between them, and he couldn't cross it on his own.

'Are you okay?' Tony asked.

Basil affected a smile. 'Fine,' he lied. It was probably obvious—he was shit at hiding the truth from his face—but he couldn't bring himself to talk about it just yet. Not with this man he hardly knew, and not without knowing what the future held for him and Derek.

> Derek: Any chance you want to change our lesson into a date? My last appointment should be done around four, and I was thinking we could go into Denver and have dinner. We can work on restaurant signs, then make out in my car.

> Basil: Blushing.

> Derek: Is that a yes?

> Basil: I'm work close but maybe after. Close tonight eight.

> Derek: What food do you feel like eating? I'll make us a reservation.

> Basil: You decides. Surprise me good thing.

> Derek: Prepare to be blown away. Then maybe just blown.

Basil jumped away from the counter when he felt his sister smack his side, and he realized she'd been reading over his shoulder. His face blushed so hot he felt a little dizzy and he pulled his phone away from her.

'Dirty,' she signed, waggling her brows.

'Do you mind?' he demanded, his hands slapping together in more embarrassment than anger.

'I'm happy for you. Finally you're getting laid!' She moved to the side of the counter where she was working on trimming one of their rose deliveries and she picked up her shears with one hand. 'I like him.'

Basil bit his lip and rolled his eyes up toward the ceiling, taking a breath for strength. 'Me too, but I don't…I don't know.'

Setting the shears down, she leaned on the counter. 'Don't ruin it before it starts. I like him, and you like him.'

Basil pursed his lips. 'All his friends are hearing. His family. The whole shop is hearing.'

'The owner's baby is deaf,' she pointed out. 'Her mom and dad both know sign. Your boyfriend is learning sign with classes. Not even YouTube, but real classes, with a real Deaf teacher.'

Basil's stomach twisted, because it was true, but it didn't mean there weren't problems with the whole situation. 'The people he works with are his family. He loves them, he relies on them. They don't sign, and I don't want to speak.'

She gave him a flat look. 'No one is going to make you speak.'

'They don't sign, Amaranth. They know baby sign language, and I want more than that.'

She walked around the counter and put both hands on his shoulders, turning him to face her and let their gazes connect for a long time. He was overwhelmed for a second by just how much she looked like their father—the dimple in her chin, the cut of her jaw, the almond shape to her eyes. Her hair held the same curl, a slight frizz in the humidity of spring which framed her face.

He missed his parents and wondered what either one of them would tell him about Derek. They had never cared he was gay, but they hated the idea of Chad, and he never got the chance to ask if it was because they could just tell he wasn't a good guy, or because they thought Basil should stick to someone in his own community. His aunt had been cut off for assimilating, and even Amaranth had gone months without speaking to them when she had chosen to speak, to attend a hearing school over a deaf one, whenever she brought hearing boys home.

Would they tell him to give it up—that although Derek was a nice boy, it wasn't enough? And if they did, would he have done it?

'I know what you're thinking,' she told him.

Basil blinked at her, feeling his eyes get a little wet. 'No you don't.'

'Yes,' she countered. 'And mom and dad would love him. They'd want to wrap him up tight and chase the pain in his eyes far away. I know they were angry at Aunt Rachel for her choices, but they got over it. And I think it was a lot more than Uncle Rick.'

Basil had long since assumed, but all four of them had died before he got the chance to ask, and he could never be sure. And really, did he want to live his life on a hypothetical answer he could never confirm? Because in the end, his parents were dead. Wherever they were, he liked to think they just wanted to see him happy.

'Go on your date tonight and stop thinking so much,' she told him. 'Let yourself be happy. Derek can make you happy.'

Basil bowed his head, but nodded, because he didn't have any plans to turn Derek down, no matter what his parents might have wanted. It still weighed on him, probably always would. The idea of being with Derek made this town feel a little more permanent, and it was in that moment he realized a small piece of him had always planned on going home. Except DC was starting to feel a lot less like home the more time passed.

CHAPTER FOURTEEN

Derek got a text from Basil saying he was late, and that he'd meet him at the restaurant. The place he'd picked—an out of the way little Moroccan shop complete with shin-high tables, floor poufs, and baskets full of bread instead of silverware—was just on the outskirts of the Cherry Creek mall to really be considered hole-in-the-wall, but it still had an old-world, almost indie feel to it which Derek loved.

The place held twelve tables, which meant they could only seat by reservation, and it meant that the entire meal wouldn't be overwhelming with noise. He found it funny—the place was dimly lit with no windows, covered in tapestries and artwork, and it should have made his claustrophobia rear its ugly head, except it never did there. Maybe it was the gentle music, or the hands-off demeanor of the service, but he was excited to be able to share the place with Basil and not run the risk of a panic attack settling in.

He arrived a little early, shedding his shoes at the door before he was seated, and he ordered some tea to soothe his nerves as he waited. He toyed with the edge of the menu, then nibbled on some of the bread in the center near the little candles, and he checked his phone obsessively like he was almost expecting Basil to cancel.

He hadn't seen him since the morning after—way too early to feel properly human. But he'd still dragged his ass out of bed to make sure Basil had breakfast and coffee and a long kiss before he had to run out and open the shop. He'd gone back to bed when Basil had gone, wrapping himself in the blanket that still held the faint echo of Basil's floral scent, and he wanted to keep the other man there every night, so he'd never lose it.

Just when twenty minutes had passed and he started to really panic, he saw Basil's head poke around the side of the wall and spot him immediately. The relief was almost visceral as he rose, beckoning Basil over, and for just the briefest second, he was captivated by the soft, socked feet padding across the floor. Derek met him with a hand to Basil's cheek, drawing him in for a soft, chaste kiss.

It felt right again, like a puzzle piece slotting into place where it always belonged. From the faint pink on Basil's cheeks, he thought maybe the other man felt it too. They settled together, side by side on their cushions, and Basil's gaze roamed around for a moment, taking it all in.

When he returned his attention to Derek, he laughed quietly and shrugged. 'New place for me.'

Derek nodded. 'No one really knows about it, but I like it. The food is good. We can share.' He held up the menu and tapped on the vegetarian five courses. 'They play music and have dancers between the entrée and dessert.'

Basil's eyebrows rose. 'You take dates here?'

Derek felt himself blush. 'No. You're my only date.'

At that, Basil's lips lifted into a pleased grin, and he nodded, tapping the menu with his long finger. Derek fought the urge to lift his hand, to bite the tip of that finger just to see if he could make Basil's cheeks go darker, make him squirm a little in his seat. But there was time for that later. Derek was feeling bold, but also romantic. He desperately wanted to give Basil a reason to say, and he knew that was his abandonment and fear talking, but it was also want.

Luckily, his swirling thoughts were interrupted by the server, and Derek checked with Basil to make sure it was fine before he ordered the five courses for them to share. Basil seemed utterly unbothered by Derek taking the lead, and when the server left, Basil even shifted a little closer and instead of saying anything more, he just leaned his head on Derek's shoulder and relaxed against him. Their hands found each other's and fingers linked, and Derek felt the soft, beating pulse in Basil's wrist against his thumb.

'Long day?' Basil finally asked, shifting so his hands could be seen properly.

Derek shrugged. 'No. I had ASL class this afternoon, but I didn't do well for my presentation.'

Basil's eyebrows lifted. 'You've been signing very well.'

Derek cleared his throat, flushing a little. 'I got nervous,' he admitted. 'I was...thinking about you.'

Basil seemed to understand, and his face pinked just the slightest bit, his mouth twitching at the corners. 'Our night?'

Derek shrugged, but he knew his face had given it away. He tried his damndest to pay attention in class that afternoon, but every time he was idle, his thoughts kept drifting back to before, to the feeling of his fingers inside Basil, to the way he surrendered with open mouth and warm tongue under his pressing kisses. The teacher had noticed his distraction and admonished him in front of everyone, and Derek wanted to care, but more than that he just wanted to get out of there and get the day over with so he could be with Basil again.

And now they were here. 'I missed you,' he said instead of answering him.

Basil looked startled, but he smiled all the same and shifted just a fraction closer. 'I met your boss today.'

Derek, who had just taken a sip of his water, choked on it.

"What?" he couldn't help but voice, then swiped his mouth with the back of his hand before he signed, 'What?' to clarify.

Basil chuckled and shrugged. 'He was nice. I met Jasmine, she is so sweet. Very smart.'

Derek felt himself puff with a little pride, and he nodded. 'So smart. She's going to be president one day. Or maybe an evil dictator. Either way, I plan to be on her good side.'

Basil laughed louder, shaking his head, but he looked so damn happy and Derek wanted to keep that look there. 'Do you want to meet my friend after we eat.'

Derek's eyebrows furrowed. 'Your friend?'

'You know him,' Basil clarified. 'Amit. He gets tattoos from your brother. He works at a bar and I've told him about you.'

Derek felt something hot and uncomfortable in his gut, and he realized it was jealousy. He knew Amit—the guy Basil had been on a date with the night the date with Niko had gone poorly. 'Your ex?' he couldn't help but ask.

It was Basil's turn to choke—just a little—on his small bite of bread he'd dipped in his soup. 'My ex?'

'I saw you,' Derek admitted. 'The night of my bad date. You were with him at gelato.'

Basil blinked, then threw his head back and laughed. 'Not a date,' he insisted with very clear signs. 'Only a friend. Promise.'

Derek hated that he'd made an ass of himself because he knew his expression had given him away, but he couldn't help it. 'Sorry.'

Basil shook his head, then laid his hand on Derek's cheek and drew him in for a kiss that was mostly chaste, but a little deeper than he was expecting to have in the middle of a restaurant. 'It's okay. But not a date. Friend only.'

Derek sighed, then nodded. 'Yes. I want to.'

Their conversation went quiet when their meal came, and he discovered that maybe this restaurant wasn't entirely the best idea. Eating with their hands and no utensils and trying to sign made the multi-tasking a little difficult. And yet, the silence between them was just as comfortable as it had been before.

After they'd finished their entrées, the little show began. It was the same every time—the dancers, the music, the routine. Derek had been coming here a while with everyone at the shop, and yet the routine still got him every time. He and Basil both leaned back as the two women began to sway their hips and balance swords on their sides. He felt Basil shift, looked over and saw that he had his hand pressed to the wall to feel the vibrations playing through the room, a small smile touching his lips.

Derek moved closer, let their thighs press together, let himself lean in and kiss the underside of Basil's jaw softly. It was nice to feel comfortable like this. Basil was shorter than him, and smaller, but he never looked at Derek like he was intimidated or afraid, never looked at him like he was some big, hulking monster. He just...looked at him.

He wasn't feeling very hungry by the time they came around to serve tea and baklava, but he nibbled anyway and then waved Basil off as he slipped his card in the bill fold. He laughed a little at Basil's disgruntled glower, so he told him, 'You can pay for drinks,' which only earned him an eyeroll.

'My friend is the bartender, we drink for free. Next time me.'

Derek shrugged, too caught up in the thrill that there was the idea of next time, that this was turning into something maybe real, and maybe great to care about arguing over money. They left not long after, and Derek let Basil take his hand and lead the way to the car.

Amit's place wasn't far, but parking was a bitch and he ended up at the curb right near a strip club which looked unsurprisingly dead for a Tuesday night. They made their way through the empty sidewalks, and up two blocks before they reached the little hipster college bar nestled between two other themed bars on the little strip.

Derek felt a small wave of anxiety as they stepped in, but the music wasn't overwhelmingly loud, and the place was spacious enough. There was a decent crowd there, at least half the tables full of patrons, though none of them looked interested in doing more than drinking their whiskey flights and talking through their curly mustaches. Derek almost wanted to people watch, but instead he let Basil lead him to the near-empty row of barstools.

Amit was there, looking frankly gorgeous in a tight mesh tank-top and dark jeans. He perked up instantly when he set eyes on Basil, then turned a curious and somewhat amused stare to Derek before raising his hands to ask, 'Date?'

Derek braced himself for Basil to minimize it, and though Basil's signs were way too fast for him to catch it all, he saw him tell Amit, 'Finished dinner,' so he didn't think there was any denial there. Especially after Basil moved into his side and tucked in a little closer.

When Amit finally approached, Derek raised his hand in a hello. 'I'm Derek.'

'Sage's brother,' Amit signed.

Derek could see hearing aids over the guy's ears, and he knew that Amit spoke, but he had no desire to break their non-verbal night now. 'I'm learning sign. Sorry I'm slow.'

Amit's smile widened, almost surprised as he gave Derek a look, then turned his attention back to Basil. 'Good. Lucky.'

Basil shrugged, but he glanced over at Derek and his face was telling. He was happy, and Derek had done that. 'Two drinks. Whatever,' Basil told him, and Amit gave a wink before he wandered off. 'Is that okay? I let him choose for me.'

Derek nodded with his own soft, easy smile. 'Whatever you want.'

Basil stepped in closer, bringing one of his hands to Derek's waist, holding him tight there. 'Thank you,' he signed with his other hand. 'Tonight was good.'

'Yes,' Derek signed in response. He fought the urge to take Basil's face between his hands and kiss him, but he didn't want to make a big show of it. When Basil licked his lips though, Derek couldn't help himself and he leaned in, just brushing their mouths together for a brief moment before pulling away. 'You're beautiful.' His bladder decided to join in on the fun right then, so he sighed and stepped back. 'Bathroom. Wait for me.'

Basil pointed out the restroom sign, and Derek made his way around the tables to the small hallway. Like most men's bathrooms, it smelled like old piss and axe body spray, but it wasn't as overwhelming as some places, and there were private stalls which always helped him feel a less anxious than the open urinals. He took his time, mostly gathering himself and he was happy to note his anxiety hadn't overwhelmed him too much in spite of subverting his routine to the point he no longer recognized his day. But it was good. It was wonderful. It was the perfect end to the shake-up, and he couldn't regret a second of it.

As he stepped out to wash his hands, he came to an abrupt halt at the sight of a man standing against one of the sinks, arms crossed, very obviously watching him. Derek swallowed thickly, feeling an urge to confront the stranger, and to turn tail and run warring equally in his head. After a beat, he broke eye-contact and walked to the sink.

"Haven't seen you here before," he said.

It was a fucking cheesy movie-line opening and he felt a rush of irritation build in his gut. "You got a problem, man?"

"I just saw you come in with Basil and I thought I'd introduce myself. Save us all from an awkward conversation at the table you probably couldn't follow." The guy's tone was smarmy and a little threatening which told Derek he was either an ex or an interested party, which he was so not in the mood for. Tonight had been going so well, he didn't know why the universe wanted to test him after all this.

"Look, man, if Basil wants to introduce us, that's fine with me," Derek told him.

The guy held up two hands. "Hey, I don't have a problem with it, I just noticed your signing is a little…slow."

Derek fixed him with a flat look as he finished scrubbing off his hands, then brushed past him for the bin of paper towels. He debated answering, debated trying to defend himself, but what was the point. This guy was going to act superior either way, and Derek wasn't going to defend his territory like some piss-happy alpha trying to protect his boyfriend.

He fixed the guy with a last, quick stare, then pushed the door open and walked out. As much as the urge struck him, he determinedly didn't look behind him. He could tell, though, from the look on Basil's face when he glanced up from his conversation with Amit, the guy had followed him out.

Derek shook off his irritation and affected a smile instead, reaching for the second, untouched beer waiting for him on a little coaster. He downed a third of it, and by the time he set the pint glass down, he could feel the guy behind him, his arms moving in rapid signs. Derek was still learning about the Deaf Community, but he was fairly sure the guy was breaking some sort of social etiquette by doing this where Derek couldn't see.

At least by the look on Basil's face, he knew it wasn't going to be well received. 'Not now,' Basil signed, and Derek recognized that one, even as fast as Basil signed it.

From his place behind the bar, Amit caught Derek's gaze and offered him a wink and smirk of solidarity. 'No worries,' he mouthed.

Derek cleared his throat, then stood up and backed away so he was no longer the physical barrier between the guy and Basil. 'Sorry,' he signed. 'I met him in the bathroom.'

Basil's hands flew, and Derek caught, 'What,' and 'you,' several times.

The guy's hands were just as fast, his gaze flickering to Derek with a smug grin because he knew Derek had no hope of following. This had to be the guy from Basil's bad date—the guy who'd ruined his night right before things had changed between them.

'Should I go?' Derek asked.

Horrified, Basil's full attention was back on him. 'No. I'm sorry, please don't go.'

Derek reached for him, touching his arm gently. 'I'll wait at the bar if you want to finish talking to him. I can't understand, so you can fill me in later?'

Basil fixed him with a fierce, determined look and nodded. 'Yes. I promise.' He gently pulled away from Derek, but then as an afterthought, surged forward and kissed him, one slow kiss followed by lingering pecks as he pulled back. 'Soon.'

Derek nodded and as much as he wanted to look back at the guy, he snagged his beer and moved to the end of the bar instead. Amit was already there waiting for him, leaning in close as he kept one eye on Basil and the dickhead who moved to a quiet corner.

"Do you want me to fill you in?" Amit asked aloud, his voice startling Derek after so much voiceless conversation.

Derek couldn't help a grin, but he shook his head all the same. "Basil told me he'd let me know everything when he was done. I trust him."

Amit considered him a long moment, then shrugged. "I think I like you. I mean, I was pretty sure I liked you before, even if we didn't properly meet, but I'm glad I was right. Do you want something else to drink?"

"No. I have to drive back," Derek told him. He was watching as subtly as he could—which wasn't really subtle at all—and he was fascinated by the way both men's hands flew. There were no spoken words exchanged, but Derek could all-but feel the way they were shouting at each other. He could see the guy's face getting redder, getting more insistent, could see Basil holding his ground. "Do you know that guy?"

"Not before he went on his one shitty date with Basil," Amit confessed. "I think he saw Basil meet me here one day, but when he realized I was hard of hearing, he backed off. With you though…"

Derek sighed. "Is he deaf?"

Amit snorted. "No. He's CODA. Like the worst kind of CODA."

"Uh," Derek said.

"Deaf parents," Amit explained. "Most CODA are chill as fuck, but there are the occasional ones like him that are total dicks. They like to speak where they're not welcome."

Derek's brows rose in understanding. "Like white dudes with black friends who think they can tell other white people about the black experience?"

Amit's grin widened. "You know those guys?"

"We live in Colorado. Everyone here knows those guys," Derek said a little flatly, though he was smiling. His grin didn't last long as he watched the guy and Basil's signs start to calm down. Their conversation looked far from over, and Basil was looking a little uncomfortable now as he glanced back at Derek a few times. "Do you uh…I mean…would Basil be better with a guy more like him?"

"Like that douche?" Amit asked, his tone surprised and a little offended.

Derek shrugged. "Okay, maybe not him specifically, but someone who gets it. Who grew up around signing and…and everything. I don't know shit."

"Saw you talking to him just fine," Amit replied.

Derek dragged a hand down his face, then drank more beer just to give himself something to do as he tried to find the words he was looking for. "It's slow, it sucks. It's like…he has to spell half the words, and I know he's not using the right grammar because I'm taking ASL right now and the grammar's still a little confusing. None of it's natural and it feels like it's going to be a hundred years before I can even get half that fast. I can't imagine how tired it must make him."

"But you're doing it," Amit said. "I don't want to overstep here so I won't say much, but I do know that the fact that you're doing this on his terms means everything. Because there have been people who wouldn't in his past."

"You mean Chad," Derek said darkly.

"He told you about that guy?" Amit asked, sounding a little surprised.

Derek snorted a laugh. "Yeah, he fucking did, and I wouldn't mind flying my ass to DC and delivering an epic beat-down if I knew where to find him." In truth, Chad was probably in politics right now. A guy like that probably would have gotten along famously with his dad. Hell, he was probably closeted and engaged to someone with high aspirations of visibility in the government. Derek had grown up with too many people like that, and he knew how their lives went.

"You and me both," Amit said. "But I wouldn't worry about it. Basil knows what he wants, and it's not that asshole."

Derek chanced a look over, and he felt something raw and possessive take over as the guy's hand grabbed at Basil's arm and touched the ink there. In the back of his mind, he supposed that was another danger of marking someone he was growing attached to— the idea that the ink was still his, that he had some right to it. He swallowed it down like a bitter horse pill and forced himself to look away.

"You're good for him, and he knows it," Amit told him softly. "Don't let that asshole get to you. He's going to walk away alone tonight, and you're not. And you'll wake up with Basil more times than you won't over the rest of your lives, and that's what matters."

He wanted that. More than anything, he wanted that, but he was still a little too terrified to hope. Before he could reply though, movement out of his periphery distracted him and he turned his head to see the guy storming off and Basil slowly making his way over.

He was still pink in the cheeks, flush and frustration clouding his features, but when he reached for Derek, his touch was soft. 'I'm sorry,' he told him again.

Derek shook his head. 'Not your fault.'

Basil looked just a little guilty, and he shrugged, taking a drink first before he answered in spelling and sign to make sure Derek caught it all. 'We had a bad date. He saw some guys from your shop at the restaurant and called them trash, so I left him there and never texted him again. Later he tried to apologize, and I let him think I might give him a second chance. I didn't mean to, I was just confused.'

'If you want to think about things,' Derek began, but Basil quieted him by gently touching the back of his hand and shaking his head.

'No. I don't want him. He's an asshole.' He spelled it first, then offered the sign, and Derek couldn't help a small grin.

'You're sure?' Derek pressed.

Basil nodded. 'I'm sure.'

Amit grinned at them both before replacing Basil's beer and then lifting his hands to sign at Derek, 'I told you.'

Derek really didn't mind that *I told you so* at all.

CHAPTER FIFTEEN

Basil let his eyes close for a minute, though it really was near impossible to relax with a tattoo needle tearing into his arm. It was worth it, and the pain wasn't unbearable, but he was learning quickly he was never going to be the kind of guy who was addicted to the process. He'd never look like Derek or Sage, he couldn't imagine coming here every week to have a new image carved on his skin.

He did, however, find himself in the shop a lot in the few weeks since the night he and Derek ended up in Amit's bar, confronted by Jay. When he let himself think about it for longer than a moment—the idea that Jay had followed Derek into the bathroom to confront him without Basil there—he found himself overcome with a rage he wasn't used to feeling. The situation had been handled, though a few days after the incident Basil found himself having to block Jay on his messenger after waking up to a novel of why the two of them should be together instead of him and Derek. It was the same drivel Jay vomited at the bar, and Basil's feelings hadn't changed on the matter.

'He's not like us,' Jay had insisted, his hands tense and pointed.

'I don't even know what that means,' Basil countered. 'Just because he has tattoos…'

Jay scoffed, his eyes rolling. 'I don't mean the tattoos, though I noticed yours and I can't believe you let someone do that to you.'

'Him,' Basil signed pointedly, his hand steady as he indicated Derek who was across the bar with Amit. 'I let him do it to me.'

Jay's cheeks pinked and he looked almost uncertain, which was what Basil was hoping for. 'I don't care. I can learn to live with it. But I won't sit by and watch you waste more time on some hearing guy who will eventually just treat you like shit. I know about Chad.'

Basil felt rage boiling in him, his hands trembling now in an effort to keep from clocking the guy in the face. 'You're hearing.'

Jay flinched like he'd been slapped. 'Not the way he is.'

'Worse than he is,' Basil told him, his face screwed up in a grimace. 'You're entitled and superficial and you refuse to acknowledge that you're part of the problem. You're more like my shitty ex than Derek will ever be, and I would rather take a thousand hours of speech therapy and never sign another word for the rest of my life than go on another date with you.' Basil took a breath for courage, then leaned in close, cleared his throat, and dredged up ancient muscles he hadn't used in years. "So fuck you," he said, and watched Jay visibly step back at the sound of his voice. "Never text me again."

He stalked off and went right back to Derek and made sure he spent the rest of the night reassuring Derek he was exactly where he wanted to be. Any doubts of what he wanted had been erased by Jay's confrontation, and in spite of knowing it would be harder as their relationship progressed, he wasn't afraid anymore.

He wouldn't start speaking now, but he had meant what he said to Jay. Not that he'd ever be in that sort of position, but he would have chosen giving up sign over dating a person like Jay, and he wouldn't have resented it for a second.

He opened his eyes after a moment, looking down at Derek's face which was drawn and almost blank in his concentration. It took some getting used to, reading far more subtle facial expressions on

Derek than Basil had grown accustomed to in his own community, but in a way, he liked it. It was like learning a private language, and when he managed to get something right, it felt overwhelmingly rewarding.

Like tonight, for example, their lesson before his next tattoo, there had been a tension in Derek most people might have missed, but he didn't. There was also a quiet, private look that begged anyone who had seen it not to ask, and Basil hadn't missed that either. So he simply gave Derek a soft, lingering kiss, and then handed over his arm to let Derek work. The profound gratitude in Derek's eyes was enough to tell Basil he'd done the right thing. Eventually Derek would trust him to share, and that's all that mattered.

It was more than an hour into the session when Basil noticed Sage—who was sitting in his periphery doing something on a woman's ankle—sat up straight. It was often startling just how much he looked like Derek, but there were differences in the way his face rested. Now though, as Basil looked between both brothers, it was difficult to see them. They wore identical expressions of worry.

It took Basil a second to realize the interruption was from Derek's phone. Sage had stood up, pointing at it, and Derek shook his head as he switched off his machine and reached for it. Basil couldn't read their lips well enough, but he did catch, 'Dad,' from Sage, and he saw the way Derek's cheeks pinked.

Basil wanted to stand up and demand that Derek let Sage take over. He knew what interacting with their father cost the man he was falling for, but it wasn't his place. He simply looked back and forth, and felt his stomach drop when Derek finally reached for his phone and pressed it to his ear.

He shed his gloves as his lips formed the words, 'Yeah, dad?' As he moved to drop his gloves into the bin, Basil watched as all the color drained from his face. There was a sudden and subtle tremor to his fingers, and he sat back with a dull expression. Basil caught, 'Yeah,' and, 'when,' but that was it, though he knew whatever else he was saying had startled Sage.

Someone else had taken over the ankle-tattoo woman, and Sage had squeezed himself into Derek's stall, touching his shoulder. The two of them stared at each other, like everything in the shop had faded away, and Basil felt a little like a voyeur as he stared at them.

After what felt like an hour, though couldn't have been more than five minutes, Sage backed away and Derek set his phone down. There was a hollowness to his eyes as he glanced back up, like he was just remembering what he was doing, and who was sitting in his chair. Then he licked his lips and raised his fist. 'Sorry.'

Basil leaned forward, reaching out to touch him, but felt his heart stutter when Derek pulled away and shook his head.

'My dad,' he signed, and then he faltered.

Swallowing thickly, Basil got his attention and focused hard. 'Say it,' he signed. 'I'll read your lips.'

Derek hesitated, like he wanted to tell him no, then he shrugged and said, "My dad died."

Basil fell back against the seat in shock. His hands lifted, then dropped down, then lifted again, but he didn't know what to tell him. What the hell could he say? When his parents had died, every word a person said or signed for months after felt trite and meaningless. The sympathies and the condolences only made him felt worse, and more alone, to the point his grief began to feel like rage, and he had to fight the urge to punch people every time they spoke.

After a beat, Derek picked up the machine again, but Basil moved to the end of the chair and gently laid a hand on his arm. 'No,' he signed. 'Stop.'

Derek looked at him with desperate eyes. "Please," he said aloud. "I need this."

Basil bit his lip, but he knew Derek would deal in his own way. He looked around, but Sage was long gone, and finally he settled back and offered his arm again. Some of the tension drained out of Derek's shoulders, and when he took Basil's arm, he stroked his thumb near an unmarked patch of skin and gave him a look of such gratitude and thanks, it made Basil's heart twist.

He felt the vibrations of the machine start up again, felt the sting of needles pressing into his skin, and he closed his eyes to let it happen. He expected Derek to take hours more, expected him to use Basil's body to work through his grief. But suddenly, he was finished. Suddenly, the machine was off, and he was being wiped down and wrapped up, and then Derek stood and walked out of the room.

Basil blinked, startled by the abrupt ending, and he glanced around to see Sam wheeling closer to him, a concerned look on his face. 'Sorry,' Sam mouthed.

Basil shook his head, feeling a little irritated that no one else in the shop spoke any real sign, and it triggered a little bit of his hesitance at continuing something more serious with Derek. This. This was the position he didn't want to be in.

Sam, however, reached for him and touched his arm, then pointed to the back door which Basil hadn't gone through before. He nodded at Basil, then pointed again, and Basil understood what he was trying to say.

His legs shook a little, his body still humming from the endorphins released by the pain, but he managed a steady stride all the way back, then through the door which led right into a small room. The walls were covered in flash, a single table in the middle surrounded by five chairs, and the top a mess of markers, colored pencils, and charcoal sticks.

Derek was there, his face in his hands, elbows shaking as they held him up. He didn't acknowledge Basil walking in, but when Basil touched his shoulder, Derek stiffened. He felt his throat tighten with what he was about to do, but all this reminded him that he was well and truly falling for this man, and this man was hurting.

"Derek," he said aloud. He'd been practicing in secret, and no real way to tell if he'd gotten in right, but the speech lessons he'd taken when he was dating Chad had been burned into his memory forever. He'd always been bitter about them. Until now. Until Derek looked up with wide, watery eyes, shocked at the sound of Basil's voice.

With trembling hands, Derek used the table to push himself up.

He hovered over Basil for a second, hands in the air almost uselessly until they cupped the sides of Basil's face and his thumbs stroked over his heated skin. He didn't say anything, just looked at him, but that look was a novel of words.

He was hurting, and he didn't know what he wanted, but there was gratitude lurking behind the pain at Basil's presence.

"I'm sorry," he said, continuing to speak.

Derek shook his head, his hands drifting from Basil's cheeks to his wrists. He squeezed them gently, raising them, before letting him go. 'Sign. Please. I know you hate voice.'

Basil went up on his toes to even their height, then he kissed him. Nothing deep, just a soft press of lips to remind Derek that he was here, and he'd do anything for him. Literally anything. He pulled back as Derek's hands settled on his waist, and he gave himself enough space to sign. 'What can I do?'

'Nothing,' Derek told him. 'I need to...' His hands fluttered to a stop, then he shrugged. 'I don't know.'

Basil knew, though. He knew what came after. The paper work and the meetings and dealing with everything left behind. There would be creditors to deal with, and debt, and any property. He knew very little about Derek's past, but he knew his father had been a disgraced politician and that meant there would be more than just the standard will. It meant things would come to light, and Sage and Derek would have to come forward after disappearing, and it meant there would be questions.

Derek would have to decide if he wanted to tell the truth—if he wanted the world to know what he'd suffered at the hands of that man.

'I want to help,' Basil told him, making sure Derek didn't break their gaze. 'Please.'

Derek licked his lips, then nodded. 'Stay with me? Tonight. Sage and I need to fly to New York. I can't ask you to come, too far, too long.'

Basil shook his head firmly. 'No. Not too far. Not too long. Amaranth can work, I can go with you. Please.'

Derek looked torn, but eventually he nodded and dragged Basil into a fierce embrace. His stubbled chin brushed along Basil's jaw as he smudged kisses all across his skin. Basil felt breath against his ear, a vibration under his fingers as Derek spoke something. Then he pulled back and repeated it in sign. 'Thank you.'

Basil cupped his cheek and held him fast. There weren't words to make this better, so he didn't try to offer any.

Basil had finally drifted off, and Derek slipped from the bed as carefully as he could. He was torn in half, desperately craving touch and comfort from the man he was half-way in love with, and desperate to fall apart on his own because he hated when people saw him at his weakest. Most of the time he didn't have a choice, but the way his father's death was hitting him was like nothing else he'd experienced.

The anxiety was there—the crushing feeling like the world was spinning out of control and there was nothing he could do about it. But beyond that was an anger. An anger, because his father died before Derek could squeeze one last favor out of him. He died before Derek could force him to look both him and Sage in the eyes and acknowledge what he'd done. The man had left the world probably feeling like he'd had every right to torture his sons—that it had done some good for them.

And there was no way to change that now.

There was no way to drag that man back from the grave, from hell, and force him to face the messes he'd made during his fall from grace.

Derek made it to the living room, back pressed to the far wall next to the window, and he sank down. He let his face fall into his hands and his shoulders shook with dry sobs. His eyes were aching and raw, but no tears came. Derek had cried enough thanks to that man, and he had nothing left to give. But the hollow feeling in his gut was eating at him and he just wanted it to stop.

He jolted when his phone began to buzz on the table, and he leapt for it before he remembered that Basil wouldn't hear it anyway. He saw his brother's name on the screen and debated ignoring it, but he wasn't that cruel. He had to face this with Sage, regardless of whatever else he planned to do.

"Hey."

Sage cleared his throat. "I just got off the phone with dad's lawyer. He said there's a lot to go over, but I...but he..."

Derek could hear what Sage wasn't saying. "He left it all to you," he said flatly.

"I don't want it," Sage said in a rush. "Fuck that old man, I don't fucking want any of it."

Derek let out a bitter laugh, letting his head fall back against the wall with a heavy thud. "I don't care."

"You took care of him," Sage growled. "The last three years, when that stupid fuck was dying, you took care of him. You answered every call and didn't say a word against the abuse he shouted at you, and you made sure he didn't suffer. He fucking deserved to suffer, Derek, but you are a better person than I will ever be. I don't want any of this." Sage let out a tiny sob, and Derek swallowed back his own.

"I don't want it either, you know," he admitted, his voice raw and hoarse. "I don't care that he left it to you. I wouldn't touch it even if it would mean I wouldn't have to use a single student loan ever again."

Sage was quiet a long moment, then he sighed, "What do we do? The lawyer says you need to be there—there's shit that involves you, and he thinks some of dad's old colleagues are going to have some questions."

"Why? Because his teenage sons ran away from home and then abuse allegations surfaced from the single teacher who bothered to give a fuck?" Derek asked bitterly. He dragged a hand down his face. "I don't want to care about any of this."

"I know," Sage said, his voice barely above a whisper. "I don't either. I'm done with him, and done with people dying and I just..." He let out a ragged sigh. "Will you come with me?"

"Yeah. I already booked us a flight," Derek admitted, because he had. It was the first thing he'd done after Basil said he was going to stay by his side. "Basil's coming too."

He half expected Sage to protest, but instead his brother just chuckled. "Thank god."

"Seriously?" Derek asked.

"I've never seen you look at anyone the way you look at him. He's...fuck's sake, I signed up for sign class last week because I'm not about to exchange notes like a fucking middle schooler to talk to my eventual brother-in-law."

Derek felt something warm explode in his chest, and it took a full thirty seconds before he could breathe again. "Thank you."

"Don't thank me," Sage said, almost furious. "Don't thank me for being the bare minimum of decent person. Just...pack your shit and let's get this over with. I want to put that man in the past for good."

"Me too," Derek breathed out. "I'm done letting him make me into this mess."

CHAPTER SIXTEEN

"Hey, kiddo." Derek almost smacked his head, startled halfway under his desk as he gathered up a group of fallen pencils. Pushing back on his stool, he spun and glowered at Tony and Sam who were barely restraining a laugh. "Thanks, fuckers."

Sam's grin turned a little sad, and Derek felt a pang of irritation because the last thing he needed was more coddling from everyone. "We just wanted to catch you before you and Sage head out." He pushed his chair a little closer and reached out his hand.

Derek was helpless against the offer of comfort, and let Sam take his arm. "We're only going to be gone like four days, man. Trust me, I'm not eager to draw this out."

"I know," Sam said, and his gaze flickered back up to Tony who had Jasmine propped up on his shoulder, her face smushed against his shirt as she slept. "And I promise we're not going to be assholes and baby you about this. We just want to remind you that this shit sucks, no matter what kind of scum he was, and if you need anything…"

"I'm good," Derek told him, and gently pulled away from his grip.

"I just want to move past this. It'll...fuck," he dragged his hand back through his hair, "it'll be nice to just bury the fucker and not have to take those calls anymore."

Except the strange thing was, knowing that weekly call wasn't coming in felt strange. Not bad—he wasn't going to miss listening to the old fuck slur into the receiver about what a disappointing homo he was, and how much he'd tried to beat the gay out of him, and some sinners just couldn't be cured. But the fact that it was over, the fact that this part of his life was irrevocably changed unsettled him. And logically he knew it was because he depended on routine. That the good and the bad were what kept him functioning. Still, he wanted to be rid of that. He wanted the newness to feel normal, and he wanted it to hurry.

"Look, you know we can close up shop and do the whole funeral thing with you, Der," Tony said, shifting Jasmine a little. "Our clients will understand, and those that don't, well we don't need their fuckin' business anyway."

Derek couldn't help a twinge of gratitude as he pushed himself up to stand, clasping Tony's shoulder. He gently rubbed his fingertips over Jasmine's curls, smiling when she nuzzled her dad's neck a bit in her sleep. "Thanks, man. Seriously, you have no idea how much I appreciate it, but we're not making a big deal out of this. We're the only family he had left, and we've already talked to the priest. It's going to be quick and dirty, and then we get to head home."

"Sage said you were bringing Basil with you," Sam told him.

Derek nodded, shoving one hand into his pocket just to keep his hand from fidgeting. "Yeah. Yeah, he...I don't even know how to feel about it, really. Like...shit. That's never happened before—someone who gave that much of a shit about me." When the pair of them looked a little affronted, he rolled his eyes. "I don't mean family, asshats. I mean...other."

"Right," Sam said, waggling his brows.

Derek kicked at his wheel gently. "I expect to come home and find all you fucks enrolled in the class Sage just signed up for, by the way. No more fucking excuses. For him, and for Jasmine. Enough bullshitting around it."

Tony's cheeks darkened a little, but his lip twitched into a half smile. "I'll see to it."

Derek nodded, then turned around to gather the supplies he wanted to bring on the plane. "I'll uh...I'll keep in touch," he promised without turning back around. "And Sam, you call me if shit goes down. I haven't given up on my promise to find you a lawyer, okay? We're going to work this out."

"Derek, right now," Sam started, but Derek spun around and quieted him with a firm stare.

"No. Now is exactly the right time for it, Sam. In the midst of all this bullshit, if I can get something good out of it, I'll feel like maybe I won't totally lose my mind, okay? So, when you get home, you kiss May for me and tell her uncle DeDe loves her and that he's going to help make this right."

Sam swallowed thickly, then nodded. "Just be safe, asshole. And don't be mad if you come back to me poaching all your clients. You know they can't resist my charm."

"Fuck off," Derek said, grinning through the words. "I'll be in touch." He hugged them both, then headed back to Sage's where he and Basil were waiting. Their flight was in a few hours, and the airport was going to be a huge pain. But it would be over. The ending was on the horizon, and Derek was more than looking forward to closing the book on that chapter of his life.

Derek felt a wave of guilt when he watched Basil pop a pill for his flying anxiety, but Basil quickly assured him it was fine, then held his hand as the plane began to taxi. Before they were at cruising altitude, Basil had dropped off against Derek's shoulder and was snoring quietly into the crook of his neck.

Sage glanced over, his mouth forming a very soft grin, and he shook his head. "This looks good on you."

"What, drool?" Derek asked, pointedly acting as though he didn't know what his brother meant. It wasn't that he wanted to diminish what Sage was saying, but there was a part of him still terrified to let himself be happy with another person in front of Sage after everything he'd lost.

Unfortunately, it was hard to hide anything from his twin, and Sage shook his head, letting out a tiny sigh. "I know what you're doing, but you need to know it's okay."

Derek swallowed thickly. "I just…I'll never forget what it was like right after Ted died, and I can't…I can't be someone who puts you back to that dark place."

"Seeing you happy is never going to send me to a dark place, Der," Sage told him, reaching out to squeeze his wrist. "And Ted wouldn't want me to be miserable and hateful just because life didn't turn out the way either of us expected. I'm…I'm good. Maybe not the best I've ever been, but I'm smiling again, and I have more happy days than shitty ones. And even in the midst of all this bullshit, I don't feel like I'm sinking. So just…let yourself have this, okay?"

Derek shifted a little and couldn't help a contented grin when Basil let out the smallest murmur and nuzzled closer. Derek's hand was tangled with Basil's, and he let himself get lost in the warm feeling of a palm pressed to his own. "I didn't think I could feel this happy."

"I knew you could, just like I knew it was going to take a really stubborn asshole to get through to you," Sage told him. "I'm glad he's here with us."

"Part of me wanted to tell him no," Derek admitted. "This is going to be a hell of a week and Jesus, I mean, I still don't know enough sign to properly interpret for him. I'm trying and I'm learning, but it's going so goddamn slow. I can't imagine what it would be like."

Sage shrugged. "I think I can. At least a little. My freshman year—remember I dated that Israeli guy and I went to spend Pesach with him and his family in Tel Aviv?"

Derek chuckled. "Yeah. You guys lasted like five months which was a record for you at the time."

Sage grinned back at him. "It was. Purim and Pesach, and by the time he invited me to temple for Shavuot, it was over." His smile was a little wry. "Anyway, I had gotten some really basic lessons from him before we went over there, and he kept telling me to chill because everyone spoke English—which was like sort of true, except that no one bothered unless they needed to address me directly. When we were in big groups for meals or shopping or whatever, it was all in Hebrew. And I picked up a few more things after two weeks, but still not enough that I wasn't totally lost unless I asked him to translate for me. I hated it, but I also didn't mind so much because it was important to him. And when we were together, he always made sure I understood what was happening. Everything important, anyway."

Derek glanced down at Basil's profile and wanted to lift him by the chin and kiss him awake. Instead he laid his head back against the seat and turned to look at his brother. "I'm going to keep working, and I hope you guys do too. I want this for him. I want him to feel safe and understood and part of us."

"We're doing it for Jazzy too," Sage reminded him. "He's not alone in this, and for you, he's worth it."

Derek allowed that feeling to take over, to eclipse the gentle simmer of badness in his gut since the night he'd gotten the phone call about his father. "I just want all this to be over, and I want to move on."

Sage nodded. "I get it, and I do too. I've uh…I've actually been giving this all a lot of thought. What to do with all this shit."

Derek raised his brows. "You mean the assets?"

"The lawyer said it'll all add up to a couple million if we decide to liquidate—which I don't see why not. I mean, I don't want any of this shit. But I also don't want to keep the cash. If anyone should have it, it should be you, considering what you went through."

Derek shuddered. "No. Fucking…absolutely not. I don't think I'd be able to live with myself."

"I have a thousand reasons why I disagree with that, but I also get it," Sage told him with a small breath. "So, I was thinking, we could start a charity—or maybe halfway house. Something to help kids like us with shitty parents so they're not squatting in abandoned warehouses and sneaking into public pool changing rooms for showers once a week." He dragged a hand down his face, his eyes closed when he pulled his fingers away. "From the day we left until I was twenty, I didn't eat a single fresh vegetable. When I got that apartment across the street from campus, I went to the farmer's market the day after I got paid and bought broccoli. I couldn't remember eating anything else, but I remember how Luisa used to make that steamed broccoli with garlic and butter, so I did it. I ate an entire plate, and fuck man, I was sick for like three damn days. My shit was weird and green, and I wanted to die, but I also refused to give up. I bought zucchini the next time I went down there, and then an artichoke, and then some spinach. And I swore to myself I wasn't ever going to live like that again. I want to do something so no one else has to go through what we did."

Derek hadn't been there when Sage took off and decided to do something more with himself. Derek was still flailing and falling apart, but he had his own moment. The first time he put his key into a lock and stepped into a studio apartment that was his and just his, without anyone telling him what to do or how to live, he almost turned around and walked right back out. Because he wasn't sure he was capable of being more to himself, or to anyone else. But he'd forced himself to step inside, and to unpack his three boxes, and to buy more things and make the place his.

He moved five more times after that—each place his own and mostly secret, and precious to him, and above all—it was freedom.

Sometimes that freedom felt like it was choking him to death, but he wouldn't let it go for anything in the world.

With Basil, it felt different, like the world tilted on its axis the other way, but the topsy-turvy felt good. It felt perfect. He wanted to keep going just as much as before.

"We can talk to someone about it," Derek finally said. "Is it something you want to do like hands on? Or do you just want to give money?"

Sage bit his lip, then said, "How insane is it that I kind of want this to be hands on?"

Derek shook his head. "It's not. It's brave and it's wonderful."

Sage ducked his head a little, then looked up at Derek through his lashes. "And if I said I wanted you to do it with me…?"

"Yes," Derek said, because frankly, there was no other answer than that. The thought might be terrifying, and more than intimidating, but the answer to something like that would always, always be yes.

CHAPTER SEVENTEEN

Derek tried to pretend like he wasn't relieved when Basil said he wanted to stay back at the hotel instead of attending the meeting with the lawyer, but it was a lie. Mostly because he'd have spent the entire time worrying about Basil not following along, and he just wasn't good enough yet to provide Basil with what he needed.

He toyed with the idea of hiring an interpreter, but Basil hadn't brought it up, and Derek didn't want to assume. At least, not with shit like this. The lawyer was a stuffy, over-dressed, weedy little man who had probably been prom king back in his hey-day, and then had let the years ravage him. His mostly-grey hair had once been black, and his mouth held a near-permanent frown.

He didn't seem to be their dad's biggest fan, either, which was the only relief Derek took from sitting in that office. "So, you're saying he left three million in cash, and his assets total four point six million," Sage said after the reading was finished. "And that bastard seriously didn't leave a thing to Derek?"

Mr. Thompson tapped his pen on the side of the desk and sighed.

"His will allowed the transfer of the home in Missouri to Mr. Osbourne. The value of the property at the last assessment was at..."

"I don't care," Derek interrupted. "Seriously, I don't care what it's worth. I don't actually want anything from him."

"I'm aware, Mr. Osbourne," Thompson said, addressing Derek directly, "that you were the sole caregiver for your father in the last three years. You were his assigned power of attorney, and both medical records as well as communication records will back that up."

"So?" Derek asked, glancing over at Sage.

Thompson licked his lips as his gaze flickered between the brothers, like maybe he was uncertain if there was conflict between them over the will. "A case might be made that your father's cognizance had been deteriorating due to the advanced cirrhosis, and he may not have been aware he had two sons near the end. However, a case might be argued that you are due at least half the inheritance—and that's a case you'll likely win if you decide to take this to court."

Derek blinked, glancing at Sage for a startled second. "Okay hold on, I meant what I said about not wanting any of this."

"If my brother wants anything my father left me, he can have it," Sage cut in. "Trust me when I tell you that as far as I know, we're both on the same page. We just want to get rid of it as quickly as possible."

"I see," Thompson said. He took up his pen again and made a note on his yellow legal pad. "As I have been overseeing your father's estate for the last twenty years, I would offer my services. However, if you find that uncomfortable, I can also recommend several good attorneys who would be more than familiar with such a situation."

Derek bit his lip, then said, "Actually I could use a good recommendation, but it's not about inheritance or anything. It's about custody, and it's in Colorado."

Thompson's eyebrows raised. "Perhaps a discussion for another time? Before you leave, of course."

Derek nodded, feeling only slightly guilty for immediately talking about Sam in spite of their present situation and dead father.

"We should probably take a day and go over all this," Derek said, eyeing the stack of folders.

"I'll arrange for you to come back in after the funeral, assuming you'll still be in the city. If not, I'm happy to come to you," Thompson told him.

Derek figured the guy had gotten a decent pay-out from his father if he was being this helpful, but he couldn't really turn his nose up at it. After making sure Sage was with him, he nodded. "One of us will call you. Thank you for all your help."

"My pleasure," Thompson said. "Let me put you in touch with the funeral home. All the arrangements were pre-made, so there's little you need to do. Your father ensured his plot would be ready, and the expenses taken care of."

Derek swallowed past a lump in his throat, then rose and he and Sage collected the folders before they headed out the doors. Neither one of them felt up for driving, so they'd hired an uber which was still waiting for them as they exited the law offices and quickly climbed inside.

"Fuck," Sage said, letting his head fall against the window. "I need a damn drink."

"Hotel bar could be good," Derek replied. "I don't really want to end up wasted somewhere like this. And Basil's waiting for me."

They fell into a silence which made Derek want to scream until he'd filled the void, and as the car came to a stop in front of the hotel, he realized he'd tensed nearly all of his muscles. He would be sore for days later, and he wondered how long he'd be suffering the repercussions of a death he shouldn't even be mourning.

Sage was out of the car first, making sure the payment had gone through, and Derek followed him in through the lobby, past the lounge seating, and they quickly found a booth in the corner of the dimly lit bar. He sent a quick text to let Basil know they were back and going over paperwork, but he didn't get a response and hoped it was because Basil was sleeping off the jetlag and flying anxiety.

Sage went to the bar to grab them a couple drinks, then sat back down with a heavy sigh as he eyed the paperwork like it might spontaneously combust. "This fucking sucks."

Derek nearly choked on his first swallow of beer, his laugh unexpected and so needed. He wiped his mouth with the flat of his palm, shaking his head with his grin. "Yeah, it really fucking does."

"I never really thought about money until we didn't have it anymore," Sage went on, reaching out to thumb the corner of the folder. "Like, we didn't really want for shit as kids—I mean, apart from the whole not wanting to get beaten and locked in a shed any time we mouthed off. But yeah, it just never occurred to me until we were on the streets. I told myself that when I got out of that fuckin' warehouse and started making money, I'd make sure I was stable and never hungry again. Now, with this shit sitting in my lap, I'd rather go back there than use any of this for myself."

"Feels like blood money," Derek murmured.

Sage sighed, then picked up his pint and gulped down half before looking at Derek again. "I don't think I could live with myself if we didn't use it to help people. I know you got student loans and shit—I mean hell, I'm still paying off mine, but..."

"No," Derek said in a rush, ignoring the queasy squirm of his stomach at the very thought of using his dad's money for that. "I got loans, but I can pay them off fine without this. I can't...I'm with you. I can't do it like this."

Sage reached over and took the second folder which detailed out all the property. He rifled through the papers, then came out with one near the bottom and spread it out between them. "This one though..."

Derek peered over and saw what it was. The Ozark cottage. "Sage," he said from behind a breath.

"Hear me out," his brother interrupted, making sure Derek was meeting his gaze. "This wasn't dad's place. Not really. It was mom's. I remember...I remember him buying this for her. Her sister had just died, and she was a wreck. I think it was the first time I'd ever seen him look at her like she was a person. It was like two in the morning, and I was sneaking down to get cookies. They were in dad's office and she was just sitting there crying and he looked so...he looked so helpless. He just kept asking her how he could help, and she just kept crying." Sage ran a hand down his face, then rolled his eyes up toward the ceiling. "He came home like five days later with the keys, and we went on our first vacation there. He didn't hit you that trip. Not once. Not that time."

Every single word was like a physical blow, and it took Derek several minutes to regain his voice. "Why don't I remember that at all?"

Sage laughed bitterly. "I don't know. I mean shit, we were like seven? Eight? And dad was already being an epic dick to you, so you had other shit to worry about. I mean, I wasn't even supposed to see that conversation, it was an accident. But I know that place was hers. Whenever shit got bad, whenever she looked like she couldn't take it anymore..."

"That's where we'd go," Derek finished quietly. "We stopped going that second year after she died."

"I just think," Sage said, touching the edge of the blurry, black and white photo printed next to the property assessment, "I think she'd want that for you."

Derek looked up at him, a bitter laugh tumbling past his lips. "She never stepped in. Not once."

Sage's eyes fluttered closed. "Der..."

"No," Derek said fiercely. "I'm not going to condemn her because she was probably getting it just as bad as we were—maybe worse. But she made me feel so alone. Like I wasn't worth making that man just...just stop. Then she went and died, and I really was alone. You were the only one," he stopped when his voice cracked, and he quickly took a drink to help regain his composure. "I don't want that because of her."

"So take it because of me. And you," Sage said, and Derek narrowed his eyes in confusion. "We can remake that place as something else—take it back, make it something good again." He rubbed his hand over his mouth, then smiled a strange, almost sad smile. "I wanted to take Ted there, but I was too afraid to ask dad for the keys. But I have these memories of…of running through the woods and climbing trees and it was one of the few times in my childhood I felt unafraid. I just…I wanted to keep that."

Derek felt a pang in his chest, almost physical pain, and he rubbed the heel of his palm up and down his sternum before looking back at his brother. "Okay," he said. His voice was hoarse, but it was strong, and he meant it because he knew what Sage was saying. "Okay. The rest…"

"The rest we fucking get rid of. We help Sam and Maisy, and I'm going to start talking to someone else because I want to do something good with this. I don't want to just dump it on some charity that's going to pay their CEO a three million-dollar bonus and give us some bullshit tax write-off. I want to know kids like us have a place to go that isn't some frigid warehouse with flea-infested blankets and cold poptarts every day for months."

Derek smiled at him, reaching for his wrist, and he squeezed down hard. "Yeah. I'm with you, okay? We can fucking do this."

Sage turned his hand over and squeezed back, and Derek knew he'd never really be alone.

Basil woke from his attempt to sleep off his migraine, a little confused by the unfamiliar smell and feel of the bedding wrapped around him. It took him a long second to remember where the hell he was and why, and then he became aware of the warm body that had woken him.

Derek was in the room, though he hadn't bothered with lights or pushing back the curtains, instead curling up behind Basil with a firm hand around his waist. Basil could feel a tension in him, and he shifted, reaching for the little bedside lamp, letting the room fill with a soft glow. Turning around, his eyes met Derek's and he saw they were red-rimmed and swollen, though long-since dry of any tears he'd shed.

Not wanting to make Derek work to understand him, he simply lifted his hand to Derek's cheek and held his palm against the flush-warm skin. 'Hi,' he mouthed.

Derek chuckled, his shoulders rising and falling with it under Basil's other hand. 'Hi,' he mouthed back.

Basil leaned in and kissed him, slow and drawn out, trying to give him as much comfort and support without words as he could manage. Derek took every second of it, his fingers a little rough and desperate as they clung to Basil's waist. But it didn't go deeper, and Basil could feel with Derek's hips pressed against him, his boyfriend wasn't hard.

When he pulled back, he dragged his hand away from Derek's face. 'You ok?'

Derek shrugged, his body going slack with a deep sigh and he rolled onto his back. Basil propped up to look at him properly as Derek struggled through his signs. 'The meeting was long."

Basil reached out, rubbing his thumb gently over Derek's wrist before pulling away. 'Tell me.'

Derek sighed. 'I'm slow, sorry. Frustrating.'

'I don't care,' Basil insisted. 'Please. I came here to help. Talk to me.'

Derek licked his lips, then pushed his hands down onto the mattress and propped himself up, scooting back to lean against the headboard. He crooked one knee up, dragged a hand down his face, then finally met Basil's gaze again. 'There's a lot of money. Almost three million in cash,' he spelled the number out, and Basil's eyes went wide. His parents had left a sizable inheritance, mostly from their life insurance policy, but nothing like that. Not even close. 'More in property. He left it all to Sage.'

At that, Basil felt himself make a noise—something of protest, maybe, or of sympathy. It got Derek's full attention, and normally he would have been self-conscious, but not here. Not now. 'I'm sorry.'

Derek shook his head firmly, his eyes going hard. 'I don't want it. Sage wants us to use it to create a charity to help people like us. Homeless teenagers. It's the only good thing we could do with that man's legacy.'

Basil felt the center of his chest go warm, and shit, he knew what that was. He might not have a lot of experience with love, but he was being bashed in the face with it. His fingers itched to form the sign, to place it against Derek's softly beating heart because he deserved to know. But now was not the time.

'He also left me a house,' Derek carried on. His eyes closed a minute, like he was absorbing pain, or maybe old memories. 'Remember that cottage by the lake I told you about? From my paintings?'

'Yes,' Basil replied.

'He left that to me. I don't know why, but Sage thinks we should keep it. Make it ours again. Make it something good.'

'Is that what you want?' Basil asked.

Derek looked at him for a long time, then a smile played at his lips. He didn't answer straight away, instead reaching for Basil, drawing him forward and into a kiss. When he pulled back, his eyes were a little clearer and a lot softer. 'I think so. Would you go there with me someday? Stay a week?'

'Yes,' Basil said, because what other answer could he give. He would say yes to damn near anything Derek asked of him, without question.

Derek swallowed thickly, then gathered Basil to his chest, and Basil didn't hesitate as he let the other man pull him back down to the bed. He octopussed his arms and legs around Basil, pinning him there, and though Basil felt like he'd slept enough for the night, he allowed this moment to carry on for as long as Derek needed it to.

CHAPTER EIGHTEEN

The day of the funeral was tense. Basil went to breakfast with both brothers, and he could feel the silence between them as neither one of them bothered to communicate with each other. They got ready shortly after, but in the lobby, Basil watched as Sage stopped Derek with a hand to his chest.

He couldn't tell what was being said, but he knew they were arguing. When people started to stare, Basil realized it was getting kind of loud, but he made no move to stop them. After a beat, Derek wrenched himself away from Sage and stormed off, but before Basil could go after him, Sage stopped him with a hand on his arm.

He held up his finger for Basil to wait, then began to type on his phone. I'm sorry. Derek's not doing well, and I don't think he should go to the funeral. It's not going to do him any good. We need to get out of this city, and I told him he should go to our dad's penthouse and finish signing off on what needs to be packed up and sold, and I'll handle the service.

Basil stared at the words and found he couldn't disagree. Derek would hate it—only because he hated having control taken away from him, but Basil knew full well that attending the funeral wasn't going to do him any good, wasn't going to give him closure. The man was dead, and the only thing that would happen was Derek subjecting himself to the lies the community told about what a great man he was.

Okay, Basil typed back. Order us a car and I'll get him to go.

Sage gave him a grateful smile, taking the phone back to do just that. Before Basil could walk away, Sage took him by the shoulder, then dragged him into a fierce hug. When he pulled away, Sage looked him directly in the eye and signed, 'Thank you.'

Basil gave him a stiff nod, then hurried out the automatic doors and glanced around for Derek. He assumed his boyfriend would have gotten further than the side alley, but he found Derek pacing, one hand in his hair, the other clenched into a fist. Basil approached slowly, not flinching when Derek looked up at him with fire in his eyes, his mouth set in a firm, angry line.

He stopped pacing the moment Basil walked up, but he didn't accept him into his arms the way he normally would. He put his palm out, then released his fist full of hair to sign, 'Stop. Please, don't.'

Basil sighed, closing the distance between them, but respected Derek's request not to be touched. 'Your brother is right,' he signed carefully, slowly, watching understanding and then anger dawn in Derek's eyes. 'You don't need to go to the funeral. Go to the house. I'll come with you and we can finish it together.'

Derek shook his head, but Basil was pretty sure it wasn't refusal, it was just the chaos swirling around his mind, and he desperately wished there was a way he could help soothe him. 'I want,' he started, but his hands just hovered there in the air between them.

'I know,' Basil replied. 'I know, but it's almost over. Sage ordered a car. It's almost over.'

Derek stared at him a long moment, then gave a stiff nod. When Basil reached for him again, he didn't pull away.

. . .

THE SILENCE WAS stony on the way to the penthouse, and he knew that was his own fault. He also knew how profoundly lucky he was that Basil wasn't taking any of it personally and was still by his side. He didn't try to communicate with Derek at all, instead keeping his hand in a firm hold, letting his thumb run soothing circles over his wrist.

Derek kept his eyes fixated on the night bloom emblazoned across Basil's forearm, and after a moment, he let himself reach over and touch it. The edges of the tattoo were fresh still and peeling a little, and the center skin was still raised around the lines. He traced them with the tip of his finger and let himself absorb just how important this ink was. They were tied together in a permanent way, and Basil didn't seem afraid of it at all.

Even after everything he'd been through, and the cruel people he'd known, he still trusted Derek enough for this. He still felt Derek was worthy enough to carry something of his for the rest of his life. Even if they didn't work out, Derek would know he meant something to Basil once. Something important. He thought maybe, just maybe, if he leaned over right then and told Basil he was falling in love with him, he might get the same back.

It wasn't the right time, but he couldn't help wondering if there ever really was one.

Switching their positions, Derek took Basil's hand and laid the back of it on his thigh, studying the lines of Basil's palm. They were smoother than his own, and he had less callouses and a little more fat deposits at the base of his fingers. His skin felt so good under Derek's rough fingertips, and he found himself wanting to strip Basil down and touch every single inch of his body with hands, with lips, with tongue.

Their intimate time together was limited to their single night of mutual orgasms, and it had been enough, right up until this moment. Derek had been taking it slow for both their sakes, but he was ready for more. He fucking loved this man and he wanted to show him in more ways than one.

When he finally glanced up at Basil's face, Basil's eyes were soft, but intense as they drank him in. His free hand lifted slowly to his chin. 'What's wrong?'

Derek couldn't help his smile, in spite of the situation. 'Nothing. I'm…' He licked his lips and shrugged. He wanted to say he was happy, because in a way, he was. But he was afraid he didn't have enough words to make himself understood and he didn't want Basil to think there was anything superficial or light in this moment. He lifted his hand and traced his finger under Basil's bottom lip, dragging it over his adam's apple, feeling across his collarbone. 'You're beautiful. So beautiful."

Basil sucked in his breath, his cheeks going faintly pink, and he leaned in for a kiss. It had the promise of something deeper, hotter, the passion inside of him threatening to consume this moment if he let it. Instead he put a hand to Basil's cheek and let the moment simmer gently in the background. There would be time for more. He just…he just had to do all this first.

They reached his father's building, a too-posh apartment he shouldn't have been able to afford after being disgraced the way he was. But like any politician, he'd managed to claw his way up from the muck and remake himself because ultimately, no one cared about the fates of two gay boys who ran away from their good Christian father.

Derek reached into his pocket and palmed the key to the lobby, then dug out his ID for the doorman who quickly gave him directions to the elevator. The keycard swipe got him to the top floor which led them to a short corridor. His father's door was at the far end, and he felt his stomach twist as he put the key in the lock and stepped inside.

The place was lit mostly from the floor to ceiling windows, and it didn't smell musty the way it should have after three years of abandonment, but he supposed the cleaning services hadn't stopped during his father's convalescence. Derek had been power of attorney for two and a half of those three years, and he hadn't known about this place, but he had ensured his father's personal business was run as usual.

He felt something ugly creeping up his spine—a sort of envy in a way, or maybe it was just fury that a man like Brian Osbourne had been subhuman and yet had lived with such luxury. Everything was new and shiny. He'd beaten his kids and driven his wife to an early grave, and he got to come home every night to a three-million-dollar penthouse. He'd never slept on a cold, concrete floor, belly empty, body filthy, unsure when the next time he'd eat.

Derek let out a shaking breath, then jolted when he felt a warm hand touch the small of his back. He glanced over at Basil who was watching him carefully, and he gave a nod to let him know he was okay. It was a lie. He wasn't okay. He was the furthest thing from okay. He was standing in his father's home with no evidence that he'd ever existed. There were a handful of photos on the wall—his father meeting presidents, golfing, on a cruise ship with a blonde woman holding a pair of drinks, looking like he didn't have a care in the world. His bookshelves were filled with the classics he'd probably never read, his walls full of art he never bothered to appreciate. His bank account was filled with zeroes he'd amassed because his wife and children disappeared from his life and he only ever had to worry about himself. His liquor cabinet was full of the poison which eventually killed him.

Derek broke away from Basil and walked to a closet door. He wrenched it open and found a set of golf clubs which looked well-polished and new. They'd probably seen courses Derek would never be able to afford, registered to country clubs who would turn Derek and Sage both away on appearance alone.

He found his hand reaching for them, plucking one of the putters from the collection. It was heavy in his hand as he twisted his wrist, testing the balance. He moved away from the closet, to a tall shelf with the most important photos of Brian on display. One of him being sworn in years after Derek and Sage left. Another of him shaking the hand of the Secretary of State.

He swung the golf club before he was aware he was doing it, not sure if the roar was coming from his chest or was in his mind. But he couldn't stop himself. The rage was taking over, and the only thing he knew was the overwhelming pain that his father had ruined lives and destroyed his soul and had gotten to leave this earth without ever taking accountability for what he'd done.

He could hear his father's last words to him blaring in his head, so loud in his memory it made his ears ring. "You were fucking useless as a child and you're even more useless now. I should have let your mother end the pregnancy before you even had a chance to take your first breath."

He was sobbing now, watching glass fall as the club made contact with figurines which crashed to the floor. The end of the club smashed into the face of the clock above the mantle, it hooked around the books in the shelf, sending them toppling to the floor. He crushed frames under his feet, tore at the curtains until the rod gave way and it all came crashing down.

He wasn't aware of when he'd dropped to the floor, or of when Basil had pulled the golf club from his fingers, but he came to with his hands pressed to the carpet, shards of glass cutting into his palms as his body was wracked with dry sobs. He didn't fight Basil when his arms came around him, pulling him back, holding him like it was the only thing keeping it together—because it was.

He knew there was no taking it back. He knew his father—dead or alive—didn't deserve a single second of his energy, his rage, his sadness. But he couldn't stop it. Now that the dam was broken, he was helpless against the flood. He turned, pressing his face into the crook of Basil's neck and let himself cry. Real tears, real emotion, anguish for himself and knowing that nothing he did would take away his past. His father's death didn't matter in the grand scheme of things. He could probably move on now—he could let the past go and know that in the future, Brian Osbourne could no longer hurt him, but he would be forced to reconcile that the man had gone to his grave without a single second of remorse.

Basil's fingers drifted through his hair, and he was humming a tuneless, deep noise in his chest which brought Derek back from the edge better than anything ever had before. He pulled back enough to swipe his hand over his face, and then he looked up at Basil who was staring at him without judgement or fear or disgust. Just affection and worry, and it meant everything.

When his hand lifted, fingers curled into a fist, Basil stopped him and shook his head. 'Don't apologize.'

Derek was about to argue that he wasn't going to, but he realized he had been, and he finally nodded, letting his hands drift back down to his lap. After a beat, he looked around at the carnage and found himself surprised he actually did feel a little better. 'At least I can afford to have this place cleaned up.'

That startled a laugh from Basil who shook his head and reached for Derek's wrists. He pulled his hands up to survey the damage—superficial cuts, a little blood, but far less pain than even his kindest tattoo. 'What now?'

Derek sighed, shrugging. 'I'm going to need to explain this to the agent coming by for me to sign papers,' he admitted. 'But I don't care.'

Basil's lips softened into a grin. 'What can I do?'

Derek shook his head, then dragged the tip of his finger across Basil's jaw. 'Nothing. You're perfect.' At the slight blush on Basil's cheeks, he knew this was it for him. This was all he'd ever want, and he meant to do everything in his power to keep it.

CHAPTER NINETEEN

Collapsing on the couch, Derek wriggled and twisted until his head was firmly planted in Sam's lap. Sam's thighs had long-since atrophied, so what was left of the muscle was hard and stiff, but the comfort of being home and with someone he considered family was enough to soothe him. Especially when Sam gently put a hand through his hair and smiled down at him.

"Was it seriously that bad?" he asked.

Derek closed his eyes and let out a slow breath. "Worse. I fucking lost it, man. We got to his penthouse and I started looking through shit, and when I realized he hadn't bothered keeping any trace of me or Sage or my mom I just—I just went batshit on the place. I grabbed a fucking putter out of the closet and broke everything."

Sam jolted a little under him, and when Derek opened his eyes, he saw the guy staring down at him with a vaguely startled expression. "Der…"

"I know," Derek said. "I had a two-hour therapy session today to work through a lot of it, and I'm doing okay but…but fuck, man. This is going to take some time."

"You knew it would," Sam reminded him gently, scratching at his scalp like he would a cat. "When you decided to take on his care, you told me yourself it was going to fuck you up in the end."

"I was hoping I'd find a way to forgive him," Derek admitted. He turned to his side slightly and Sam's hand dropped to the back of his neck. He wondered if other people got this kind of comfort from their friends and family. Or maybe he was just a freak. Maybe they all were. He realized even if that was the case, he couldn't care less. "I told Leila today that I don't want to forgive him."

"What did she say?"

Derek shrugged. "She said I don't have to, that people who are abused aren't obligated to forgive their abusers, and that it's not true that the only way to live a healthy life is if you can bring yourself to do that."

Sam's mouth lifted into a grin. "I like her."

"Me too," Derek said quietly. "If she wasn't married, I might give her your number."

Sam rolled his eyes. "I don't have time for dating right now, Der. And even if I did..." He trailed off, and by the tone in his voice, Derek realized he was keeping something back.

Pushing up on his elbow, he lifted to sit and stared at his friend. "If you did?" he pressed.

Sam shook his head, dragging both hands down his face with a groan. "It's fucked up."

"Look man, unless you're like in love with me or my brother which would be so weird..."

"No," Sam said in a rush, then laughed. "I mean, no offense. You know you're both hot as hell, but you're my brothers. No, I...it isn't either one of you."

"Then who cares," Derek said.

Sam licked his lips. "Bro code, Derek."

Derek frowned. "I...what? Bro code?"

"You don't fucking date your friend's ex," Sam clarified, and blushed so hard the tips of his ears went pink.

Derek leaned forward. "Who the fuck has an available ex?"

Sam shifted, looking uncomfortable. "Well...maybe not ex, necessarily, but it was pretty obvious you liked him and..."

Derek's eyes widened. "Wait. Niko?"

Sam licked his lips, then nodded. "He's...we've gotten together a couple of times, and he co-hosted a wheelchair yoga session at the gym last weekend. He's also really great with May and I just...I'm sorry. I already told him I'm not in a place where I can date, but I would never do that to you."

Derek tried to hold back his laughter, but he couldn't. He covered his face, his body shaking with it, and when he regained some control, he dragged Sam into a hug before righting him back on the sofa. "Fucker. I'm so fucking in love with Basil, Niko never had a chance. I only went on that one date because Sage begged me to, and it didn't end well."

Sam's eyes flickered down. "Yeah. He told me. Honestly part of me can't help but wonder if he's only interested because he wants to prove he's not some ableist asshole. I mean shit, it's not like I have a whole helluva lot to offer."

Derek's jaw tensed. "First of all, he was kind of an ableist asshole, but he's the kind of guy who could learn to be better. Secondly, you're a fucking catch, Sam, and if you want to argue, we can take this shit outside and duke it out."

Sam laughed, rolling his eyes. "The last time you tried to fight me, I floored your ass."

"I had like half a bottle of tequila, that doesn't fucking count."

Sam grinned for a second, but it didn't last long. "I just mean... I'm...I come with a lot. It's more than just a chair, and it's more than just a kid. It's pain and sometimes it's me pissing myself and not being able to maintain a fucking erection, and it's also constant court battles for my girl, and never-ending scrutiny by people who will never see me as an able parent—and sometimes that constant questioning makes me believe it. I can't saddle someone with that, Der."

"A person who loves you for you—all of that shit is just going to be part of what they love about you," Derek told him fiercely.

"Believe me, okay? I didn't think I'd ever meet anyone who'd be willing to put up with all this fucking mess," he waved his hand up and down his body. "And Basil and I are still new so who the fuck knows if it's going to end up too much for him, but right now it isn't. Right now, he just wants me for exactly who I am, and I'm learning to accept that."

Sam worried his bottom lip with his teeth, then sighed. "I get it, because that's the shit I'd be telling you if you were freaking out about Basil, but it's...I just..."

"I get it," Derek said. "But trust me, if it's right, it'll happen. And more than anyone I know, Sam, you deserve it."

BASIL WAS JUST FINISHING COUNTING the drawer when the lights flashed. He looked up, irritated that he'd forgotten to lock the door, but his entire body lit up with relief when he saw Derek making his way through the rows of spring flowers they'd set out earlier that day. He was a strange juxtaposition—massive and hard angles and sharp ink in contrast to the soft petals and rounded edges of the flora he was walking through, but it looked right. He looked perfect there.

Basil was still a little shaken from his experience in New York. Derek had eventually been able to calm down and sort out the paperwork for his father's estate. The agent who came by didn't seem entirely surprised by the chaos that greeted him and didn't make mention of it that Basil could see. The whole process was done in less than an hour, then they went to a kosher deli for lunch, and eventually met Sage back at the hotel.

The trip was meant to last another two days, but the brothers looked flayed raw and exhausted, so Basil didn't put up a fight when Sage changed their tickets to that night, and they hopped the red-eye back to Denver. Basil immediately went home with Derek and they curled together under his threadbare blanket and held each other for hours as they slept the day away.

Then life got on as normal. Derek went back to work, and Basil went back to the shop and they still texted and still got together to work on sign, and Derek kept a close watch on the tattoo, his eyes telling Basil more than his words that the image wasn't finished.

Basil couldn't stop thinking about the cottage the brothers had decided to keep and wondered if Derek had meant it about wanting to go there and spend some time. Basil couldn't imagine it would be soon—couldn't imagine Derek being ready for it in the near future, but the thought of spending a week away from everyone and everything made him crave with a fierceness he wasn't expecting.

Now, seeing Derek making his way across the shop floor, he wanted it even more. He smiled as Derek laid his hands on the desk and leaned in, and Basil turned his face up for a kiss.

'How was your day?'

Basil waved the question off. 'Fine. Boring. Amaranth booked three weddings next month, so I'll be crazy then.'

Derek's shoulders shook with his chuckle. 'I booked a long-term job. Two grand total and he prepaid.'

Basil's eyes went wide. 'Wow. You happy?'

Derek shrugged. 'It's a long commitment, but it means I can ask you...' He stopped and licked his lips. 'I need to...can we spend the night at yours? I want to talk.'

Basil felt his stomach twist with worry. Logically he knew Derek wouldn't be asking for a night over, or anything intimate, if he was about to end things, but Basil's heart was still a little raw and a little afraid. 'Are we okay?'

'No,' Derek signed, but there was a playful smile tugging at his lips. 'We're perfect, I think.'

Basil let out a breath, then smacked him on his shoulder. 'Asshole.'

'I know.' Derek tugged him in for another kiss. 'I'm going to get food. Meet you there?'

Basil nodded, and Derek reached over, curling his hand into the front of Basil's shirt and pulling him in for a third lingering kiss.

'See you soon,' he signed, then he went right back out the way he'd come in. Basil followed to lock up, and maybe his numbers weren't super precise as he hurried through the last of his closing duties, but Amaranth could yell at him for it tomorrow.

He made the drive back to his place in less than five minutes, and was just getting out of the shower when the lights flickered, letting him know that Derek had come in. Amaranth had gone into Denver with friends and had already told Basil not to expect her back, which meant they had the place to themselves. It was good, unless Derek had been lying about why he wanted to talk, and things were not perfect. Yet, he reminded himself, Derek wore his heart on his sleeve and Basil could see it plain on his face—Derek was in it. This was solid. It was good.

In Derek's words, they were perfect.

He threw on a pair of sweats and a t-shirt, then walked into the living room to find Derek setting a pizza on the table. He looked over his shoulder when Basil entered the room, and his cheeks immediately went pink as he straightened and walked over like he couldn't help but take Basil into his arms and kiss him. When they broke apart, Derek didn't let him get far, his eyes roaming over Basil's face like he just couldn't get enough.

Finally, he dragged them to the sofa, but where Derek might have immediately put his feet in Basil's lap and dug into the food like they'd been doing that together a hundred years, instead he turned to face him.

'I've been practicing this,' he said in perfect ASL. 'I want to get it right, and I want it to be said in a way you understand without having to try. My teacher helped.'

Basil blinked at him, his throat a little hot and a little tight. 'Okay.'

Derek nodded, and his chest puffed and deflated with his breath. 'The night we met, I was a mess. My father had spent an hour telling me how worthless I was, and I didn't feel like my life was going anywhere. I will always be a mess. Part of me will always be the terrified teenager locked away in a garden shed not sure if he was going to die in there.'

Basil felt white-hot rage course through him and wished he could drag the old man out of hell just to put him back there himself. But he didn't say any of that, because he knew what this was costing Derek, and he knew how hard Derek had worked on this.

'The night I was trapped in the bank, I went right back to that dark place. But then you touched my arm and you pulled me out. You bought Kevin and you let me give you a piece of me on your arm that you'll carry forever. And then, when I was falling apart, you held me together.' Derek swallowed thickly, his eyes darting away only for a second, and when he looked back, there was fire and purpose in them. 'I love you,' he said, signing the full sentence instead of using the three fingered sign for it. 'I'm falling in love with you, and I'm terrified but I don't care anymore. If you think it's too much, I understand, but I need you to know that this is everything.'

Basil waited several beats after Derek's hands dropped, just to be sure he was finished. He had wanted to interrupt more than once, wanted to just take his hands and kiss his palms, then slowly undress him and meld their bodies together until he wasn't sure where one began and the other ended. But he also knew how hard Derek had worked to perfect everything he wanted to say, and he wasn't about to take a single second of that way from him.

'I love you too,' he signed. A simple gesture, the I love you sign, and same, signed in the short space between them. Derek's eyes were fixed hard on his hands, and then looked up into Basil's eyes and his face erupted into a grin.

'Yeah?' he mouthed.

Basil chuckled. 'Yeah,' he mouthed right back.

Then Derek's hands were on him, pulling at him, searching for skin under his shirt and below the waistband of his bottoms. He had Basil pinned to the sofa in seconds, a knee between his legs gently pushing up against his balls with just enough pressure to feel good. Derek's mouth barely left his, tongue sliding across his own in wet, hot, gorgeous strokes and Basil's eyes rolled back in his head with want and desperation.

Somehow, moving in tandem, they managed to stand and stumble down the hall without losing their grip on each other. Derek had Basil's shirt off and flung into the corner of the room the moment they got inside, and Basil could feel the vibrations in his feet as Derek kicked the door shut.

'I want you,' Derek signed.

Basil nodded frantically, let Derek drag him back toward the bed. They were barely dressed by then, the last of their covered skin separated by loose, thin boxers, Derek still in his socks. His hands were warm and a little rough as they brushed down the center of his chest, his fingers pinching at his nipples, drawing little gasps and moans from Basil's throat.

He felt Derek hesitate, and when he opened his eyes and looked down, he saw Derek's hand hovering just over the place where his dick was growing rock hard and throbbing. His gaze was fixed on Basil's face, eyes questioning, asking for permission.

Basil reached between them, gently pulling his hand down until it made contact with his hard cock, and he thrust into it. Derek let out a puff of air, then he shoved his hand into the waistband of Basil's boxers and took Basil's cock into the palm of his hand. It was rough, and a little too dry, and also perfect enough Basil wanted to cry—or maybe scream and then come.

But he wanted more than this, he wanted everything. He wanted to feel Derek on top of him, and inside him, and he wanted to be inside, and he wanted Derek's mouth on him. He felt his lips forming a word, his throat vibrating with it. "Please."

Derek's entire body jolted at the sound, and then he used both hands to tug Basil's boxers to his knees, over his ankles, flinging them across the room with purpose. He nosed up his thigh, his moan vibrating against Basil's skin, and then wet heat enveloped him as Derek swallowed him down in one go.

"Uhgf," Basil groaned, his head tipped back. It took everything in him to keep from thrusting as Derek used his tongue to draw a line up the underside of his cock. He pulled back, suckling the head for a minute, eventually drawing away as he licked precome off his bottom lip.

'I want,' Derek signed, then dragged his hand down the back of Basil's crooked thigh and palmed the side of his ass.

Basil nodded frantically, turning on his side to dig out his lube and condoms. They were new, and he saw the slight amusement in Derek's eyes as his nails tore at the packaging, sending the plastic wrap to the floor. Basil's breath stuttered in his chest as Derek's fingers went shiny with the silicone slick, and then his eyes slammed shut at the first press of a finger.

He expected Derek to take a long time, to torture him, to ignore the desperation of the moment and be sweet—which would have been fine, though it wasn't what he wanted. He appreciated being wrong in this case when, after only a moment, a second finger joined Derek's first. Then a third after only a couple of strokes. Basil felt stretched out and sore and on the verge of begging if Derek didn't get on with it.

He lifted his leg higher, trying to telegraph his wants, and he let Derek grip the back of his thigh and push his leg higher, resting his calf over his shoulder. His free hand lifted the condom to his mouth, tore the wrapping, then finally pulled his hand out to hold his dick steady so he could roll it on.

Basil braced himself, willing himself to relax as he felt the first push of Derek's cock head. He reached for him, gripping him by the hips, refusing to break eye contact because he wanted to drink in every single second of Derek's blissed-out expression. The way his cheeks were pink, the way his eyes were half-lidded and all pupil. The way his mouth hung partway open like he was trying to catch his breath.

Basil urged him in further with a tug, and Derek complied with a firm thrust. The lube made the way slick and easy, even if it was impossibly tight, even if he felt impossibly full, and god…god, this was the moment he'd been waiting for. It wasn't angels singing or the heavens parting with holy light. It didn't even really feel that good—except that it was Derek and he was joined with him, and that—that—was what he'd needed all this time.

"Yes," he felt himself say. "Derek."

Derek's cock throbbed inside him, and his hips stuttered midway through his thrust, and his eyes flew wide open to meet Basil's. He lifted one hand away from where he was pressing his palm to the bed and he curled his two middle fingers toward his palm, the other three out. 'I love you.'

Basil returned the sign, then put one hand on Derek's shoulder, drawing him down for a kiss, and curled the other around his dick and stroked as Derek's tongue fucked into his mouth. The sensations from all sides were enough to send him careening over the edge. He felt the orgasm tear out of him along with the moan which Derek caught in his mouth.

As Basil's body tensed, his cock spurting between them, he felt Derek's hips slam against him again, and again, and again. And then he was coming too. Derek slammed his lips down over Basil's, his hands holding Basil by the hips as he pressed in deep—deeper than anyone had ever been—and filled the condom.

Basil was only half aware when it was over, still trying to regain his composure as Derek gently pulled out and rolled to the side. He came to fully when he felt a warm, wet cloth brushing over his chest and stomach, and his bleary eyes searched out Derek's face. He found the love there, still flushed from passion, his eyes soft. It was like every remaining wall between them had crumpled, and though Basil wasn't foolish enough to think it would be perfect forever, he knew that as long as they worked for it, they would be able to keep it.

Derek tossed the towel to the floor, then let himself curl into Basil, both of them facing each other with a scant few inches for signing space, but it was fine. They didn't need words—spoken with mouths or hands—to know that this was right. They would always be a bit of a mess, he knew. Derek would likely never heal—not completely—from the cruelty his father had shown him for far too many years. And Basil would never fully trust the world Derek belonged to. But there was a common ground between them, and it was right there in that bed, right there with each other. When one stumbled, the other would reach out a hand, and that was exactly enough.

EPILOGUE

Derek felt something rising in him—a sense of nostalgia he had experienced so few times in his life that it almost frightened him. Almost nothing had changed about the cottage built right on the banks of the lake, down to the pale rocks that lined the driveway, or the sea-foam green his mother had painted the front door.

It had been maintained over the years, and rented out, he suspected. Yet it was like stepping back in time to his childhood and the brief escape from being terrorized by his angry father at home. He could almost hear his mother's laughter—such a rare oddity that as a child, he wasn't sure how to feel about it. He could even see the softness in his father's eyes, and he remembered thinking once— only once—that maybe the man actually had loved her.

Derek had stopped wondering a long time ago whether or not his father was capable of real human emotion, but he knew that there had been someone other than a monster once, long before his father had decided what family he wanted to present to the world. Maybe the old man always knew where to hit him that no one else would see, or exactly what to whisper which would make Derek instantly quiet and too terrified to talk back, but maybe not. Maybe it was a carefully cultivated goal and trial and error that he just never understood growing up.

Whatever it was, it didn't exist here. Not now. Not with Basil's hand gently wrapped around his. The noise of their feet on the gravel was enough to overwhelm him, but it was a short walk from the rented car to the front porch, and inside was blissfully quiet. A faint floral scent lingered in the foyer, a long-dead bouquet waiting to be swapped out with a new one, but Derek had dismissed the caretaking staff for the week because he wanted this to be them and only them.

Part of him felt a pang of grief that Sage wasn't there to share in this moment with him, but his brother was caught up in the building of the new halfway house, and interviewing staff and organizations that would help with the caregiving for teens needing a place to go. They didn't have enough money or resources for what Derek and Sage both really wanted—to ensure no teen in their position ever went hungry, but it was a start. At the very least, it was a start.

He felt a slight tug on his hand, and he looked over at Basil who was staring out the front window which overlooked the massive lake. There were a handful of people out on jet-skis, and a couple of rowboats toward the middle. He could see five other cottages on the right side, and three to the left. But the woods were thicker and obscured most of the side-view, giving them a sense of privacy which was what he was craving.

It had been eight long months since his father died. Eight long months since he'd pinned Basil to the bed and pressed inside him and told him he loved him for the first time. He'd always been warned not to say it during sex—it would mean less, it wouldn't be real. But Derek had come to discover that most advice about love was bullshit, and he was done following what other people thought he should do. His heart had stopped leading him astray the night he met Basil, and he was willing to give his instinct the benefit of the doubt.

Which was why he had a little box tucked away in his case, buried under a pair of ugly yellow socks Basil wouldn't go near. He wouldn't take it out right away. No, not immediately. They'd do other things first. Like he'd set up his easel and paints and try to capture how the place made him feel—the good and the bad, the cowardly and the brave. He and Basil would take out a pontoon boat and try to fish. They'd go into town and shop at the farmer's market and hold hands in public and kiss, and Derek would give exactly zero fucks about what anyone else thought.

Home waited for them just on the horizon—with obligations, with his degree just around the bend, and with Basil trying to figure out if the shop really was his end-game. Derek would keep taking his ASL classes in spite of using it every day with Basil because he was dedicated, and he wanted to encourage everyone else in the shop to keep going.

He'd keep putting his mark on random strangers he'd never see again and go to bed knowing that he'd made a difference in the world, even if it was superficial in the form of an infinity symbol on the inside of a twenty-year-old's middle finger.

It was just life. Everyone had their paths to walk, and that was fine.

'You okay?' Basil asked, interrupting his thoughts.

Derek smiled as he grabbed Basil by the waist, spinning him and pressing him to the glass which led to the wrap-around porch. He loved the quiet, unassuming noises Basil made with him now that he wasn't trying everything in his power to keep from letting his throat give way to involuntary sound, and he couldn't help but lean down and kiss him.

Their gazes locked, and Derek traced his finger down the side of Basil's jaw before nodding his fist. 'Yes. Yes. I'm perfect.'

Basil smiled at him, the sun glinting off the side of his face, and Derek smiled back.

ALSO BY E.M. LINDSEY

Broken Chains

The Carnal Tower

Hit and Run

Irons and Works

Love Starts Here

The Sin Bin: West Coast

Malicious Compliance

Collaborations with Other Authors

Foreign Translations

AudioBooks

ABOUT THE AUTHOR

E.M. Lindsey is a non-binary writer who lives in the southeast United States, close to the water where their heart lies.

For a free serial novel, join EM Lindsey at their newsletter or join their Patreon and get access to ARCs, teasers, free short stories, and more.